'NO PLAN B, MALCOLM!'

Mervyn S. Whyte

A M.S.W. Press Productions

ABOUT THE AUTHOR: Mervyn S. Whyte was born in Lancaster in 1972. His main influences are P.G. Wodehouse and Des O'Connor. 'No Plan B, Malcolm!' is his first book.

M.S.W. Press Production Original

Published 2023 by M.S.W. Press

Copyright © Mervyn. S. Whyte 2023

Cover design by Ken at Creative Covers

Formatting by Book Polishers

For Linda. For getting it.

'It's a comic novel, and a comic novel is not about, it's just something.'

(Saul Bellow on More Die of Heartbreak)

CONTENTS

CHAPTER ONE

MALCOLM MOVED THROUGH the shop floor at top speed. Still wearing the pink, fluorescent tracksuit and lime green running shoes he always jogged to work in, he passed into the foyer and out into the car park. As he was forever preaching, the perfect form for a long-distance runner is head forward with a natural gaze, shoulders low and relaxed, fists unclenched with arms at ninety degrees and a straight, running tall torso. But the way Malcolm was moving suggested something else altogether. Instead of straight, his torso, like his head, turned this way and that, his shoulders high and tight. Meanwhile, his gaze, far from appearing natural, had a haunted, dumbstruck look about it. Malcolm wasn't so much running sloppy as running scared.

He leaned against the crash barrier to catch his breath, the heat from the latter reacting with the icy-cold January air to form cumulus clouds of condensed air. In his hand were two pieces of paper. He glanced down at the first.

BURN DOWN THE STORE!!!

Perspiring heavily, Malcolm looked across the almost-empty car park with unseeing eyes. A company man, he couldn't believe that anyone would want to burn down the store. But it was what was written on the second piece of paper that was really making him sweat. He glanced down at it.

KILL FRANK!!!

Frank was his department manager. The person he received all his instructions from. And who spent all his time in the car park helping customers with their shopping or collecting trolleys. The thought of somebody wanting to *kill* him…

Malcolm felt the hairs on the back of his neck stand up. Remembering the breathing exercises he'd been taught at the Lunestone Running Club, he placed both hands on his stomach and began taking deep breaths. As he slowly inhaled, then exhaled, his thoughts turned to what his store manager, Derek, had said in yesterday's staff briefing. That retail was about one thing, and one thing only. Trends. Sales trends, seasonal trends, economic trends: Malcolm was worried that if you killed one department manager, you might start off another of these mysterious trends. Before you knew it, there would be dead department managers everywhere. And then where would the Lunestone branch of Whiting's Supermarket Plc be?

'Sliding down the league table faster than a greased monkey down a drainpipe.'

That's what Derek would say. What Malcolm said, out loud so strong was the currents of his thoughts, was:

'Ask Victor.'

This was Malcolm's solution to everything. To him, Victor was the oracle, the all-seeing, all-knowing one. If he could get to him before Victor got too drunk, everything would be okay.

Malcolm looked at his watch.

8.25 a.m.

It would be a close-run thing.

II

MALCOLM WAS WRONG. Victor didn't know the answer to

everything. He didn't know what the capital city of Mongolia was, he didn't know when he was going to finish the book he was supposed to be writing and he didn't know how he was going to persuade the bus driver to let him on with just twenty-six pence.

He gazed down at the grubby coins in his hand.

Not even enough for a cheap can of lager. The bottle of whisky he'd bought the day before had been finished off at breakfast. Another hour or so and the shakes would start. Then the pink elephants. Then the tantrums, usually aimed at the other members of staff, but which sometimes spilled over to the customers. Only a few days before he'd upbraided some old timer who'd got in his way after spending ten minutes rummaging through the bananas. Running on empty at the time, Victor had turned to the customer and said, 'You're going to die one day and you've just spent ten minutes looking for the perfect fucking banana!' It was enough to put him on a final written warning. One more transgression and that would be it.

Gone.

Dismissed.

Given his marching orders.

It wasn't the job that he'd miss. It was the wages. Badly paid, it still kept him in whisky for the first week or two.

He jiggled the coins in his fist.

Well, the first week anyway.

With the cash and booze situation so serious there was only one thing to do. Get to work and borrow some money from Malcolm. That was if Malcolm had remembered to come into work and hadn't been distracted by one of his obsessions. The latest were marathon running and UFO spotting. Malcolm would combine the two by scanning the sky for flying saucers while out jogging. By the time Victor got to work Malcolm was as likely to be on his way to Area 51 in Nevada or off to Melton Mowbray for the Belvoir Marathon Challenge then stacking shelves at Whiting's.

Victor put the collar of his overcoat up. First, of course, he had to get to work. With just twenty-six pence on him he had to persuade the driver to take him all the way to Cannon Hill. And for that he would require two pounds and seventy pence. There was only one thing for it.

Richard Burton or Luciano Pavarotti?

Richard Burton. A tad old school, but it would give him the necessary oratorical umph that was required. A thought came over him. He'd tried to pull the same trick yesterday. Unsuccessfully. What if it was the same driver? He took a crumpled blue polyester face mask from his pocket and put it on. Masks were no longer mandatory on buses, but many people still wore them.

After turning up the collar of his coat, Victor pulled the mask over as much of his face as he could manage. It wasn't much of a disguise, but it was better than nothing. Wetting down his bouffant black hair with saliva-slicked hands, he got himself into character.

III

BACK AT WHITING'S Malcolm was trying to keep himself alert. With Victor nowhere on the horizon it was important that he didn't forget about the two slips of paper. Rather than stand with them in his hand he folded them up and put them in his pocket. He then started to do a stretching exercise. Not the usual one he would do after a run – hamstring, or quadriceps or piriformis – but a yoga exercise. The one he chose was called the Khatu Pranam, or 'Greetings to Khatu'. Not only was it supposed to harmonise body, mind and spirit, but it also helped with concentration.

Pushing out his left leg and pulling his right as far back as it would go, Malcolm arched his back, then stretched his arms heavenwards and pressed the palms of his hands closely together. Closing his eyes tight so he could 'visualise' the slips of paper, he proceeded to let out a series of deep 'Oms'. He had no sooner started his greetings to Khatu when he heard:

'Morning, Malcolm.'

Thinking for a moment it was Khatu sending his greetings back, a shocked Malcolm's eyes popped open. Instead of Khatu it was Violet from Customer Services. Buck teeth, strawberry-blonde hair and bottle-rimmed glasses, she was holding a book in one hand and a charity collection tin in the other.

'Morning,' said Malcolm holding his position.

'It's so sad,' said Violet, shaking her head at the small group of customers waiting outside for the store to open.

'Sad?' said Malcolm, screwing up his eyes as he tried to concentrate again on the two slips of paper.

'We don't open for another hour.'

'Forty-nine minutes,' said Malcolm, letting his arm drop momentarily so he could check his watch.

'You'd think they'd have something better to do than hang around supermarkets on Sunday mornings.'

Violet's words made Malcolm lose his balance. 'What could be better than waiting outside a supermarket for it to open?' he said, regaining his composure. He nodded over at the customers. 'They've probably run out of milk. Unless of course they're vegans. Or parrots. Or is it canaries that don't drink milk? Something to do with the shape of their beaks probably.'

'Mercedes Heartbeat would never hang around outside a supermarket on a Sunday,' said Violet, stroking the front cover of the book she was carrying. 'Or any other day, come to think about it. She'd be too busy watching the Prince of Wales play polo. Or waking up at the Ritz Hotel in Paris.'

'Hotels never run out of milk,' said Malcolm. 'Against the law, apparently. Or is that fire extinguishers?'

'Or she'd be at Doctor Willoughby's house. Yes, that's it. He invited her over to discuss her daughter's heart condition and ended up staying the night.'

'Who's Doctor Willoughby?'

'He's the man who saved Beauty's life, of course,' said Violet, holding the book up so Malcolm could see it closer.

'*Love by Proxy* by Amy Lovelace,' said Malcolm, taking hold of the book and reading the front cover. Forgetting about sending any more greetings to Khatu or visualising the two slips of paper, he turned the book over to read the back cover. 'Who's Beauty?'

'Beauty is Mercedes Heartbeat's daughter, silly,' said Violet, snatching the book back. 'Her illness was caused by Doctor Willoughby's evil wife, Stella, who was hired to look after her following her accident in the swimming pool. But suffering from Munchausen's syndrome by proxy, Stella kept on making Beauty worse. Mercedes suspected Stella from the start, of course, but it was only after Doctor Willoughby performed an emergency operation on Beauty and found part of a necklace belonging to his wife blocking Beauty's throat that he realised Mercedes was telling the truth.'

'A sharp slap on the back,' said Malcolm. 'That should clear any blockages when it comes to the throat. Failing that try the Heimlich Manoeuvre.'

By this point Malcolm had stopped sending even the briefest

of greetings to Khatu. So intently was he listening to Violet's story about Doctor Willoughby and Beauty that all memories of the two slips of paper were slipping from his mind like sand through a child's fingers.

'But don't worry,' said Violet, 'there's a happy ending.'

'Oh, good,' said Malcolm, pushing his glasses back into place. As he did so the two slips of paper made a brief reappearance. Until…

'I don't want to spoil it in case you read the book, but it ends with Stella in a psychiatric hospital, Mercedes and Doctor Willoughby – Edward – married, and Beauty becoming the youngest-ever winner of an Olympic gold medal for swimming.'

'Front crawl or backstroke?'

'I wonder where I'll find my Doctor Willoughby?' said Violet, clutching *Love by Proxy* to her ample bosom.

'You could try your local swimming baths,' said Malcolm. 'Or the hospital. I hear they have lots of doctors there.'

'Oh, I can't go swimming,' said Violet. 'It would damage my nails.'

'Because they'll rust, you mean? Coat them in some grease.'

A puzzled look on her face, Violet glanced down at her three-inch crimson fingernails. 'Anyway, Malc,' she said, 'what are you doing out here?'

This time it was Malcolm's turn to have a puzzled look on his face. With his head now a confused mess of doctors and necklaces and greased nails he had forgotten why he had come out into the car park. As for the two slips of paper, the last grains of sand were long gone. Blown away into the vast, swirling desert of lost memories. Scratching his head, he looked blankly at Violet and said:

'Just, erm…'

IV

'CANNON HILL, DRIVER, please,' said Victor, behind his mask in a booming Richard Burton voice.

'Single or return?' asked the driver.

'Return. "No man is a friend to his friend if he does not love in return." Plato.'

'Three quid,' said the driver, staring impassively out of the window.

'Three pounds?' said Victor, dropping the Richard Burton impersonation. 'It was only two pounds seventy yesterday.'

'I don't set the prices, mate, I just collect the money.'

Victor went through the charade of taking his wallet from his trouser pocket. 'That's hyperinflation, that is,' he said. 'Monday, you're paying for a loaf of bread with your spare change. Tuesday, it's gone up so much you need a wheelbarrow to transport the cash. That's how Nazi Germany started.'

'It's those politicians you should be having a go at, mate,' said the driver, sorting some coins in the tray in front of him.

'I'm working on it,' said Victor, opening his wallet. 'Ah, yes,' he said, checking his pockets, 'I've left my money on the mantelpiece. Yes, I remember now,' he continued, taking a large book from his coat pocket. 'I was rereading Russell's *A History of Western Philosophy* – have you read it? A little bit dated now, or, as we philosophers would say, *non à la mode*. Anyway, as I say, I had just finished the chapter on Cynics and Sceptics and was about to move to the Epicureans, when -'

'Three quid.'

'I haven't got three pounds. I've got twenty-six pence and two safety pins in the whole world.'

'Then I can't let you on the bus.'

Victor raised himself up to his full height. 'Do you know

who I am?' he said.

'Let me guess,' said the driver. 'Richard Burton? Luciano Pavarotti? That's who you told me you were yesterday when you tried to get on with no money.'

'How did, did -?'

'Your tits,' said the driver, pointing at Victor's 36-DD breasts. 'They stand out a mile. You can't hide them with a mask. Couldn't hide them with a marquee.' He slammed shut the coin tray. 'That's what happens when you start mucking about with nature. When are you getting the other half done?'

Victor placed a protective hand over his chest. 'I am not, sir, in the middle of gender reassignment,' he said. 'I happen to suffer from a serious medical condition. Gynecomastia is not for the faint-hearted.' He noticed his right hand quiver slightly. The shakes had started early. If he didn't get any booze down him soon they would get quickly worse. Much worse. 'In some countries it's illegal to hold up a man on his way to work,' he said, removing his mask.

'In this country it's illegal to let a man, woman, or anything in between, ride on a bus without a ticket,' said the driver. 'And while we're talking laws, what about God's law that says the Sabbath is holy and whoever does any work on it will be put to death? Exodus 35:2.'

Victor stroked his beard in nervous surrender. He wasn't used to having theological debates with bus drivers. Especially ones with such an intimate knowledge of the Scriptures. All he could think of by way of a rejoinder was:

'And Jesus wept. He would've done if he tried to get on your bus without any money.' He stepped off the bus. 'Imagine what would've happened if his parents had tried to catch the number 42 to Bethlehem and the driver refused to let them on because they didn't have any money. They'd never have got to that stable in time.'

'I'm a Buddhist, mate,' said the driver. '"The greatest patience is humility." They'll be another bus along in an hour. If you're lucky, the driver might be a Jehovah's Witness. Or someone who doesn't know that Richard Burton and Pavarotti are both dead.'

As the bus drove off, Victor kicked the bus stop in frustration. Another defeat in a lifetime of disappointments. He recalled the time he'd sat on his mum's knee as she told him about his name. '"Victor". It is a Roman name, meaning champion, hero, winner.' Not for the first time did he feel like he was coming down with a bad case of irony.

He took his flying hat from his pocket and put it on his head. The walk to work was two miles. No distance at all for someone like Malcolm who was fit and healthy and flat chested. But for a Pavarotti lookalike with melon-sized breasts it felt like Mao's Long March. With the shakes spreading to his other hand Victor put his best – and least shaky – foot forward and set off down the road with a 'No Plan B.'

'Just waiting for me, that's it, isn't it, Malcolm, you old romantic?'

Malcolm stared blankly at Violet. At the back of his mind he had some vague notion that he was waiting for someone. Violet was as good a person as any.

'Probably,' he said.

'Well, don't forget tonight,' said Violet.

Malcolm didn't want to admit it, but he had no idea what it was he wasn't supposed to be forgetting that night. He thought, maybe, that Violet was referring to the meeting of the Lunestone UFO Society – the Lunnies as they were known around town. But they only met on Wednesdays.

'And don't forget your costume.'

A light went on in Malcolm's head. The Lunestone Marathon. That's what Violet must be referring to. He always wore a costume when he ran marathons. At the last pre-Covid Bungay Black Dog marathon, he'd donned a full suit of armour (time: fifteen hours and four minutes). He couldn't remember agreeing to don the plate mail for the marathon he had coming up next week. But with thirty-two pounds in sponsorship money already pledged, he didn't want to run the risk of people asking for their cash back just because he'd forgotten to line up in a suit of armour.

'I won't,' he said.

'Just so you know,' said Violet, 'it's not Covid Aid anymore, it's...' She shook the tin that hung from her wrist like an oversized bracelet. On it scrawled in black eyeliner across a COVID AID sticker were the words MUNCH BY P.

But Malcolm had stopped listening. Having noticed that both of his shoelaces had come undone, he bent down to tie the first.

'I'm collecting through the day as well,' said Violet. 'So...?' She dangled the tin in front of Malcolm's face.

Pausing his shoelace-tying, Malcolm stared up at the tin with a confused look.

'So...?' said Violet, again, shaking the tin.

Malcolm's mind flashed back to the staff suggestion box in the canteen. In the flashback he saw himself take two slips of paper out of it. He also saw himself pick something up from the floor...

'Malcolm!'

'Hmmm?' Despite the slips of paper making a reappearance in Malcolm's mind, it was what he'd picked up off the floor that was dominating his thoughts.

'Have you any idea how much people with Munchausen's syndrome by proxy suffer?' said Violet. 'Not to mention the people around them?'

'No,' said Malcolm, resuming his shoelace-tying.

'Look at what happened to Beauty Heartbeat! Having part of that amethyst necklace stuffed down her throat. So...' Violet shook the tin for a third time. 'Are you going to make a contribution or not?'

Relieved at finally being able to work out what Violet was after, Malcolm took a coin from his pocket and handed it to her.

'Oh, Malcolm!'

Malcolm looked up from tying his second shoelace to find Violet holding an engagement ring. Platinum-coloured with a single diamond set in a rose-shaped claw, *that's* what he had picked up from the canteen floor.

'And you're down on one knee,' said Violet, putting the ring on her finger. 'Oh, it's perfect! I can't wait to tell everyone we're engaged!'

Violet skipped off towards the store.

A puzzled Malcolm stood up and pushed his glasses back into place. With everything that had happened in the last twenty minutes – greeting Khatu, listening to Violet's story about Doctor Willoughby and Beauty, Munch by P, getting engaged – his brain was starting to short-circuit. It's what always happened when he had too much information to process. The only thing he could do was wait until the wires uncrossed themselves. Hopefully by then Victor would've turned up.

He had a lot to tell him.

If he could remember any of it.

CHAPTER TWO

KURTZ WALKED DOWN the Beers, Wines and Spirits aisle and stopped in front of the bottles of whisky. Taking a checklist from under his arm, he began to count.

'*Een*, twee, *drie*, four, *vyf*, six…*vyf, six*…'

He stamped his foot in irritation and started again.

'*Een*, twee, *drie*, four, *vyf*, six, *sewe*, eight, *nege, nege*…'

This time he kicked the bottom of the shelf. Noticing his reflection in one of the bottles, he stopped to straighten his tie. Meticulous when it came to his appearance, that morning he'd made a special effort. His shoes shone like licked plates, the creases in his pants ran down his legs like metal bands, while his collar-length, swept-back salt and pepper hair, together with his Eugene Terre Blanche-drooping moustache and bushy beard had been neatly washed and trimmed.

'*Nege*, ten, eleven, *twaalf, dertien*, fourteen…'

What he couldn't do anything about was the film of sweat on his permanently creased forehead.

'Fifteen, *sestien, sewentien*, eighteen…'

Every time he wiped the sweat off it would reappear again a few minutes later. Nerves, of course, in case something went wrong. He'd planned everything down to the minutest detail. But that hadn't stopped the sweat. Or the little man in his stomach – who since the Brexit vote he'd christened Jacob, after

Jacob Rees-Mogg – from rumbling. Back home on the force in Pretoria it always used to rumble when something didn't add up. And it hadn't rumbled like this since he'd caught the Faerie Glen Flasher red ended.

'Nineteen, *twintig,* twenty-one.'

Twenty-one?

It said twenty-two on the checklist.

Kurtz's eyes narrowed.

Victor! He's a dronkie after all.

Kurtz picked a piece of gristle from out between his front teeth. Back on the force he'd met a thousand Victors. They were the ones who annoyed him the most. The ones who never stopped yakking when they were being questioned.

He swallowed the piece of gristle. Even if Victor hadn't stolen the bottle of whisky, Kurtz was still going to get him. For what, it didn't matter. Two hundred arrests, two hundred convictions, Kurtz always got his man. Cheered by the thought, he broke into song.

'Mijn lieve Sarie is ver weg mij maar ik hoop om haar weer to zien…'

He went through all the different options he could use to get Victor.

Stabbed to death while resisting arrest.

Bludgeoned to death while resisting arrest.

Strangled to death while resisting arrest.

Poisoned. Pick-axed. Buried alive.

Best to keep it simple and stick to the old favourites.

Tripped and fell down the stairs.

Found hanging in the toilet cubicle.

Died from natural causes.

Kurtz swaggered off swinging his keys.

'In de Mooi River County…' He stopped and slapped his

20

face. '*Ag sies*, man.' He'd got so caught up with Victor he'd forgotten the other thing. Running over the words he was going to say – over the Tannoy, so everyone in the store could hear – he wiped the sweat again from his brow. Reaching into his trouser pocket, he took out a heart-shaped velvet ring box. Inside was a one carat De Beers solitaire engagement ring. Kurtz took the ring out of the box and held it up to admire.

Violet wouldn't know what had hit her.

II

VICTOR CROSSED THE bridge at Charles Street and came to a halt at the crossroads of Valby Park and Caulkeld Road. The shortest route to work from there was through the park itself. But that would mean running the gauntlet of the Visigoths. That was the name Victor had given to a group of layabouts who seemed to frequent the park on a permanent basis and whose only role in life appeared to be teasing him about his breasts. Two days ago they'd spotted him coming down the path and stood in a chorus line along the verge and sang *Swing low, sweet chesticles* to the tune of *Swing Low, Sweet Chariot*.

The town hall clock struck nine. The time Victor should've been clocking in at work. If he took the Caulkfeld Road route he wouldn't get to his destination for another half an hour. The short cut through the park would have him there in less than ten minutes. There was no choice. Having been late four times already that week he couldn't afford to be so again.

Moving like a man who expected to be ambushed at any moment, he darted through the main gates and scurried along the tree-lined path with his head down. The Visigoths usually congregated at the wooden bench near to the duck pond. As he approached it, Victor lifted his head. The only person there today was a man in a raincoat and white visor carrying a clipboard. As Victor rushed past the man reached out. '*Lunestone Gazette,*' he said. 'I wonder if you'd mind answering a few questions about the council's proposal to turn the park into a carpark?' Victor screeched to a halt.

'A carpark?' he said, forgetting that he was in a hurry. 'No, no, no, that way is the way of folly.'

'So, you're against it then?' said the man.

Victor took a deep breath. When talking to the nation it was vital that he got his words in the right order. They were bound to be quoted at the highest level. And for decades to come. 'Against it on principle and on philosophical grounds,' he said. '"In all things of nature there is something of the marvellous". Aristotle. "If one way be better than another, that you may be sure is nature's way". Aristotle again.'

'So, you think it'll be bad for the environment?'

'My dear sir, cars are like gases, in that they will expand to fill all the available spaces. The more carpark spaces we build, the more cars will be built to fill them. Very soon there will be no more green parks left. The world will be a mass of concrete carbuncles.'

'The council's plan is to build a carpark at the north end and one at the south, leaving some of the original park intact. So, in your mind that would mean two carbuncles?'

'Indeed it would.'

'Two monstrous growths?'

'Yes.'

'Two big, bulky, mammoth mommas?'

'Eh?'

The man ripped off his vizor and raincoat and threw the clipboard over his head. At the same time three other bodies came tumbling out of the bushes. Lining up alongside the first man, they dangled their hands in front of them like they were holding enormous breasts.

'Swing low, sweet chesticles/ Coming for to carry me home…'

III

KURTZ SAW VIOLET behind the Customer Service desk and broke out into a soppy smile. Not usually one of life's romantics, when it came to buck teeth and ginger hair, he was smitten. He checked his collar and tie and ran a nervous hand through his well-brushed hair. He'd faced many tense situations in his time. Marauding bands of assegai-wielding Zulus. Machine gun-toting bank robbers. Shoplifters attacking him with frozen legs of lamb. But he'd never felt this afraid before.

He plucked a single red rose from the floral display. Hiding it and the engagement ring behind his back, he tiptoed up to the Customer Service desk.

'I'd like to make a complaint, please,' he said in his deep Transvaal-trill.

Violet spun round clutching her chest. 'Oh, you made me jump!' she said.

'You want a jump, *bokkie*, I'll give you a jump.'

'Now, don't start any of that,' said Violet, coquettishly.

'Any of what, *bokkie*?' said Kurtz, handing her the rose.

'Oh, how lovely,' said Violet, holding the rose under her nose. She put it down on the counter. 'But I'm afraid I can't accept it.'

'Why not?' said Kurtz, keeping his hand with the ring in it behind his back.

'Accept a flower from another man? What would my fiancé say?'

The soppy look fell from Kurtz's face. 'Fiancé?' he said.

'Yes, I'm engaged now,' said Violet. 'Didn't you know?'

'E-E-Engaged?' said Kurtz, his eyes bulging. His mouth remained open, but no more words would come. Until, staccato-like, they tumbled from his mouth. 'What? How? When?'

'This morning,' said Violet, clasping her hands together. 'Isn't life wonderful?'

Catching a shoplifter stealing a bottle of whisky. That's when life was wonderful for Kurtz. Or eating a full English breakfast with extra black pudding. But finding out that the woman he was about to propose to has already gotten herself engaged to another man...Just then life seemed about as wonderful as an earful of Swahili spit.

Still unable to form fully coherent sentences, Kurtz spat out the word 'Who?' No sooner had he done so then a shiver ran up his spine. 'It's not Tubby *Tets*, is it?' he finally managed to say.

'No, it's not Victor,' said Violet. 'It's Malcolm.'

'That *domkop*!' said Kurtz, picking up the rose and smashing it on the Customer Service counter. Petals scattered everywhere. '*Bladdy* hell, he's probably forgotten he's even asked you.'

'Good job I didn't cancel the church,' said Violet, picking up the rose petals. 'I booked it, remember, after Roger from Online promised to marry me.' She dropped the petals into a nearby bin. 'Funny him running off to Peru like that. But when Pachacuti Inca Yupanqui, King of the Incas, asks you to be Keeper of the Royal Llamas, you can't very well turn him down. Well, instead of me and Roger getting married tomorrow, it'll be me and Malcolm.'

Tomorrow! Kurtz grabbed hold of the Customer Service desk to steady himself. The last time he'd felt this dizzy he'd had Covid. But a respiratory disease invented by Bill Gates and made in a lab in Wuhan was nothing compared to how he was feeling just then.

'Malcolm's proposal was so romantic,' said Violet, clasping her hands together again. 'He even got down on one knee.'

'He'll be getting down on one knee when I've finished with him,' said Kurtz, through gritted teeth.

'Sorry?'

'I said, erm...' Kurtz's gritted teeth turned into a forced smile. 'Down on one knee, you say? You sure he wasn't praying?'

'No, he wasn't praying,' said Violet, folding her arms. 'He was asking me to marry him.'

'Let's see your ring, then.'

'You know I don't like wearing jewellery on the shop floor. I might lose it.'

'Who said anything about jewellery?'

'Oh!' said Violet, picking up the petal-less rose and whacking Kurtz on the arm with it. 'And I bet you stole this flower.'

'*Moi?*'

'And you the security guard! You'll have to arrest yourself.'

Violet's rutting rhinoceros laugh reminded Kurtz of being back home on the veldt. It was one of the reasons he found her so attractive. The best thing to do was to laugh along with her and sort out her fiancé later. Without her knowledge, of course. She'd hardly be likely to say 'I do' if she found out he'd nobbled her intended. No, a quiet word with Malcolm would do it. Preferably at the top of a steep set of stairs.

'Here's someone who wants arresting,' he said, as a sweating, red-faced, Victor tried to sneak past.

'I, I, missed my bus,' said a panting Victor, collapsing on top of the Customer Service counter.

'I'm missing a bottle of whisky,' said Kurtz. 'Know anything about it?'

'Why should I know anything about it?' Fortunately, Victor's face was too beetroot red for the guilty blush beneath it to be detected.

'You were in yesterday. And for someone who's supposed to be putting out *bladdy* potatoes you seem to spend a lot of time on the spirits aisle.'

'Helping customers.'

'Helping yourself, more like.'

'How dare you, sir! I pay my way like everyone else.'

'*Ja*, using other people's money.' With Violet checking herself in a compact mirror, Kurtz pulled Victor to one side. 'Just so you know, I'll be keeping a close eye on things today.' He prodded Victor in the gut. 'And on you in particular.' He sniffed Victor's mouth. 'Against company policy to drink on the premises. Get caught one more time and...' He drew a finger across his throat.

'Don't forget tonight,' said Violet, putting down the mirror.

'Tonight?' said Victor, stepping away from Kurtz. 'What's tonight? A bring-a-gun party, or a sponsored witch hunt, or are we all going to stand around a fire and throw books into the flames?'

'You know perfectly well what's tonight,' said Violet. 'The charity gala.'

Victor looked up at the ceiling in despair.

'And don't fall off the stage this year,' said Kurtz.

'I didn't fall,' said Victor. 'I slipped.'

'*Ja*, slipped as a fart.'

'And come as someone we've heard of this time,' said Violet, checking herself again in the mirror. 'There's no point doing fancy dress if no one knows who you are.'

'How was I to know nobody had heard of Wat Tyler?' said Victor. 'Maybe this year I'll come as Jimmy bloody Saville.'

'You haven't got the hair,' said Kurtz. Making sure Violet

wasn't listening, he pulled Victor nearer to where he was standing. 'Suit you that dressing up as a pervert.'

'Wat Tyler was a roof tiler,' said Victor, trying to put some social distancing between himself and Kurtz.

'I'm talking about what happened between you and Violet at last year's do, you *verdraai*.'

'What's a *verdraai*?'

'Pervert. Degenerate. *Broekie*-sniffer. Dragging Violet into that broom cupboard.'

'Dragging her into the broom cupboard...Have you seen how big she is? It would be like a mini trying to pull an articulated lorry.'

'There's nothing mini about you, tubby.' Kurtz prodded Victor in the gut a second time. 'If it happens again it'll be me doing the pulling. Your head off your shoulders. Understand?' Kurtz lifted a clenched fist under Victor's chin. 'And tell that *mompie* Malcolm to keep his paws off too. Or else...'

Victor turned to go. Coming the other way was Baz the cleaner. Bald, toothless and covered in a gallery of tattoos, he was rushing outside for probably his hundredth roll-up of the morning.

'Morning Baz,' said Victor.

'Fuck off,' said Baz.

To be fair, it was the best advice Victor had heard that morning. Under the evil eye of Kurtz, he gathered his breasts under his arm, and with a 'I knew it was a mistake to join the working classes,' set off towards the staff changing rooms.

IV

VICTOR WALKED THROUGH the back area and up the stairs.

Ignoring the chorus of 'Morning, fat tits' and 'Look who it is, it's Charlie Chesticles', he made his way to the clocking-in machine outside the men's changing room. His hands were shaking so badly by now that it took him three goes to clock in. The shaking wasn't just from the alcohol withdrawal. Victor had also been badly shaken by his assault by the Visigoths. If a man with a clipboard asking questions about carparks was no longer safe, what was? Dangers lurk around every corner for the strange, indeed. Including at work. No matter how many Respect campaigns Whiting's ran it was always the same. Nudge-nudges, wink-winks and a barrage of innuendo. There was only one remedy. To write his book and show them just how mightier the pen was to the slander.

Blurry of eye and hazy of thought, Victor stumbled half-blind into the changing rooms to his locker. Changing into his crumpled, stain-splattered work shirt, he's eyes scanned the half dozen or so empty whisky bottles. In one a couple of mouthfuls remained. Sending up a silent prayer of thanks to his mother, he grabbed the bottle, unscrewed the top and guzzled down the contents. The change was immediate. Gone were the shaking hands and fuzzy vision. Gone too were the blurry thoughts, replaced by ones that were as clear as they were confident.

Revitalized, he stood in the middle of the empty changing room and in a loud, defiant voice declared: '*A History of Western Philosophy: Volume Two.*'

He removed his trousers to reveal a pair of 'I Luv Philosophy' boxer shorts.

'*A New History of Western Philosophy.*' He hung up the trousers in his locker. 'Yes, that's better. *A New History of Western Philosophy* by Victor Porter, BA Hons Cantab, DPhil, FBA. Chapter One: Aristotle.'

He paused to put on his creased work trousers.

'Aristotle…Aristotle…' He plucked the Bertrand Russell book from the pocket of his hung-up coat and flicked through it. 'Here we are, Aristotle…' Mouthing the words as he silently read, he reached halfway down the page and looked up. 'So, Russell thinks that too, does he? Well, you know what they say: great minds and all that.'

Grabbing a pen and piece of paper from his locker, he wrote: "Aristotle's metaphysics, roughly speaking, may be described as Plato diluted with common sense."

He was about to cross out the quotation marks – he could always put them back in later – when the dressing room door flew open and in came Kevin.

With his bulging eyes and carnassial grin, Kevin reminded Victor of a piranha fish. Or a cross between Nosferatu and Uncle Fester. All topped off with what appeared to be a bad hair transplant and a mishmash of pestilential skin complaints and pockmarks. Never mind Covid, Kevin looked like he'd either just got the bubonic plague or was in the process of recovering from it.

'What's been going on here, then?' he said, looking Victor up and down.

'Nothing,' said Victor. Folding up the piece of paper he continued to get dressed. As he did he noticed that Kevin was smiling in that unusual way of his. Like a demented shark with toothache. It usually betokened some bestial carnal design.

'Something amusing,' said Victor, pinning on his name badge.

'Just given Malcolm a load of bluies,' said Kevin, pulling a packet of Monster Munch from his pocket.

'A load of what?'

'Bluies. You know, dirty movies. The real under-the-counter stuff as well.'

'What are you trying to do? Get him arrested?'

'Hey, these are some quality titles we're talking about,' said Kevin, with a serious face. 'And I put some special stuff in there for him.'

A shadow seemed to fall across Victor's soul. 'What do you mean "special"?' he said.

'You know, with him not being right and all.'

'That skiing accident didn't leave Malcolm retarded, Kevin,' said Victor in an irritated voice. 'Just a little…forgetful.'

'He's not going to forget the films I've just given him,' said Kevin, munching on a crisp.

'Why, what have you given him?'

Kevin leaned in. '*Midget Mayhem*,' he said grinning.

Hiding his face with his hands, Victor let out a howl of anguish.

'You know,' continued Kevin, lifting his hand to just above his waist and thrusting backwards and forwards, 'midgets getting fucked.' He reached in the bag for another crisp. 'It's not all dodgy. I put some incest in there as well.'

Victor let out a second howl.

'And a bit of gay porn to mix things up. You never know today who's into what. One thing I don't understand,' said Kevin, holding the crisp in the air and examining it.

'What?'

'When one homo's bumming another homo, why would he give him a reach-around? You'd think he was already pulling his weight.'

An inane and homophobic question, even by Kevin's standards. And one that Victor wasn't about to contemplate for very long. There was that bottle of whisky he still had to acquire. And now he had to get those dirty movies from Malcolm and cast them into outer darkness. Or at least into the bushes in the car park. He quickly put on his work shoes and headed towards the door.

'Where are you going?' said Kevin, clearly amazed that anyone would want to leave when such an important question was being asked.

'To find Malcolm.'

'Why, does he know anything about reach-arounds?' Kevin put the crisp in his mouth. Hey, he will when he's watched those films.'

VICTOR DECIDED TO try the canteen first. Malcolm was often in there stuffing his face. Not because Malcolm was greedy. But because he'd forget that he'd already eaten and end up having three breakfasts or lunches.

When Victor entered the canteen, everything appeared to be normal. Chef was in his usual place behind the counter, swinging a meat cleaver and adulterating whatever culinary nightmare he had dreamed up the night before. The familiar smell of burnt toast, old cooking fat and stale food still pervaded the room. The grey chipboard tables were their usual mess of dirty plates and used serviettes. And Angel – aka Big A, aka The Angel of Death – was still smashing the place apart. Yesterday, it was because her sausages had been undercooked. Today, it was because she had lost something, or somebody – a very foolish somebody – had stolen something from her. Victor was able to discern the latter by the way Angel was hurling cups and plates across the room while shouting.

'Dirty! Robbing! Bastards!'

Victor glanced over at Chef, who was trying to look relaxed

by loudly whistling the theme tune from *Match of the Day*. Chef was no slouch when it came to the weighing scales. But even he resembled a pygmy when it came to a physical matchup with Angel. Built like a 200-pound gorilla, and just as hairy, she was more Australopithecus than winged messenger of God. Indeed, any wings trying to lift her off the ground would first need to be fitted with at least ten Rolls Royce engines. Woman born, but not fitting into any recognisable gender group, she required a pronoun of her very own.

With the salvo of cups and plates increasing in intensity, Victor tried to beat a hasty retreat. He had almost made it to the door when he felt Angel's Mike Tyson-stare fix itself on him. Frozen to the spot, Victor returned the stare with a rictus grin.

'P-Perhaps madam requires some assistance?' he said.

'Wot did you say?' said Angel, charging towards him like an angry bull.

'I, I, was merely offering to lend a hand.'

Like a dog chasing a cat that refuses to run, a brain-fogged Angel stopped dead just inches away from Victor's face. She looked him up and down, her basilisk breath breaking over him like brown clouds.

'Lost me mam's engagement ring,' she said. 'She gave it me just before she died of the Chinky.'

Victor tried to stop himself from looking surprised. After all, even Grendel had a mother. But a creature of darkness exiled from happiness and accursed of God or not, he couldn't let the Sinophobia pass without comment. 'Erm, Coronavirus-Nineteen is a terrible illness,' he said, sympathetically, 'but I'm not sure it's right to call it "The Chinky".'

'She didn't die from Chinky flu,' said Angel. 'She died from *the* Chinky. The Chinky takeaway. Normally, she only ate numbers one to twenty-three on the menu, but that night she went right up into the thirties. Her arsehole dropped out of her like shit from a goose. I tried to push it back in, but it was like trying to push a used balloon through an uncooked sausage. She just had time to take her ring off – her engagement ring, I mean – and give it to me.'

'I'm very sorry for your loss.'

'Why? It's 'ow she wanted to go. I remember her last words. "I finally did it, our kid. I got to the beef chow mein". It's what's written on her gravestone. "She Got to the Beef Chow Mein, Now She's Got to Heaven. R.I.P. Mandi-Shandi Rose Hole".'

'Very poetical. What, erm, what does the ring look like?' said Victor. 'The engagement ring,' he added quickly.

'It's platinum with a big stone in a flower.'

'A flower?'

'A rose. It's me mam's middle name. And mine.'

'Angel Rose,' said Victor, mouthing the word 'Help' over Angel's shoulder to a smirking Chef.

'Angel Rose Sarah Elizabeth Hole,' said Angel.

'Very pretty.'

'Like me ring. If someone's pinched it, I'll tear them limb from limb when I get hold of them.' She moved even closer to Victor. 'Or marry them.'

Getting nothing back from Chef but a wave of a hand and a big grin, Victor closed his eyes and wondered how long it would take for Angel to tear him limb from limb. However long it was, it was still better than being married to her.

'Or marry them,' she repeated.

Recoiling from the toxic fumes emanating from Angel's mouth, Victor started to edge his way towards the door. 'Well, I hope it turns up,' he said, reaching behind him for the door handle. Peering down at him with a raptor's gaze, Angel looked like she was about to pounce. But then her features changed as a lightbulb moment flashed up inside her head.

'Might've dropped it in the back yard,' she said. 'I was out there this morning chucking pallets into the skip.'

Swatting one of the tables to one side, she barged past Victor and out the canteen.

'Cowards die many times before their death,' said Victor, flashing Chef a V-sign. He leaned against the wall to catch his breath. Forget about a global pandemic or war in the Ukraine. An encounter with the Angel of Death was enough to test the health of any person. As for the person who had stolen Angel's ring…Victor let out a nervous laugh. Never mind *Midget Mayhem*, it would be Monster Mayhem.

CHAPTER THREE

MAKING HIS WAY back downstairs, Victor spotted his department manager, Frank, on his mobile phone near to the Produce desk. Short, squat and sporting a monk's haircut and a pair of thick round glasses, he reminded Victor of the cartoon character Penfold. Usually a department manager would expect some kind of explanation as to why one of his staff was late. But Frank was not your normal manager.

'There she is,' he said, showing Victor a picture on his phone of a broken-down caravan. 'Nineteen Ninety-Seven Avondale Mayfly.'

'Sorry I'm late,' said Victor. 'MI5 stopped me outside my house to warn me of an incel plot to kidnap me and sell me to Andrew Tate.'

'I'm going to do her up when I retire,' said Frank, scrolling through some more photos of the caravan. 'Isn't she a beauty?'

'Yes, I'd just discovered that Hilary Clinton was about to sacrifice a reincarnated Shirley Temple and drink her blood with Elvis Presley.'

Frank took his glasses off and rubbed them on the front of his shirt. 'New aluminium shell, new inside wall panels, two settee berths with quilted upholstery...'

'But then Jeffrey Epstein grabbed me and flew me to Little St James Island on Robert Maxwell's private jet. Fortunately

I managed to escape. Thanks to David Ike. Say what you like about Dave, he certainly knows how to handle a jet ski.'

'Four point one eight interior – over thirteen feet in old money – kerbweight of eight seventy kilos, seven nine three-centimetre awning...She'll be a little cracker when she's finished.'

'I asked Ikey to give me a lift to work, but he had some shape-shifting alien reptiles to uncover at Buckingham Palace. God bless him. That's when MI5 warned me about the incel plot.' Victor glanced over at the pallets of fruit and veg outside the chiller. 'Malcolm not working the delivery?'

Frank looked up from his phone. 'What?'

'Malcolm working the delivery?'

'Malcolm?'

'Yes, Malcolm. You know - glasses, Aardman Animations smile, probably sporting a garishly coloured sweatband?'

'Isn't he on holiday?'

'He told me yesterday he would be in.'

'Are you sure?' said Frank, putting his mobile phone away.

'Unless he's forgotten he's off and come in.' Victor pointed at the rota pinned up above the Produce desk. 'Check the schedule.'

Frank glanced over at the rota with a look that reminded Victor of a man about to face a firing squad. His department manager then took a packet of cigarettes and a lighter out of the Produce desk drawer. 'I'll look later,' he said, shuffling off.'

'Sisyphus eat your heart out,' said Victor, taking the rota down from the wall. He ran his finger down the list of names.

M. LEGG 09.00 to 18.00.

Bingo!

After putting the rota into his pocket, Victor noticed his hands were shaking. The slug of whisky from before was beginning to wear off. Setting off in search of his friend, a list of priorities started to form in his head:

1. Borrow some money off Malcolm.
2. Buy some whisky.
3. Drink the whisky.
4. Relive Malcolm of *Midget Mayhem*.
5. Get Malcolm to work the delivery.
6. Drink more whisky.
7. Have an existential crisis.
8. Drink even more whisky.
9. Pass out (preferably at home).

II

VICTOR FOUND MALCOLM at the self-scans helping a customer. Despite beckoning his friend over, Malcolm continued to show the customer – an old woman with a walking stick and twinset – how to operate the self-scans.

'You take it like this…' said Malcolm, picking up a jar of Marmite from the old woman's basket.

'…yes…'

'…and do this…'

'…yes…'

'…and then this…'

'…yes…'

'…and then go like this…

'…yes…'

Despite the 'yes's' the old woman was too busy staring at Victor to take much notice of what Malcolm was saying.

'…and then you take the next one…'

'…yes…'

The old woman reached into her handbag for her glasses. Putting them on, she peered even closer at Victor.

'Perhaps you'd like to take a picture?' said Victor.

'I beg your pardon?' said the old woman.

'What's the matter, never seen breasts on a man before?'

'I'm sorry?'

Malcolm tried to get in between Victor and the old woman. 'Victor…'

'I'm sorry, too,' said Victor, pushing Malcolm out of the way. 'Sorry that nosy old bags can't keep their eyes to themselves.'

'Victor…'

'I'll go through the checklist for you if you like. One. No, I'm not transitioning, I was born like this. Two. Yes, they do give you backache. Three, no I don't get black eyes when I run. And four…'

'Victor…'

'And four, no I can't crack coconuts between them. Anything else you'd like to know?'

Malcolm whispered into Victor's ear. 'Your flies are undone.'

Victor looked down at his crotch. Not only were his flies undone, but a piece of his shirt was poking through them and drooping down like a flaccid penis. He pushed the flap of shirt back into his trousers and zipped up his fly. 'Spam,' he said, picking a tin up from the old woman's basket. 'A fine standby, I always find. Got us through the war. Well, not us, I'm too young, but you…I hope you managed to find everything you were looking for today. And that you will find time to go online and leave positive feedback about your shopping experience.' The old woman quickly packed up her shopping and hobbled off at top speed. 'Thank you for shopping at Whiting's.'

'Nice woman,' said Malcolm. 'Helps out at my local church.'

'Well, let's hope to God she understands the Christian concept of forgiveness,' said Victor, checking his flies again. 'Otherwise I'm going straight to the bowels of hell. Or

Personnel, which is the same thing.'

'It's this having breasts thing. It's given you a complex.'

'That and chapped nipples.'

'You should celebrate being different, not keep getting hung up about it.'

'Celebrate it? By doing what? The *Hokey Cokey. You put your left breast in/Your left breast out/In out, in out/You shake it all about...*I shake one of these puppies about and I'll be knocking folk over like nine pins.'

'You need to get over them.'

'I'd need a dozen sherpas to get over them.' He pulled Malcolm to one side. 'Anyway, I need to talk to you.'

'That's odd,' said Malcolm.

'What's odd?'

'I need to talk to you.'

'What about?'

Malcolm thought for a while. 'I've forgotten,' he said eventually. 'I think it had something to do with doctors. Or was it parrots?'

'You'll need a doctor when I tell you what's up.'

'You look like you need one yourself. Have you been running? You probably didn't keep your head level. It keeps you balanced and stops you from bouncing up and down.'

'Listen, Malcolm!' said Victor, bouncing up and down. 'We've got an emergency.'

'A pen emergency or a health and safety emergency?'

Victor ignored the question. The last thing he needed just then was to get Malcolm on to the subject of pens. Or health and safety. They'd be there all day. 'Remember that work's day out just after the Covid restrictions were lifted and we went to Blackpool?' he said.

'When you fell asleep on that park bench and got sunstroke?'

'I did not fall asleep. I was resting my eyes.'

'Kurtz said you passed out after drinking that bottle of whisky on the coach.'

Victor licked his lips at the mention of whisky. 'Never mind that now,' he said. 'Remember the old woman on the log flume who had her skirt tucked in her knickers?'

'I remember being sick after eating all that candy floss. I kept forgetting I'd had one and…'

'Nobody told her she had her skirt tucked into her knickers. They just let her walk around with her bloomers on show for everyone to see. And you said if anything like that ever happened to you…'

'I don't wear bloomers. Or a skirt.'

'If anything like that ever happened to you, you would want someone to tell you.'

'So?'

Victor took hold of Malcolm's arm. 'We've got a knickers-tucked-in-the-skirt situation.'

'David Starkey hasn't been in again, has he?' said Malcolm, looking around.

'No, David Starkey has not been in again,' said Victor, letting go of Malcolm's arm.

'Because the last time he came in, you soiled yourself. You were so excited when you saw him that you followed through.'

'I had food poisoning, Malcolm. I don't start filling my pants every time I see a TV historian doing their shopping. The situation I'm talking about is those films Kevin's given you.'

'Oh,' said Malcolm. 'What films?'

'You know, *those* films.' Victor tapped the side of his nose. 'The under-the-counter ones.'

'Under-the-counter?' said Malcolm, tapping the side of *his* nose.

Victor puffed out his cheeks. Time was pressing. There was still whisky to be bought. And drunk. 'Kevin gave you some films this morning,' he said.

'Did he? Oh, yes. Three on one DVD. Training films, I think.'

'Training films?'

'He said they'd make me sweat. One thing I don't understand though…'

'What?'

'Where does the counter come in?'

'Never mind about the counter, Malcolm. Put the counter right out of your mind. It's a red herring.'

'Oh, you mean the fish counter?'

Victor grabbed Malcolm by the shoulders and shook him. 'What have I told you about taking things off Kevin. The man's a walking Sodom and Gomorrah.'

'He said they would broaden my horizons.'

'Go on holiday if you want to broaden your horizons or learn a foreign language. It'll do more for you then *Midget Mayhem*.'

'*M-M-Midget M-M-Mayhem*?'

'You didn't read the titles of the films on the DVD cover? I've told you before, beware of geeks bearing gifts. Now, where did you put it?'

'Put what?'

'The DVD. We've got to get rid of it before they put your name on the Sex Offender's Register.'

Before Malcolm could answer, the electronic tones that always proceeded an announcement on the public address system rang out.

Ding-dong!

'Margaret to Checkouts, please.'

Malcolm lifted a Eureka finger. Turning away from Victor, he made his way over to the Customer Service desk.

'No, Malcolm!' said Victor, trying to pull Malcolm back.

But it was too late. Making his way behind the desk, Malcolm pressed the button on the Tannoy.

Ding-dong!

'Good morning, ladies and gentlemen,' said Malcolm into the mic. 'We have another fantastic offer for you here today at Whiting's. A thirty-six-inch, flat screen TV. It was three-nine-nine-nine-nine-nine-nine-nine-nine-nine-nine-nine…' There was a short pause while Malcolm tried to gather his thoughts. 'Was three-nine-nine-nine-nine-nine-nine-nine-nine-nine-nine-nine. Now two-nine-nine-nine-nine-nine-nine-nine-nine-nine-nine-nine.'

Some price, thought Victor, *some reduction*.

'On offer now. Also on offer…' Malcolm reached into his pocket, pulled something out and read the words written on the front. '*Back Door Boys, Fathers and Daughters, Midget M-M-Mayhem…*'

OVER ON THE Beers, Wines and Spirits aisle, Kurtz was watching an old man with a shopping trolley who he thought he recognised from the day before. The day the bottle of whisky went missing.

'You wanted to see dirty movies in my day you had to jump through bleeding hoops,' said the old man. 'Through bleeding hoops. Now you can buy 'em in supermarkets. You young 'uns don't know you're born.'

Kurtz watched the old man shuffle off.

'Fool me twice, shame on me,' he said, following the old man.

III

NEAR TO VICTOR a sea of stunned customers surrounded the Customer Service desk. He pushed his way through them until he reached Malcolm.

'Mystery solved, Doctor Watson,' he said, taking the DVD from Malcolm. Victor was just putting it in his pocket when Violet charged behind the desk and started jabbing a finger in his face.

'What do you think you're doing giving my fiancé rude films?' she said.

'F-F-Fiancé?' spluttered Victor.

'What have I told you, Malcolm, about going on the Tannoy?' It was Jackie, the Customer Service supervisor.

'Fiancé?' repeated Victor.

'Didn't you know?' said Violet, linking her arm through Malcolm's. 'Me and Malcolm are getting married.'

'Congratulations,' said Jackie. 'But Malcolm, don't do it again.'

She moved off to deal with the cacophony of complaints – and one or two enquiries – from the crowd of customers congregating around the desk. Leaving the future bride and groom and a set-to-implode Victor. Struggling to focus properly because of the shock, the latter gripped hold of the desk for support and said:

'When did this happen?'

'This morning,' said Violet. 'He proposed to me in the car park. It was so romantic.'

If Victor needed a drink *before* hearing the news about Malcolm and Violet's engagement, then *after* hearing about it he needed one – or two – or several – even more. Midget porn was one thing. But marriage! And to Violet!! Malcolm must've gotten his wires crossed again. It was the only explanation. No person would *willingly* allow themselves to become engaged to Violet.

'Is this true, Malcolm?' said Victor. But Malcolm was too busy staring into the far distance, lost in thought, to hear. 'Malcolm?'

'Of course it's true,' said Violet. 'He gave me a beautiful platinum engagement ring. You should see it. It's a one-carat diamond set in a rose.'

Angel's ring!

Victor made a noise that sounded like air escaping from a punctured balloon. Thinking his last moments on Earth had come, he felt his legs turn to jelly.

'I'm sorry, Victor,' said Violet, sounding anything but. 'I didn't want to tell you like this. Not after everything that happened between us in that broom cupboard.'

If Victor's life wasn't quite flashing before his eyes before, it was now. To have to relive the broom cupboard brouhaha was enough to finish off any man.

'Violet!'

It was Jackie. Unable to deal with all the customers still gathered round the desk, she waved Violet over for support.

'Coming!' said Violet. When she turned back round it was to find Victor sliding down the side of the desk.

'I think this is it,' he said, clutching his chest. '"Into the jaws of Death, into the mouth of Hell."'

'Oh, bless,' said Violet, 'you're devastated, aren't you? I did warn you. When you've got a face like mine you're not going to be on the shelf for very long. I just hope that in time we can be friends.'

Violet moved across to help Jackie.

Almost prostrate on the floor by now, Victor was blowing

like a stranded whale. *Malcolm engaged to Violet! Using Angel's ring!!* Devastated wasn't the word. It was more like the Eleventh Plague of Moses. With Victor's mother dead, Malcolm was all he'd got. If his friend disappeared down the aisle with Violet, he'd have no one left. No one to be part of his bubble, should the country go into lockdown again. And no one to buy him whisky. Victor shook his fists at the ceiling.

'For fuck's sake, let my people go!'

He pulled himself to his feet. Even the Ten Plagues of Moses – Eleven – were nothing compared to what was going to happen when Angel found out about the ring. When she did, Malcolm would be about as dead as a dead dodo on the doomed deck of the Marie Celeste. Even if Malcolm hid out in the Bermuda Triangle Angel would find him.

'If you were called Lazarus we might get away with it…'

Victor was thinking out loud. What he was forgetting was for the Lazarus thing to work you needed some kind of Jesus Christ turning-water-into-wine, walking-on-water figure. Victor's thaumaturgical talents began and ended with his ability to pass water into a wine glass from ten feet.

The important thing, Victor told himself, was not to panic.

'Maybe there are two engagement rings with roses?' he said, continuing his external monologue. 'Maybe they *all* come with roses? Maybe, maybe, maybe…'

It was no good. However much he tried to build an edifice of self-deception, reality soon knocked it down. Rather than fight it any longer, he lost complete control of his senses. Skipping wildly round the floral display, red-faced and tits a-flapping, he kept repeating the words, '*Ring-a-ring a roses, a-tishoo, a-tishoo, we all* fucking *fall down*' over and over. Only after catching his foot in one of the struts did the performance come to an end. Bellyflopping like an overstuffed goose, he landed amid a sea of safety-slip mats and buckets filled with water and flowers. Drenched in water and covered in a garland of lilies and violets, Victor was brought back to his senses. The only thing to do now was to start with the basics.

'Where did you get the ring from, Malcolm?' he said, picking himself up from the floor.

'What ring?' said Malcolm.

'The engagement ring you gave to Violet, dumbo!' said Victor.

Malcolm screwed up his face in concentration.

'Did you buy it?' said Victor, closing his eyes and crossing his fingers for luck.

'I don't think so.'

'Did someone give it you?'

Malcolm shook his head.

'It belonged to your old mum – that's it, isn't it? She left it to you on her deathbed and told you to give it to someone special?'

Victor knew that Malcolm's mother was still alive. But like any other drowning man, he was ready to grasp at any passing piece of driftwood Just to keep afloat.

'Mum's still alive,' confirmed Malcolm. 'At least she was this morning when she made me my packed lunch. Tuna sandwiches with extra mayo. She knows they're my favourite. Perhaps it was her way of saying goodbye. But I doubt it. Although she did say goodbye…'

'If your mother was alive this morning, Malcolm, I'm sure she's still going to be alive when you get home this evening.' Victor was about to add, 'If you get home', but held off at the last moment. 'If you didn't buy the ring and no one gave it to you and it doesn't belong to your mother, who isn't dead, then where did you get it?'

'Where?'

'Yes, where?

46

Malcolm paused for a moment. 'Out of a Christmas cracker?' he said eventually.

Victor winced. Even for a desperate man this was a straw too slight. 'They don't put diamond rings in Christmas crackers, Malcolm,' he said. 'They put plastic rings and silly hats and crap jokes in them. And then everybody has to sit around and pretend to enjoy themselves.'

'They're very clever though,' said Malcolm. 'The jokes I mean. What do you get if you cross a duck with Santa? A Christmas quacker!' He bent double and guffawed. 'But the little gifts are a health and safety disaster waiting to happen. All it took was for grandma to have one too many eggnogs and she nearly choked to death on her plastic whistle...'

'Malcolm...'

'Even at Christmas safety is a must.'

'Malcolm!'

Malcolm jumped.

'Okay, let's start from the beginning,' said Victor, picking off some of the petals that still stuck to him like coloured confetti.

'Beginning of what?' said Malcolm.

'The day.'

'Which day? They all have a beginning.'

'Let's start with this one, shall we? But if we don't hurry up it's going to be Monday by the time we finish.'

'I'm off on Mondays.'

'What time did you get in this morning?'

'Erm, let's see. It's Saturday...'

'Sunday.'

'Sunday? Oh, well why didn't you say? Sunday, I always start at...' Malcolm started counting on his fingers, '...three o'clock. No, that isn't right.'

'Where's your little black book?'

Malcolm rummaged through his pockets. 'I can't remember where I've put it,' he said.

'You got up this morning, had your breakfast…'

'Porridge with full fat milk,' said Malcolm, clicking his fingers. 'I always increase the dairy when I'm training. Helps up the calories.'

'Jogged to work?'

'That's right. Fifty-seven minutes. Nearly a PB. I listened to Luciano Mello's *'O Samba me Cantou'* on my MP3 player…'

'Then what?'

'I warmed down, went inside, went up to the canteen…I remember now, I was early. I was supposed to start work at…'

'Nine o'clock.' Having remembered it was in his possession, Victor had taken the rota from his pocket and consulted it.

'I got in at eight,' said Malcolm.

'So, then what did you do?'

'I went to sleep on an easy chair,' said Malcolm, clicking his fingers again.

'Yes?' said Victor, pleased that progress was finally being made. 'And then what happened?'

'I was woken up by aliens.'

'Help a lame dog over a style!' said Victor, holding his hands up to the ceiling in exasperation. 'Can we leave aliens to one side just for five minutes?'

'We're going to have to deal with them one day.'

'Not today, please.' Victor was desperate by this point. Desperate for a drink.

'There are four hundred billion galaxies in the observable universe…'

'Yes, and I had to end up in this one.'

'So did I. Lucky coincidence, eh?'

'You went to sleep in an easy chair, and then…?'

'And then someone came into the canteen.'

'Who?'

'I can't remember. Whoever it was started throwing things about for a bit. I was going to point out that it was against health and safety, but I was too busy hiding under one of the chairs. They laughed at me at the Colleague Council when I suggested hard hats and body armour to protect staff from difficult customers, but if I'd been wearing them...'

'Stick to the story!'

'What? Oh. Then everything went quiet. I waited under the chair until I heard the canteen door slam shut. Then I made my escape. I was just about to run out of the canteen and lock myself in a toilet cubicle when I spotted this pen on the floor.' Malcolm took a pen from his back pocket. 'It was under the table that has the staff suggestion box on it. It's a Parker IM red fountain pen with gold trim.'

'They always leave a pen near the box for members of staff to fill in the slips,' said Victor, trying to move things along. Pens were one of Malcolm's obsessions. The last thing the conversation needed then was a mention of them.

'They glide beautifully across the paper, the Parker IMs. Smooth as silk.'

'Malcolm! You found the pen...?'

'I found the pen, that's right. Then I saw something shining. At first, I thought it was the pen lid.'

'But it wasn't?'

'No, the lid was on the table next to the suggestion box.' Malcolm shook his head. 'When will people learn? With fountain pens you've got to keep the pen lid on at all times when you're not using it. Otherwise the ink dries out and the pen won't write smoothly. I remember once...'

'If it wasn't the pen lid, then what was it?'

'Hmmm?'

'The shiny thing on the floor. What was it – Frank's toupee? Sammy Davis Junior's glass eye?' The Koh-i-Noor diamond?'

Diamond. The word seemed to set something off in Malcolm's mind. 'Oh, it was a ring,' he said.

Although he was expecting it, Victor still looked like a man who had just been punched in the stomach. 'And that was the ring you gave to Violet?' he said.

'Was it? Oh, good. I'm glad she got it back.'

'There's just one problem.'

'What?'

'The ring doesn't belong to Violet.'

'Who does it belong to? Oh…'

A look of horror fell across Malcolm's face. It reminded Victor of the look he'd had on his own face when he was seven years old and he'd put his grandmother's glass eye in his mouth after his brother told him it was a gobstopper. It meant one thing. Malcolm had remembered who was in the canteen with him that morning. And who the owner of the ring was.

'That's right, Malcolm,' said Victor, placing a consoling hand on his pal's shoulder, 'it belongs to Angel.'

Malcolm stared out of the window and said in a quiet, flat voice, 'How far is it to Canada?'

'Not far enough, I'm afraid, Malc,' said Victor. 'You can't run away from this. No matter how much training you do, Angel will always catch up with you. The only thing we can do is get that ring back to her before she finds out you gave it to Violet. Are you listening to me, Malcolm?'

Victor gave Malcolm's arm a gentle tug.

'It's started to rain,' said Malcolm.

'Courage, Malc.' Victor put his arm around Malcolm's

shoulder. 'Come on. We've faced tougher odds than this before and come through.'

'Have we?' said Malcolm, his face brightening slightly.

'No. But if we stick together we will prevail. Who was it that said, "Together we can face any challenges as deep as the ocean and as high as the sky"?'

Tears of gratitude filled Malcolm's eyes as he shook Victor's hand. 'Thank you,' he said.

'First thing we need is a plan,' said Victor. 'Violet's probably put the ring in her locker.'

'Or her car.'

'Even if it's in her car, we're still going to need to get into her locker to get her car keys.'

'How do we get into her locker?'

'We'll have to steal the master key from Personnel…'

'Human Resources.'

'Personnel! There's nobody in there on Sundays. After that, one of us will have to infiltrate the ladies' changing room.'

Malcolm puffed out his cheeks. 'The ladies' changing room…'

Victor could read Malcolm's thoughts. Ten years he'd worked at Whiting's, and not once had he so much as stepped a single step into the ladies' changing room. It would be like entering another world. 'There's just one problem,' he said, pacing up and down.

'All the toilet seats will be down?'

'We don't know which number locker it is.'

Malcolm joined Victor in his pacing up and down. 'I know,' he said, coming to a halt, 'why don't we ask her? "Excuse me, Violet, which number locker is yours?"'

Victor also came to a halt. 'I think we're going to have to be a bit more subtle than that, Malcolm.'

'"Excuse me, Violet, which locker numbers *aren't* yours?"'

Victor put a fingertip on each temple. 'I'll think of something so long as I'm not disturbed.'

'Excuse me.'

When Victor turned it was to find himself looking at a middle-aged woman with sharp eyes and an even sharper face. 'Yes?' he said.

'Can you tell me where the Brussel sprouts are please,' said the woman.

'Up past the carrots and then left at the cauliflowers,' said Victor, turning his back on the woman.

'Would you mind escorting me?'

'Escorting you?' said Victor, turning back around. 'This is a supermarket, madam, not a bordello.'

'I really must insist…Victor,' said the woman, looking closely at Victor's name badge.

'Sorry,' said Victor, 'I can't escort you. We have a staff emergency.'

'Emergency? What kind of emergency?'

Victor pointed at Malcolm. 'This man has just got engaged.'

The woman looked Malcolm up and down. 'That's not an emergency.'

'You haven't seen who to,' said Victor. 'Now if you'll excuse us…'

The woman stormed off with a 'Well, really!'

'Bloody cheek,' said Victor. 'Right,' he said, rubbing his hands together, 'give us a tenner.'

'How's that going to help?' said Malcolm.

'We're stuck behind the eight ball, kiddo,' said Victor in his best James Cagney impersonation. 'If I'm gonna find out Big V's locker number I may need to grease a few palms.'

'Grease a few palms?' said Malcolm, taking his wallet out of his pocket and handing Victor a crisp, new ten-pound note.

'That's right,' said Victor, pocketing the money. 'After which, I will infiltrate the ladies' changing room.'

CHAPTER FOUR

DEREK TOOK HIS Ray-Bans from the top drawer of his desk and put them on. He'd gone with the Aviator's because he'd read in the December issue of *Rodeo Magazine* that they were the easiest to see through when lassoing cattle. Of course, that was for cowhands in the American Midwest who worked outdoors. Not for store managers in the north of England who worked indoors in an office with no windows. But to Derek it made perfect sense. As he was always telling them down at the managers' conference in Milton Keynes, 'As a branch manager you've got an image to project.' The one he'd chosen combined the coolness of Steve McQueen with the ruggedness of John Wayne. And when they said he was too old, too paunchy, too Home Counties, and – standing only five feet five in Cuban heels – too short? Well, then he would rest his elbows back on the bar, spit a gob of tobacco into the nearest wastepaper basket, and give it to them straight.

'Retail is all about presentation, partner,' he would say. 'So, either saddle on up, or mosey on outta here.'

Derek put a toothpick in his mouth. Twenty years of retail had taught him all about presentation. Taught him a few other things, too. The first rule is that there are no rules. That it's a jungle out there. That only the fittest survive.

Survive! Shoot! That was for losers. Reaching the top was

all that mattered. And you only did that by hitting your targets. Cost of living crisis, or no cost of living crisis.

He put his feet on the desk and his arms behind his head. Pinned up on the wall opposite were tables of graphs and columns of figures. With his Ray-Bans on and the light off he couldn't read what was on them. But then he didn't have to. He already knew them off by heart. Right down to the last decimal point.

Best on the region.

Third year running. Even through the plague years of coronavirus-19 he'd managed to keep his end up. Despite the Chinese concocting some virus in their laboratories to get their revenge for all the railway-building, rice-frying and dry-cleaning they'd been forced to do over the years.

He'd heard all the bitching down at Milton Keynes. 'You're only best on the region because there's no real competition in Lunestone'. 'Shoot,' he would tell them in reply, 'Lunestone's nothing more than a dusty cow town at the back end of nowhere. One church, one doctor's surgery, one (decent) supermarket, and a one-way road that leads to no place. Like to see you rack up those kinda numbers in a dead-end town like that.' And when they asked him how he did it, he'd tip back his cowboy hat, down his whisky in one, then give it to them with both barrels. 'It's all about leadership,' he'd say. 'Jesus H. Christ, everyone knows that. Let a horse jump a fence when you're loose in the saddle and all you're gonna get is a mouthful of grass. Knowing when to crack the whip. That's what counts.'

There were always the sceptics, of course The nay-sayers. The Fancy Dans. The six footers. That's when he would take a sheet with his like-for-like sales on and shove it under their noses. Double-digit year on year. As for this financial year…

'BANG!' Derek used his fingers to fire an imaginary pistol.

He'd be giving them both barrels at this year's conference. 'BANG! BANG!' He'd turn that Royal Hotel in Milton Keyes into the Gunfight at the OK Corral.

His thoughts turned to the little chocolates they left on your pillow at the Royal Hotel. That's what a stay at the Royal was all about. That and the free breakfasts. A mess of eggs followed by cinnamon rolls.

He picked up an imaginary machine gun. 'RATATATATATATATATATAT!!!!' That was his plan. Eat the pillow chocolate, down the free breakfast, then turn the conference hall into a war zone. He'd hit them with so many figures it'd be like the Alamo. Except this time, with the numbers on his side, it'd be Texans: one, Mexican Managers: zilch.

There was a knock at the door.

'Yeahhh?' said Derek in an American drawl.

The door opened and in came Kurtz. 'Sorry to bother you, boss,' he said, 'but I've got a guy here who I caught pulling moves on the booze aisle.'

'A shoplifter, eh?' Derek took the toothpick out of his mouth. He was just in the mood to dole out some frontier justice.

'Get in there, you.' Kurtz pushed the old man into the office.

'I can't see a bleedin' thing!' said the old man, stumbling over a chair.

Derek switched on the desk lamp.

'Who the bleedin' hell are you?' said the old man, as Kurtz pushed him down into the chair.

'I'm your worst nightmare,' said Derek. He sat on the edge of the desk and shone the lamp into the old man's eyes. 'Okay, pops, tell us where you stashed the lolly and we'll let you outta here.'

'I didn't come in for any bleedin' lollies,' said the old man, covering his face with his arm.

'Hear that, Kurtz? He didn't come in for any bleedin' lollies.'

'It's a missing bottle of whisky I've bought him up for, boss,' said Kurtz, 'not lollies.'

'I can't eat lollies with my teeth,' said the old man.

Kurtz took a notebook and pen from his pocket. 'What time did the lollies go missing, boss?' he said.

Behind the Ray-Bans Derek's eyes tightened. Kurtz was supposed to be his deputy. Surely he knew what 'lolly' meant. As for the old man…Derek knew he was stonewalling. Acting dumb. Playing for time. If that's how the son-of-a-bitch wanted to play it, that's how they'd play it. Shoot! He was prepared to sit in the saddle all day if it meant catching his man. He bent down and put his face an inch away from the old man's. 'Where's the sauce, pops?' he hissed.

'What sauce?'

'The beef jerky? The overland trout? The boggy top?'

'Our Maureen only sent me out for a packet of Jaffa Cakes and half a dozen slices of honey roast ham. I don't know nothing about bleedin' overland trout. Or boggy tops.'

Derek looked over at Kurtz. 'Time to play bad cop,' he said.

'Right, boss.' Kurtz hesitated. 'What does that mean, boss?'

'Goddam it!' Derek lifted his Ray-Bans and rubbed his eyes. Twelve shot dead back in South Africa for resisting arrest, if anyone should know about playing bad cop it was Kurtz. 'Imagine you're back in the township.'

Kurtz frowned. 'You mean you want me to shoot him in the head with a rubber bullet, throw him in prison and let him bleed to death?'

The old man began wailing. 'No! No! Please! I'll tell you everything. Don't shoot me! When I was seven I stole half a crown from the collection box at Sunday school. I once took some scrap metal from work without asking the foreman. And…and…when I broke my lawnmower by running over a hedgehog I claimed it on the insurance. That's everything! I swear! I don't know who's got your lollies. Or your boggy tops. Just don't kill me! Please…!

Derek broke out into a satisfied smirk. However tough they were – and this leathery son-of-a-bitch was a tough one – they always broke in the end. 'By rights I should have you strung up,' he said. He looked over at Kurtz again. 'Got twelve feet of good, stout rope and some gallows about your person, deputy?'

'Not on me, boss,' said Kurtz, checking his pockets.

'Looks like it's your lucky day, mister,' said Derek to the old man.

'The old man stopped sobbing. 'You mean you're not going to shoot me with a rubber bullet?' he said. 'Or throw me into prison and let me bleed to death?'

'That's right, partner.' Derek took off his Ray-Bans. 'But if I ever see you round these parts again…'

'Thank you, thank you,' said the old man, kissing Derek's hand. Derek pulled it away and glanced over at Kurtz.

'Get this lily-livered trash outta here.'

'Right, boss. And if I hear anything about those lollies, I'll let you know.'

Kurtz dragged the old man out of the office. Alone once more, Derek opened his desk drawer and took out a five-pointed silver star.

'That's how we do things round these parts,' he said to himself as he pinned the star to the lapel of his jacket. Etched on the star was a single word:

SHERIFF.

II

VICTOR COVERED THE quarter bottle of whisky with his sleeve. If he was going to infiltrate the ladies' changing rooms, he first needed to top up with the old Dutch courage.

As he moved forward one in the self-scan queue his thoughts turned to the small glass of sherry he used to share with his mother before they went to bed. Those started when he was about eleven. To keep the cold away, his mother told him, as they sat in front of a roaring coal fire. The amount increased over the years until he and his mother were drinking a full bottle between them. Then a full bottle each. Since her death he'd switched to whisky. Stronger than sherry, there was more kilowatt to the mouthful. During lockdown, the number of bottles had increased to two. Not because Victor had grown more depressed about having to stay home and not see anyone. As a food retail worker he had still had to attend work. And he had still had to see everyone. *That's* what he had found depressing.

'Busy already,' he said to the self-scan supervisor. Getting nothing back in return but a grunt, Victor took a barcode for *Softsuds* washing powder from his pocket. It was this he would scan when he got to the checkout. That way the supervisor wouldn't have to authorise the sale. Drinking on the job was a sackable offense. Especially for someone like Victor, who had form in this area, and who was already on a final written warning.

He completed the transaction successfully using the *Softsuds* barcode and Malcolm's tenner.

'Cheers, mum,' he said, lifting his head heavenward.

'Victor.'

'I wasn't doing anything wrong,' said Victor, shoving the

bottle of whisky into his pocket. When he turned around it was to find himself face-to-face with a grey-haired man in a brown suit. 'Oh, hello, Mr Macintyre.'

'Some things don't change,' said Mr Macintyre, chuckling.

Victor placed a hand over the pocket with the whisky in. 'I don't know what you mean,' he said.

'It's what you always used to say when you were up to no good. That "I wasn't doing anything wrong". Every time I heard that I always used to think, "Hello, what's the little beggar been up to this time?"'

'I haven't been up to anything.'

'We're not back at school, Victor, you don't have to explain yourself to me anymore. Although some of your explanations were certainly very creative. What was that one about not bringing your homework in because of the millennium bug…?'

'The Y2K Problem. The electronic equivalent to El Niño, I believe it was referred to by some top officials at the Pentagon. Certainly a big enough problem to prevent a sixteen-year-old from completing his history homework.'

'It was Nineteen Ninety-Eight, Victor. You were two years too early.'

'And what was my reward for such foresight? A mark of nought and a Saturday detention. You wouldn't have treated Nostradamus like that.'

'Nostradamus only predicted the death of Princess Diana. You claimed you were actually *there*, remember? Which was why you couldn't come into school that Monday.'

'Blame the French Brigade Criminelle. I told them I had history periods one and two. But by then I'd been tagged as an eye-witness.'

A chuckling Mr Macintyre put some bananas into his basket. 'So, you're still here, then?'

'Oh, yes. The work-life balance is such that it allows me to focus almost full-time on my writing.'

'Ah, yes, the great work. How's it progressing?'

'*Education and Psychopathy: One Student's Fight Against Pedagogical Brutality*? It was suppressed by the authorities. Too revolutionary. They were worried the *Grange Hill* contingent would storm the Houses of Parliament. I'm now working on a sequel to Bertrand Russell's *History of Western Philosophy*.'

'You certainly never lacked ambition,' said Mr Macintyre, putting a cantaloupe melon into his basket. 'Just application.'

'"The roots of education are bitter, but the fruit"' – Victor pointed at the melon in Mr Macintyre's basket – '"the fruit is sweet". And buy-one-get-one-free.'

As he turned his back Victor heard in his head Mr Macintyre say, 'When it comes to melons, you should know', followed by a long chuckle. But when he looked over his shoulder Mr Macintyre was quietly sorting through the loose new potatoes. The paranoia and anxiety was starting to seep in. And the only thing that would wash them away was the bottle of whisky in his pocket. The sooner he became acquainted with it the better.

III

TO TAKE HIS mind off Violet and Malcolm's impending nuptials, Kurtz decided to go hunting for more shoplifters. The capture of the old man earlier had whetted the appetite. But he was just some starter-pack, scaredy-cat senior. The cost of living crisis had brought in his kind by the bushel-load. But all they got was a slap on the wrist and a verbal warning. What Kurtz really wanted was to grab one of the pros. The ones with the tinfoil-lined bags and false pregnant bellies. They were a catch worth landing. Especially if they tried to wriggle away. Then gratuitous violence was permitted. Kurtz licked his lips. Angel aside, nobody knew gratuitous violence better than him.

Like a shark with the scent of blood in his nostrils, Kurtz's whole being was set to seek-out-and-destroy mode. His eyes bulged, his nose flared, his mouth salivated. A former member of the paramilitary *Afrikaner Weerstandsbeweging* – the *AWB* – he marched with military precision through the general merchandise department. Chest out and long arms tucked neatly by his side, he counted quietly to himself. '*Een, twee, drie*, four, *een, twee, drie*, four…' He left-turned at the Food-to-Go counter. '*Een, twee, drie*, four, *een, twee, drie*, f…!' He came to an abrupt halt. Flipping the handle on one of the fire exit doors was a child of about ten. Kurtz's eyes narrowed. He had a simple rule when it came to children. That they should be beaten and not heard. That's how he'd been brought up by his father on the farm in Ventersdorp. Beaten every day with a paddle made from Chamfuta wood. Not that it did him any harm.

Kurtz folded his arms and glared at the child. But instead of running off the child glared back and carried on flipping the handle.

'Keep touching that handle, sonny, and I'll touch you. Right across the head.'

'Paedo,' said the child, flipping the handle even faster.

'What did you call me?' said Kurtz, turning red with anger.

'Oliver!' It was the child's mum. 'Come on, darling, you have your creative dancing class at one.'

Creative dancing! Kurtz didn't know whether to laugh or cry.

'Coming,' said the child. After flipping the handle a few more times, he ran off. Kurtz went over to the fire door to make sure the seal on the handle was still intact.

'Paedo!'

By the time Kurtz spun around the child was gone. Fuming with anger, he resumed his patrolling. As he did his thoughts turned to Violet and Malcolm's engagement. And how he was going to split it up. One problem was Malcolm's faulty memory. If Kurtz took Malcolm to one side and had a quiet word along the lines of, 'Break off your engagement to Violet or I'll break off your head', then Malcolm would forget in five minutes that a quiet-wording had ever been had.

'*Een, twee, drie*, four, *een, twee, drie*, four…'

Kurtz marched along the back wall towards the bakery. The only solution was to get Victor to split up the happy couple. Victor and Malcolm were *bra's, bru's*, real bum *chommies*. The last thing Victor would want was Malcolm disappearing up the aisle with Violet. Malcolm was Victor's meal ticket. Or, more accurately, bar tab. It would mean no more borrowed tenners. No more quarter bottles of whisky. *Ja*, that was the answer, have a quiet-wording with Victor along the lines of, 'Get Malcolm to break off his engagement to Violet or I'll break his *and* your head off'. That would work better. Especially if beforehand he had caught Victor up to no good, say, stealing a bottle of whisky off the shop floor, or finding a stolen bottle of whisky in Victor's locker…

Cheered up by his plan, Kurtz's thoughts turned to how, when he was having a bad day back home in South Africa, he'd put a prisoner in a small holding cell and throw in a cannister of tear gas. He'd then watch through the spyhole in the door as the prisoner did a funny kind of spasmodic dance as the tear gas took hold.

Moving over to the bakery, Kurtz fantasised about throwing a cannister of tear gas into Oliver's creative dancing class. Boy, would that *boykie* breakdance then!

Chuckling to himself, Kurtz pushed open the door to the bakery. His jolly mood evaporated the moment he stepped through it. For standing before him, covered in cream and flour, and brandishing half a baguette with wild-eyed derangement, was Angel. Around her was an Eton mess of smashed strawberry tarts, mangled meringues, and broken cream cakes. Behind her, whole racks of unbaked bread lay overturned, their contents now nothing more than a sticky mess of misshapen goo. Breathing heavily, Angel growled at Kurtz with teeth bared.

Kurtz took a step back. A seasoned big game hunter, he'd faced everything in his time. A lioness protecting her cubs. Packs of marauding buffalo. Charging rhinoceroses. Pussycats compared to an angry Angel. Thinking for the moment he was back on the veldt, Kurtz reached instinctively for his gun. All he found was his bunch of keys. He licked his lips nervously. With an elephant gun he might've stood a chance. But with a set of keys...

'What's been going on here, then, *bokkie*?' he said, keeping one eye on the baguette.

There was a tense pause as Angel mulled over Kurtz's words. Wiping some cream from her eyes, she lowered the baguette and said, 'Lost me ring, haven't I?'

'What ring's that, then, *bokkie*?' said Kurtz, keeping up the soft talk.

'My engagement ring.'

'Engagement ring?'

'Yeah, engagement ring. Don't they have them in Venezuela?'

'Sure, *bokkie*, sure.' Kurtz ran a finger across his moustache. Engagement ring? It was the second time that morning he'd had a conversation about one. 'I didn't know you were engaged, *bokkie*. Congratulations.'

'I'm not,' said Angel, twisting the baguette like she was wringing a neck. 'I carry it in case I meet Mr Right.'

'Very sensible,' said Kurtz, trying – and failing – to imagine who Angel's Mr Right might possibly be. 'Tell me what it looks like and I'll keep an eye out for it.'

'It's platinum with a big stone in a rose.'

'A rose you say? Bet it looked a picture on your finger, *bokkie*?'

'It did. And if somebody's pinched it...' Angel started breaking the baguette into pieces. '...I'll tear them to bits.'

'Sure, *bokkie*, sure,' said Kurtz, edging his way towards the door. 'If I hear anything I'll let you know.'

He slowly backed out onto the shop floor. Having escaped from the jaws of death his policeman's mind went into overdrive. Violet had already told him that Malcolm had given her an engagement ring. And now Angel has lost one. A coincidence? Kurtz didn't believe in coincidences. What he did believe in was the little man in his stomach. Like indigestion, Jacob always started grumbling when things weren't right. And right then 'he' was bellyaching like some irate customer who had just been overcharged at the checkouts.

'Don't worry, Jacob,' said Kurtz, placing a protective hand on his gurgling gut, 'I'll look into it.'

IV

AFTER DRINKING THE quarter bottle of whisky in the men's changing room, Victor made his way downstairs. Red of cheek, bloodshot of eye, his legs wobbled like jellied eels on a waterbed. On his top lip he wore a superior smirk. In no fit state to retrieve engagement rings or dispose of DVDs, he lurched down the corridor like an aging gunslinger. As he did, his thoughts turned to an encounter he'd had recently with a new member of staff – Tarquin Travers-Booth – a student who had started at Whiting's over the Xmas vacation. When Victor had asked him what he was studying, Tarquin had replied, 'Have you ever heard of a subject called philosophy?'

To be condescended to by some snotty-nosed know-nothing who no doubt passed ideas he'd read in some book off as his own, and thought that René Descartes was the wing-back for Paris Saint-Germain…

Victor slapped the wall. '"Ever heard of a subject called philosophy?"' he said, the smirk on his top lip growing smirkier. 'Phi-los-o-phy. Philo – love – osophy – of knowledge. Love of knowledge.'

He gripped hold of the dado rail to stop himself from falling over. The next time he saw Tarquin, he would ask him, 'Ever heard of a subject called love of knowledge? Hmmm? No? Well, it's philo – o – theosophy…philately – stick that up your categorical imperative!'

Leaning against the wall, he nodded off for a few seconds. Coming to with an abrupt start, he counted himself in – 'One, two, three' – and broke into song. *'I'd like to get you on a slow boat to China…Get you and keep you in my arms ever more/ Leave all your lovers weeping on…*on a subject called love of knowledge…'

He stopped in front of the staff noticeboard. Running a drunken, myopic, eye over it, he fixed on a sheet of paper advertising a poetry performance evening that was scheduled to take place next week. Those wishing to partake were invited to write their names in the boxes on the sheet. Steadying himself by holding on to both sides of the noticeboard, Victor looked down the list of names. At the top was written T.

TRAVERS-BOOTH. The next sheet was for a reading group. Headed by T. TRAVERS-BOOTH. An amateur dramatics' group. T. TRAVERS-BOOTH. Five-a-side football. T. TRAVERS-BOOTH. Choir singing. T. TRAVERS-BOOTH. Creative writing. T. TRAVERS-BOOTH. 'The Origins of the Ukraine-Russia War: a short lecture by T. TRAVERS-BOOTH'.

'Imposter!' said Victor, spinning around and addressing himself to an imaginary audience. 'Charlatan! Mountebank! Plagiarist! Ladies and gentlemen, *I* am a writer.' He bowed theatrically. '*A New History of Western Philosophy*, Chapter One, Aristotle…oof!'

Feeling like he'd been hit by a horse, Victor fell to the floor. Winded and dazed, all he could see was a huge set of yellow teeth chomping down at him.

So, it was a horse!

'Watch yourself!'

A talking horse!

The situation needed careful handling.

'I am a writer,' said Victor, by way of introduction. 'I am a writer with a love of philosophy, I mean, knowledge. Have you heard of it? Knowledge I mean, not philosophy. *Everyone's* heard of philosophy. Kant…'

'No need to be like that,' said the horse.

'Immanuel Kant has heard of philosophy, Bertrand Russell's heard of philosophy, I've heard of philosophy, I bet even fucking horses have heard of philosophy. Right?'

'I don't know about that,' said the horse, 'but whatever you do, don't go downstairs. They're about to start the daily briefing.'

Victor scratched his beard. What would a horse know about the daily briefing? His head having cleared a little, he squinted up again at the huge set of yellow teeth. Attached to them was a face that looked a lot like Kevin's. What a horse was doing with a face like Kevin's Victor couldn't work out. He couldn't work out what Kevin was doing with a face like Kevin's, but that was a problem for another day. Right then he had a horse to talk to.

'You know, you look exactly like someone I work with,' he said. 'Kevin's his name. Short, pasty fellow. Likes films with midgets.'

'I *am* Kevin,' said Kevin. 'Actually, I prefer films with lesbians, but midgets – lesbian or otherwise – will do.'

The horse was right. It *was* Kevin. Victor picked himself up from the floor. 'What are you doing charging about the place like the offspring of Poseidon and Demeter?' he said.

'It's the daily briefing,' said Kevin. 'I'm going to hide in the bogs until it's over. If you had any sense, you'd hide too.'

Victor watched Kevin disappear into the men's changing rooms.

The daily briefing?

An opportunity for every man, woman and cheese-slicer to have their say.

Here was a chance for Victor to stake his claim. To show the T. Travers-Booths of this world that he was a philosopher to be reckoned with. Dusting himself down, he staggered forward a few feet, then with a rousing shout of 'No Plan B!', half-fell down the stairs.

BY THE TIME he'd got to the bottom of the stairs, Victor's mind was made up. He would wait until the end of the briefing and then give it to them straight. A personal statement of his intellectual and artistic credentials. Never again would anyone ask him if he'd ever heard of a subject called philosophy.

Flinging open the door at the bottom of the stairs, he walked into the warehouse like a man with two wooden legs. By the baler, other members of staff had already started to gather. Among them was Kurtz, who was stood near the front patting his stomach; Tarquin Travers-Booth, who was sporting a Parisian Left Bank goatee beard and reading Baudelaire's *Les Fleurs du mal*; and a beaming Malcolm.

'Over here, Victor,' said Malcolm, waving his friend across.

Conscious of Kurtz watching him with a suspicious eye, Victor straight-legged it over.

'Hope it's going to be a good one,' said Malcolm. He put both of his arms in the air and started swaying. *'We are the champions, my friends"* – come on everybody! – *and we'll keep on fighting 'til the end –* '

Instead of joining in, the rest of the staff either gazed at their feet or talked quietly among themselves. The more enterprising found places at the back where they could fall asleep or play on their mobile phones without being seen.

While Malcolm switched from Queen to D:Ream's *Things Can Only Get Better*, Victor, thinking his moment had come, tried to gather his thoughts. But his mind was clouded by the alcohol swirling around his system, and by Kurtz staring at him with a piercing, policeman's, eye. As a consequence, his words came out a little mangled.

'Friends, countrymen and ears, lend me your Romans…' Like Brutus outside the Theatre of Pompey, he decided to have a second stab. 'Romans, countrymen and ears, lend me your friends…' Annoyed at himself for not getting his words out properly and by the people around him whispering and coughing, he let rip with a loud, 'SSShhh!' Coinciding with the arrival of Derek and Frank, the whispering and coughing subsided. Victor tried to push home his advantage.

'Friends, Romans and country – '

'This is a mighty fine posse you've rounded up here, deputy,' said Derek.

Imagining that Derek was speaking to him, Victor spun around. 'I am not a deputy,' he said, 'I'm a philosopher.'

Derek put his arm around Frank's shoulders. 'Instead of ol' Sherriff Braithwaite running the show today, I'm gonna hand you over to Deputy Frank Sherwood. Give 'em both barrels, deputy. Yee-hah!'

'Yee-hah!' said Malcolm, waving an imaginary lasso.

The only other participants in the hoedown were Violet, who shouted 'Yee-hah!' and spun the charity collection tin around her head, and Baz, who shouted 'Get fucking in there!' while banging the handle of his broom on the concrete floor. Everyone else carried on looking at their shoes, playing on their mobile phones, or – in Tarquin Travers-Booth's case – reading decadent Nineteenth Century French poetry.

Looking like a man whose caravan has just uncoupled on the motorway, Deputy Frank Sherwood stepped forward clutching a piece of paper, and in an out-of-gear-Vauxhall-Astra monotone said, 'Total sales last week: eight hundred and forty-seven thousand five hundred and forty-two pounds…'

'Yee-hah!' said Malcolm and Violet together, backed up by Baz's broom handle banging.

'That's a one point one percent increase compared to last year,' said Frank.

The Broom Handle trio broke into song once more, with Malcolm adding a 'Ride 'em, cowboy!' for good luck.

'Breaking down the figures by department. Grocery: one hundred and four thousand and sixty-nine pounds, a nought point nine percent increase. Fresh: one hundred and twelve thousand four hundred and thirty-seven pounds, a one point eight percent increase…'

By the time he'd finished even the Broom Handle Trio had hung up their spurs. And except for Tarquin Travers-Booth muttering in French as he read his Baudelaire, there was a deathly silence. One that Victor was about to fill. Until Frank started up again.

'As some of you know, I'm retiring in twelve months' time…'

'Number one on the region for the third year running!' said Derek. 'And that includes the plague years, the cost of living crisis, *and* Environmental Health finding that cannabis in the bread mix. Think you cowboys and cowgirls should give yourself one hell of a round of applause. Come on, now, give it up like a Balmorhea barn dance.'

Except for Malcolm and Violet, who whooped and clapped and shouted 'Yee-hah!', the noise from the rest of the staff reminded Victor of a slowly dripping tap. Thankfully, he was about to hit them with a piece of oratory of such power and eloquence, they'd be clapping until Christmas.

'Mister Chairman,' he said, raising a finger.

But once more he was thwarted, again by Derek. 'Now for the serious stuff,' his store manager said. Derek waved a piece of paper in the air. 'The latest directive from the boys over at head office. They now want us to work smarter and not harder. That's smarter *not* harder.' He tore the piece of paper in half. 'Horseshit! Bull! Balderdash! I see a single one of you working smarter and not harder and I'll cut you off at the knees and feed you to the hogs. Last thing we want round these parts is folk working smarter and not harder. Might go down some with the liberal elite over in Milton Keynes. But here in Lunestone it don't add up to a hill of beans. *Harder* not smarter. That's how we stay number one on the region.' Violet bent down to whisper in Derek's ar. 'Oh, yeah,' he said, 'don't forget the charity gala tonight. See Violet if you don't have a ticket. It's for…' Derek looked up at Violet. 'What's it for again?'

Violet glanced at the charity tin. The eyeliner had smudged, making it impossible to read the words. 'Oh, it's for a good cause,' she said.

'You can't say fairer than that,' said Derek.

Violet rattled the tin. 'I've already collected thirty pounds,' she said.

'Yee-hah!' said Malcolm, as Baz banged his broom handle on the floor.

'Let's hope it doesn't go missing like it did last year,' said Violet. All eyes turned to Victor.

'Okay, partners,' said Derek, clapping his hands together. 'Any questions?'

'Here, Mister Speaker,' said Victor, lifting a hand. He paused for a moment to collect his thoughts. 'Mister Speaker,' he said again. 'As someone once said, some time or another – I forget who and when, but I know it was someone and he definitely said it, some time. Or another.'

There was another pause as Victor cast a drunken eye over his audience. Had he not been so sozzled he might've noticed their bored and confused expressions. But with a quarter of a bottle of whisky sloshing around inside him, all he could see was a sea of captivated faces. Even Tarquin Travers-Booth was listening. *That's* how well it was going! The only thing to do now was to continue.

'We all know there are known knowns. That is, there are things out there we all know we don't know, I mean know. Then of course there are unknown unknowns, that is to say there are things we don't know, I mean do know, we don't know…or do I mean we do know…?'

To help him regain his thread, Victor rummaged in his pockets in a desperate attempt to find it again.

'What's that doing in here?' he said, pulling out a DVD. '*Midget Mayhem…*?' Victor looked to the heavens for inspiration. 'Mayhem! Ah,' he said, stroking one of his breasts, 'but do you know there are also unknown unknowns…? That is, there are things we do not even know we don't know. Well, I know this. However many known knowns there are, however many unknown knowns or unknown unknowns, I know one thing.' He wagged at finger in the direction of Tarquin Travers-Booth. '*I* have heard of a subject called philoso – philo – theosophy. If anything is known, known known, that is. That is.'

Victor performed a small bow.

'Three cheers for Whiting's Supermarket!' said Malcolm. 'Hip hip!'

'Hooray,' said those few members of staff who bothered to remain.

'Hip hip!'

'Hooray,' said even fewer voices.

'Hip hip!'

'Hooray,' said the solitary voice of Violet. She moved closer to where Malcolm was standing. 'Hip hip.'

'That's four,' said Malcolm.

'An extra one for my baby,' said Violet, gazing lovingly into Malcolm's eyes.

'Oh, hooray,' said Malcolm, patting Violet's stomach like he was patting a child's head. Violet kissed him on the cheek and skipped off. 'She's expecting a baby,' he said to Victor and Kurtz, the only other members of staff remaining. 'I wonder who the father is?'

'Donald Rumsfeld,' said Victor, 'that's who it was.'

'Donald Rumsfeld?' said Malcolm. 'Is that him from the cigarette kiosk?'

But for Victor the moment had come. Three cheers for his oration. And in front of Tarquin Travers-Booth. Overflowing with a swaggering self-confidence he was ready for anything. Including infiltrating the ladies' changing room. Pushing Malcolm out of the way with a slurred 'No Plan B!', he disappeared up the stairs, leaving Malcolm and Kurtz alone.

'Congratulations,' said Kurtz, handing Malcolm a hirsute hand.

'Thank you,' said Malcolm, shaking it. 'Thirty-two pounds in sponsorship is a lot of money.'

'So, tomorrow's the big day, eh?' said Kurtz, keeping a firm grip on Malcolm's hand.

'I thought the big day was next Wednesday?' said Malcolm. 'Weather permitting.'

'I think you'll find it's tomorrow, *boykie*.' Kurtz leaned in closer to Malcolm's ear. 'Health permitting.'

'Well, thanks for reminding me,' said Malcolm, shaking the hand that still had hold of his. 'The Lunestone Running Club said it was next Wed – '

'You're a lucky man.'

Malcolm nodded his head. 'Real lucky. If you hadn't told me it was tomorrow and not next Wednesday I'd be like the groom waiting at the altar at that start line.'

'Violet's a real *bokkie*.'

'Is she, is she.'

'Nice ring?'

'Nice eyes, too.'

'Where did you get it?'

'Hmmm?'

'The ring?' Kurtz pulled Malcolm closer to him. 'Where did you get it?'

Malcolm tugged his hand free so he could concentrate better. Hadn't Victor asked him about a ring earlier?

'Malcolm?' said Kurtz.

'Yes, Victor?' said Malcolm, confusing the two conversations.

'Victor? You got the ring from Victor?'

'Oh, right,' said Malcolm, breathing a sigh of relief. 'I wondered where it came from.'

'I *bladdy* knew it,' said Kurtz, rubbing his stomach.

'Oh, good,' said Malcolm, beaming. 'Yes, he gave it me this morning and told me to give it to, to, to…'

'Violet?'

'Was it, was it.'

'So, it was him who put you up to this?' Kurtz started pacing up and down. 'Probably found out I was about to do the same thing and decided to *fok* it up for me.' He stopped his pacing. 'Does it have a flower on it?'

'Violet's *bokkie*?' said Malcolm.

'The ring – does it have a flower on it?'

Malcolm shrugged his shoulders.

'It's alright, *choppy*,' said Kurtz, slapping Malcolm hard on the back. 'I'll find out myself. But if it does…' – he gave Malcolm a Spaghetti-Western smirk – '…then you and Victor are in the *kak* right up to here.' Kurtz lifted his hand to just under his chin. Flinging open the door he disappeared up the stairs.

'It's a suit of armour I'll be wearing,' Malcolm shouted after him.

CHAPTER FIVE

BY THE TIME he'd charged up the stairs Victor's alcoholic haze had started to lift. Not disappear altogether but settle down enough for him to unclog his mind and regain his coordination. The latter enabled him to reach the top of the stairs without falling over; the former, to recall a conversation he'd had with Kevin the week before. It'd taken place by the noticeboard, just outside the ladies' changing room. Surprised to find Kevin engrossed in notices about choral evenings and book clubs, Victor had stopped to find out more. Kevin had given him one of his toothy grins and said a single word: 'Cracks.'

'Cracks?'

Kevin pointed to the door of the changing room. 'They haven't fitted the door properly,' he said. 'Stand in the right spot and you can see everything. And I mean everything. Cracks. Don't you just love them?'

What had seemed disgusting to Victor at the time now seemed heaven sent. His plan was simple. Lunchtime was approaching. He would position himself by the noticeboard and wait for Violet to come upstairs to get her purse from her locker. Then, peeping through the crack, he would be able to find out the locker number.

Victor stopped at the top of the stairs to catch his breath. He didn't like the idea of turning himself into a peeping

Tom. But this was an emergency. Anything else he saw when looking through the crack he would keep to himself. He was a philosopher, after all. Not the Wordsworth sort, who would peep and botanize upon his mother's grave, but the gentleman sort, who sees all but reveals only what is necessary. Ladies' parts or no ladies' parts, he resolved to keep his mouth well and truly shut.

But after making his way to the noticeboard his mouth fell well and truly open. For already there, whistling softly, hands in pockets, pretending to look at the posters on the noticeboard, was Kevin. Victor let out a frustrated sigh. It was going to take all his negotiating skills to oust Kevin from the crack. And time was running short.

'Anything interesting?' he said, sidling up.

'Been one or two shots,' said Kevin, 'but the real action won't start until twelve thirty.' He looked at his watch. 'Six minutes until show time.' He flashed Victor a vampiric grin.

Victor smiled back. It was important that Kevin thought he was on his side. 'Stroke of luck finding out about this,' he said.

'It's like winning the 'effing lottery,' said Kevin. 'Or waking up and finding out you're married to Kerry Katona. Never mind "Mum's been to Iceland", I've reached the Promised Land!'

Victor puffed out his cheeks. This was going to be even more difficult than he'd thought. He decided to start with the subtle approach. 'Listen, Kevin, have you ever heard of a book called *A Tale of Two Cities*?'

'No,' said Kevin, keeping an eye on the crack. 'But I've got a DVD at home called *A Tale of Two Titties* – is that anything to do with it?'

'Not really.' The mention of DVDs reminded Victor of the one he was carrying in his pocket. He would dump it in the bushes as soon as he'd found out the number of Violet's locker. 'In the book *A Tale of Two Cities*, there's this bloke called Sydney Carlton who sacrifices his life to save someone else's…'

'In *A Tale of Two Titties* there's this woman called Busty Divine who smothers criminals with her knockers. It's not your usual dirty movie, there's a real story to it.'

'Sounds like a classic.'

'It is. I can't wait for *A Tale of Two Titties II*.'

Victor looked up at the clock on the wall. Lunchtime was fast approaching and here he was still stuck on titties. 'Anyway, this Sydney Carlton…'

'Who?'

'Sydney Carlton, the bloke I've been telling you about from *A Tale of Two Titties* – I mean, *Cities*…'

'What about him?'

'He sacrifices his life for someone else, and just before he's about to die he says, "It is a far, far, better thing that I do, than I have ever done; it is a far, far, better rest that I go to, than I have ever known."'

Kevin looked up from the crack. 'Sounds like me when I've knocked one off.'

With the subtle approach not working, Victor decided to fight fire with fire. 'I need access to the crack this lunchtime.'

'Hang on a minute…!'

'There's…something I need to see.'

'We've all got our needs, mate. What's so special about yours?'

Victor hesitated. If he told Kevin the truth it would be all over the supermarket in five minutes. If he told Kevin a lie that would be all over the supermarket in five minutes too. He had to tread carefully. 'We're both men of the world,' he said, putting his arm around Kevin's shoulder. 'We both know how these things work. You scratch my back, I scratch yours.'

'Here, you haven't been watching *Backdoor Boys*, have you,' said Kevin, pulling away.

'I'm talking about making a deal.'

'What're you offering?'

Victor knew himself to be a terrible negotiator. The only other time he'd tried to barter was in Tenerife during his first (and last) trip abroad with his mother. He'd ended up paying more than twice the original price for a stuffed camel that smelt like the real thing. Being skint he couldn't offer Kevin any money. 'What do you want?' he said.

Kevin thought for a moment. 'A pair of those sunglasses the boss wears.'

'How much are they?'

'Hundred nicker.'

'I can't afford that!'

'I'm not asking you to buy them.'

'You mean…?'

'That's right,' said Kevin, nodding. 'I want you to steal them.'

Before Victor could answer a gaggle of early lunch-goers rushed past him and disappeared into the changing room. Violet wasn't among them, but Victor knew she would turn up soon. When there was food about she was usually first in the queue. Well, behind Angel. There was no time to lose. 'Alright,' he said, 'I'll do it.'

Kevin stood his ground. 'How do I know you won't change your mind?'

'What do you want? A contact signed in blood?'

Kevin waited until the coast was clear. 'Look through that,' he said, pointing at the crack.

A reluctant Victor put his face to the crack. What Kevin had said earlier was true. You could see everything. A full two-hundred-and-seventy-degree panoramic view.

'Closer,' said Kevin.

Victor pressed his face against the frame of the door. He was taking in the sights when he heard a clicking sound followed by a flash. He looked behind him to find Kevin pointing a mobile phone at him.

'Insurance,' said Kevin, pocketing the phone. 'No sunglasses and I start making copies. Enjoy the show!'

Kevin disappeared into the canteen.

Victor chewed on his bottom lip. What with the engagement ring, the DVD, the boss's sunglasses and now a peeping Tom picture, his problems were beginning to mount up. But at least he'd got access to the crack. All he had to do now was wait until Violet went to get her purse from her locker. Then he could get the number. So long as he wasn't disturbed...

'Victor.'

II

It was Frank. He was standing in the open doorway of Derek's office across from the changing room. 'Victor.'

'What?' said Victor, not turning around.

'I wonder if we could have a quick word.'

'I'm busy.'

'It won't take a minute.' This time it was Derek who spoke. Victor spun around.

'Certainly, boss,' he said. 'What can I do for you?'

'In my office, please.'

Victor glanced at the crowds of lunch-goers filling the corridor. 'Now?'

'Now.'

After a moment's hesitation Victor slouched into the office.

'Goddammit, son, you born in a barn or something. Close the goddam door.'

Victor was about to when he spotted Violet in the corridor. She was stood by the clocking-in machine talking to another member of staff. Victor let out an involuntary squeal.

'What in jumpin' Jack's the matter with you, boy?' said Derek. 'You sound like a hog at a pig pickin' roast.'

'Erm, it's just my claustrophobia, boss,' said Victor. 'This room's a bit on the small side. I wonder if you'd mind me leaving the door open a few inches.'

'Read this.' Derek slid a piece of paper across his desk.

With half an eye still on Violet, Victor picked up the piece of paper and pretended to read it. 'Excellent news, boss,' he said, 'excellent news.'

'Excellent news?' said Derek. 'Are you shitting me, boy? Why, that's the lowest score we've got this quarter.'

Rattled by Derek's raised voice, Victor glanced again at the paper. In bold letters at the top were the words 'Mystery Shopper', with 'Forty percent' written at the bottom in red ink.

'Eighty percent!' said Derek, taking his sunglasses off and throwing them on the desk. 'That's our target!'

Victor glanced down at the Ray-Bans. With the room so dark, maybe it was possible for him to snatch them without Derek and Frank spotting him...?

'You've got nothing to say, boy?' said Derek.

'Terrible news, boss,' said Victor, giving up on the sunglasses and turning his attention to the corridor once more. 'Really terrible news.'

'Have you seen what the Produce department got?' said Frank, moving behind Derek's desk.

Wishing someone would just tell him the answers to all

these questions instead of him keep having to look, Victor cast a moody eye down the paper. In the section marked 'Produce' was written 'Zero percent'. Victor lifted the piece of paper and said, 'It hasn't been filled in.'

'It's been filled in, alright!' said Derek, jumping to his feet and slamming his palms on the desk. 'You got zero! Zilch! A big fat nought! And do you know why?'

'Erm, no paper bags for the mushrooms?'

'Because someone couldn't be fucking arsed to take a customer – the Mystery Shopper no less – to the fucking Brussels sprouts!'

'Ah, yes. Let me explain…'

'Tell me, boy,' said Derek, sitting back down, 'how in the name of Miss Nancy do you expect me to go down to the managers' conference in Milton Keynes with a Mystery Shopper score of forty percent?'

'Oh, my God!'

'"Oh, my God!" is right. I'll be a goddam laughingstock. All those six-footers and five-feet-niners looking down at me.'

But Victor had moved on from the Mystery Shopper score. Violet had stopped her chatting and was now moving at top speed towards the changing room.'

'None of this surprises me,' said Frank, still hiding behind Derek. 'Only this morning a customer was telling me how you'd told her how the fruit and veg was better at Costbuster's…'

'Costbuster's?' said Derek. 'Jesus H Christ…you seen their fish counter. It's like a goddam Vietnamese market stall.'

Victor hadn't seen Costbuster's fish counter. Or a Vietnamese market stall. What he did see was Violet taking her keys out of her pocket.

'I can't remember the last time you showed any real interest in your work,' said Frank.

'Hmm?' said Victor, his focus on Violet as she pushed open the changing room door.

'I said, I can't remember the last time you showed any real interest...'

'Sorry,' said Victor, 'got to go.'

He rushed out of the office.

FRANK CAME OUT from behind Derek's desk. 'You see what I have to put up with. It's enough to drive you to early retirement.'

Breathing heavily and twisting a pencil in his hand to stop his anger from boiling over, Derek flashed an eye at Victor's HR file on the desk. 'What's his disciplinary status?' he said.

'Final written.'

'FW, eh?' Derek broke out into a smirk. 'So, one more wrong move and – aaargh!' He snapped the pencil in half. 'Way I see it that boy's been drinking in the last-chance saloon for too long. Time he was shut down permanently.'

'Well, I can't do anything,' said Frank, shrinking to about nine-inches tall, 'I'm retiring soon.'

'You're not gonna be the only one,' said Derek. He threw the broken bits of pencil onto the desk. 'By the time I've finished with ol' Mister Mammary Glands he'll be retired all the way up to Boot Hill. I'm gonna stack rank his ass outta here faster than you can say Calamity Jane.'

He swept the broken pieces of pencil into the bin.

'And you can take that to the bank.'

III

VICTOR MADE IT to the crack just in time. Violet had taken her purse from her locker and was turning the key. A few seconds later and he would've missed it. As it was, he was able to see the number. Thirteen, of course. His attention switched to Angel, who was standing across from Violet's locker shaving her armpits with a Stanley knife. Mesmerized by the tufts of black, wiry, hair cascading to the floor, he didn't see Violet leave the changing room. But suddenly she was there, glaring down at him like a disappointed headmistress who has just caught one of her pupil's looking through the dictionary for rude words.

'Perving through the crack, Victor?' she said, folding her arms. 'How could you?'

Discombobulated both by being discovered and by Violet's knowledge of the crack, all Victor could do was stammer a 'I-I was p-p-putting, erm, my name d-down for the poetry, erm, poetry p-performance evening.'

'Oh, Victor, look at you.' Violet looked him up and down. 'Stains down the front of your shirt, nipples like battleship rivets, breath stinking of booze and now this. If your poor mother was still alive...'

'What's going on?' It was Kevin.

'I've just caught Victor trying to peep into the ladies' changing rooms,' said Violet.

'Bit dodgy that, isn't it Vic?' said Kevin.

'I was looking at the noticeboard,' said Victor.

'You're gonna have to do better than that.' Kevin flashed Victor a knowing grin and disappeared into the canteen.

'Did you hear that?' said Violet. '"A bit dodgy". Oh, Victor, and that's from *Kevin*. It's a bit like Harvey Weinstein calling you a pervert.'

'What's happening?' This time it was Kurtz.

'Victor's been trying to peep into the ladies' changing rooms.'

'I was not trying to peep into the ladies' changing rooms,' said Victor, 'I was putting my name down for the poetry performance evening.'

'Where's your pen?' said Kurtz.

'What?'

'Your pen? You can't put your name down if you don't have a pen.'

Victor gawped like a goldfish.

'Oh, Victor!' said Violet, for what seemed like the hundredth time.

'Back home in South Africa we'd take a man like him, cut off his *piel* with a blunt *iklwa* and feed it to the lions,' said Kurtz, holding the canteen door open for Violet.

'I think it's his mother's death catching up with him,' said Violet, walking through the open door.

'Don't make excuses for him, *bokkie*,' said Kurtz, following her. 'The man's a degenerate. We all know it was him who stole last year's charity money…'

'Shit!' said Victor, kicking the wall in frustration. He turned to find Derek and Frank staring at him in disgust from the office opposite. 'I was looking at the noticeboard! There's a poetry performance evening…!'

Frank closed the door to the office.

Victor was just working out how to get hold of a second bottle of *Softsuds* washing powder, when the canteen door opened a few inches and Kevin's head poked out.

'Don't forget the sunglasses,' said Kevin, waving his mobile phone in the air.

The only hard evidence that Victor *had* been peeping into the ladies' changing room and *not* putting his name down for the poetry performance evening was on that phone. Victor made a lunge for it. But Kevin was already gone.

'Now then, Victor, what's been going on here?' It was Baz, back from one of his cigarette breaks.

Enraged by the injustice of it all – all he was trying to do was help a friend – Victor snapped. 'I was looking at the fucking noticeboard! Alright?!'

'Alright, alright,' said Baz. 'Quick tip for you, though. If you stand in the right spot, you can see right into the ladies' changing rooms. It's like fadge fucking city.' He tapped the side of his nose. 'Keep it to yourself, though.'

IV

STEAL ONE OR borrow another tenner from Malcolm to buy one. That was the only way Victor was going to get hold of another bottle of *Softsuds*. What with Kurtz keeping an even keener eye on him than usual, and the stain of sexual deviancy clinging to him like a cheap suit, he decided to go with the least risky option. The borrowing-another-tenner-from-Malcolm option. He found him on the shop floor stocking the shelves.

'Did you know,' said Malcolm, picking up a bag of oranges he'd just thrown on top of the satsumas, 'that there are over six hundred different varieties of oranges and thirty-five million orange trees in Spain?'

Victor didn't know. More to the point, he didn't care.

'But the truly amazing thing,' said Malcolm, 'is that they're full of carpet.'

A weary look on his face, Victor took the bag of oranges from Malcolm and looked at the label. 'Carpels,' he said. 'They're full of carpels.'

'That's even more amazing! What's a carpel?'

But Victor had more than oranges on his mind. He knew his Saki, and that, after all, scandal is merely the compassionate allowance the gay make to the humdrum. But for someone who aspired to be one of the great minds of his time. Who dreamed of libraries filled with books written by and about him. Who hoped to have his words quoted for generations to come. For someone like that to be caught perving into the ladies' changing room…He could see the headlines: *'Nice Arius!' says Pervert Philosopher. 'Adelard of that!' 'Gross-Mann!' 'What a Kant!'* Some Tarquin Travers-Booth-type academic would write a treatise about him: pervert or philosopher? The debate would go on until the end of time.

Unable to stand it any longer, Victor leaned his head against the shelf. 'Everyone thinks I'm a pervert,' he said.

'At least they don't think you're a mass murderer,' said Malcolm, doing some sideways arms swings.

Victor let out a weak chuckle. It was typical of Malcolm to try and look on the bright side; his glass was always half full. Victor of course measured his life in bottles. And they were always half empty at best.

He threw the bag of oranges onto the shelf. 'Every been beaten down by the vicissitudes of life, Malcolm? Smacked in the teeth by the cruel hand of fate?'

'I lost my headband the other day,' said Malcolm, switching from arm swings to trunk rotations.

'Is it really Nobler to suffer the Slings and Arrows of outrageous Fortune, to bear the Whips and Scorns of time?'

'Funny thing was it was on my head all the time. Last place I suppose you'd look for a headband.'

'I need another tenner,' said Victor.

'To grease a few more palms?' said Malcolm, doing a few arms-behind-back reaches.

'This is more along the lines of drowning sorrows.'

Malcolm frowned. 'Drowning – whether it be sorrows or anything else – should always be avoided. Stick to the shallow end is my advice. That way the water won't ever go above your head.'

'Too late.'

Malcolm reached into his pocket for his wallet. Instead he pulled out the two slips of paper. After reading them, he handed them to Victor. 'This is what I wanted to tell you about earlier.'

'BURN DOWN THE STORE!!!' said Victor, reading the first. 'KILL FRANK!!!' He looked up. 'Where did you get these?'

'The staff suggestion box. Do you think we should take them to the Colleague Council?'

'The Colleague Council? Why?'

'That's where all staff suggestions are supposed to be discussed.'

'And what do you think they'll say about a suggestion to burn down the store?'

'"Let's vote on it"?'

'And what about killing the Great Leader? Think that might get through?'

'Fifty-fifty, I'd say. Or sixty-forty.'

'For or against?'

'Against.' Malcolm thought for a second. 'Or for. It'd certainly be one or the other.'

'Not that it would make much difference. Whichever way it went, you'd still get the same amount of work out of him. The question is, who wrote these...?' Victor examined the handwriting. The words looked like they'd been etched in the paper rather than written. They were spread unevenly across the page and slanted this way and that. 'Looking at how they've been written and the excessive use of the exclamation mark, I'd say our suspect has all the signs of mental instability combined with a psychopathic personality disorder.'

'Hmmm,' said Malcolm. 'It could be anyone.'

'What do you mean it could be anyone? There's only one person who fits that description.'

'Betty from Bread and Cake?'

'Betty's nearly eighty, Malcolm. The only thing she's killed is time.'

'We've all got a past.'

'They were written by Angel.'

'That's it!' said Malcolm, clicking his fingers.

'That's what?'

'That's what she was doing in the canteen this morning. Filling in these suggestion slips.'

'I didn't even know she could write. Amazing what you can teach ogres to do.' Victor folded up the slips of paper. 'How come you removed them from the box?'

A guilty look on his face, Malcolm stared down at his shoes. 'I know only the Human Resources manager -'

'Personnel manager.'

'- is supposed to check the suggestions box. But when I saw Angel filling in the slips I wanted to make sure she was taking it seriously. Usually all you get are silly suggestions about making Chef eat his own food. Or was it faeces?'

'Same thing. You mean instead of sensible suggestions like burning down the store?' Victor put the two slips into his pocket. 'She must've put them in the box when she dropped her ring?'

'What ring?'

'I better keep hold of them.' Victor rubbed his hands together. 'Maybe we can use them against her if things get rough. And I better get rid of this.' He took the DVD from his pocket. 'I mean, can you imagine Whiting's number one pervert – the scourge of the ladies' changing room – getting caught with *Midget* sodding *Mayhem*.'

'Oh, yeah,' said Malcolm.

As HE STOOD in the self-scan queue with a second quarter bottle of whisky, Victor looked up at the heavens and said, 'It's an emergency, mum, trust me.'

The customer in front of Victor turned around.

'Just talking to my mother,' said Victor. 'She's been dead four years.'

'Right,' said the customer edging a few feet further away.

CHAPTER SIX

WITH THE SECOND quarter bottle of whisky safely secreted in his pocket, Victor made his way out into the back yard. Weaving his way through the stacks of empty pallets and bales of cardboard, he hid himself behind the rubbish skip and took the whisky from his pocket. Unscrewing the top, he lifted the bottle to his mouth and drank deeply. The warm glow that had started to wear off from the first bottle suddenly returned. And for that moment he didn't care about Angel's engagement ring or the photograph of him on Kevin's phone or whether someone thought he hadn't heard of a subject called philosophy. For that moment he was…happy.

It couldn't last, of course. For one thing, he'd have to save some of the whisky for later. He couldn't keep going to the Bank of Malcolm for loans. And however much whisky he drank he wasn't going to wash away the problem of Angel and the ring forever. Finding out Violet's locker number had been the easy part. He still had to get inside the locker and steal the ring back. Then there was the boss's sunglasses. News of his peeping Tom performance would be all over the store by now. But he would still have to honour his agreement with Kevin. Office gossip was one thing. But office gossip backed up by photographic evidence was something else altogether. He had to get Kevin to delete that picture.

After another swig from the bottle his thoughts turned to the book he was supposed to be writing. The main problem was that although he'd *heard* of a subject called philosophy, he didn't really know what it *was* and what you were supposed to *do* with it. The three thousand pages of notes he'd made during lockdown were merely the fragments of dozens of failed attempts to find out. Three thousand pages and he was still only on A for Aristotle. If Tarquin Travers-Booth had asked him if he'd 'Ever heard of the Renaissance?'

Check.

'The novels of Patrick Hamilton?'

Check.

'The plays of Peter Barnes?'

Check.

'The art of guzzling whisky while hiding behind a skip?'

Victor took another slug.

Checkmate.

As he put the bottle of whisky back into one of his pockets, Victor became aware of the DVD in the other. He pulled the DVD out and look around for somewhere to hide it. Somewhere where it would never be found again. There was a small clump of trees just outside the yard. Maybe he could bury it there? He quickly dismissed the idea. For one thing it was January. The ground would be too hard. And he didn't have a shovel. But the main reason was, as a man of learning, he didn't want to bequeath future generations fossilized filth. He could see it all now, some archaeologist hundreds of years in the future digging up a DVD with *Back Door Boys*, *Father and Daughters* and *Midget Mayhem* on it. Then it being displayed in a museum as a relic of an ancient civilization brought down by midgets and incest.

He next considered hiding it under the piles of rusted metal cage rollers or bales of cardboard that littered the yard. Or better still, throwing it in the rubbish skip where the non-recyclable waste went. It could still be dug up by future archaeologists. But they'd first have to dig through tonnes of other shit to find it. Maybe after uncovering their millionth Coca-Cola bottle they would simply label the Twenty-First Century the Age of Plastic and call it a day.

Even entire eras were becoming disposable now.

He was about to fling the DVD into the skip when he heard what sounded like a giant wearing clogs tap-dancing in a tin bath. Peering over the top of the skip he saw Angel stomping about inside. Slinging pieces of trash in all directions, she reminded Victor of some deranged shot-putter. What she was doing, of course, was looking for her ring. Which Victor knew she wasn't going to find. Because instead of it being under two tonnes of non-recyclables, it was in locker thirteen in the ladies' changing room.

Victor lowered himself down from the skip. There was no way he could throw the DVD in there now. Angel was already in one of her homicidal rages. Her mood was hardly likely to improve if the sky suddenly started raining pornos. The only thing he could do was beat a hasty retreat and lose it somewhere else.

The DVD, that was.

II

THE SOMEWHERE ELSE Victor decided to try was the bushes in the car park. It had been his original plan after all. He could stash the DVD there until the end of his shift and then take it home and dispose of it properly.

As he made his way from the yard to the car park he formulated his plan to access Violet's locker. It wasn't going to be easy infiltrating the ladies' changing room. Not given that he was a man. Albeit one with women-sized breasts. All it would take was for one person to see him and that would be it. There weren't many good reasons for a man to be in the ladies' changing rooms, especially one who by now had probably been dubbed the Lavatory Lech. Even if he managed it there was a second problem. How to get inside the locker itself. The only way was by stealing the locker Master Key from Human Resources.

Personnel.

That was a special forces mission in its own right. For if there was one golden rule at Whiting's it was that no one should ever enter Human Resources without a member of that department being present. The information centre to the whole organization, it contained employees' personnel files, sensitive business documents and all the master keys. Which was why no one was allowed to enter without permission. Never, ever, ever. Not even if your life depended on it. So sacrosanct was the rule that the powers-that-be didn't even bother to lock the door. Fear of the consequences was deterrent enough.

One advantage Victor had was that Personnel was always deserted on a Sunday. The joke being that Personnel were such God-like figures that on the seventh day they rested. But – as with the ladies' changing room – it was still going to be difficult to infiltrate. Any sign of human activity would automatically be a code red. And the part of the corridor where Personnel was situated was often like Piccadilly Circus.

He had to find another way.

By the time he got to the car park Victor thought he'd found it. He would tell Violet that Malcolm wanted the ring back so he could inscribe the date of the wedding on it. As a romantic gesture it was something Violet would probably go for. Then, once he'd gotten hold of the ring, he could return it to Angel. How, he would decide later. When Violet asked him where the ring was he would tell her that Malcolm had lost it. Given that Malcolm *was* always losing things the plan was a good one.

'What could go wrong?'

Pulling the bottle of whisky from his pocket to toast his brilliant idea, he took a celebratory slurp. After pocketing the bottle, he took the DVD from his other pocket and prepared to throw it into the bushes. First, he had to wait for the right moment. Not easy given the number of customers who were bustling about. He tried to look inconspicuous by folding his arms and whistling the aria *Nature Immense, impenetrable et fière* from *The Damnation of Faust*. Eventually a window of opportunity presented itself. He was about to fling the DVD into the bushes when Kurtz burst forth from the thicket covered in leaves and twigs.

'What's going on here, then?' he said.

'Nothing,' said Victor, hurriedly putting the DVD back in his pocket.

'Nothing?'

'That's right, nothing.'

Kurtz picked some bits of leaves and twigs from his beard. 'In South Africa when someone says they're up to nothing, it usually means they're up to no good.'

His senses lifted by the whisky, Victor immediately saw the flaw in Kurtz's argument. 'This is England, dear boy,' he said. 'When an Englishman says he's up to nothing, he's up to nothing.'

'Nothing, eh?'

Tired of Kurtz's police tactics of trying to turn nothing into something, Victor decided to go on the attack. 'I believe we've established that. Besides, it wasn't me who appeared from the bushes looking like the Wild Man of Borneo.'

'It's where they stash their ill-gotten gains.'

'Who?'

'Shoplifters, who do you think?' Kurtz glanced down at Victor's bulging pocket. 'Anyway, what are you doing out here? I thought you spent all your time trying to look into the ladies' toilets?'

'I was putting my name down for the poetry performance evening. I suppose someone with such barbarian tastes as you wouldn't understand that?'

Kurtz let out a snort. 'With *tets* like yours you probably got confused which crappers were yours. All you've got to do is tell HR you've changed sex. Then you can go into the women's toilets as often as you want.'

Victor cupped a protective hand over one of his breasts. 'I happen to suffer from a serious medical condition,' he said.

'You'll be suffering from a serious medical condition when Angel finds out you've stolen her ring.'

Victor felt his mouth go dry.

'What did you do,' said Kurtz, picking some foliage from his hair, 'give it to Malcolm to clear your drinking debts?'

'I haven't laid a finger on Angel's ring,' said Victor, raising himself to his full height.

'You'd lose your hand if you did,' said Kurtz, grinning at his own joke. 'But don't worry, *bra*, I'm not going to say anything. I'm going to wait until she's really foaming at the mouth. Unless…'

'Unless what?'

'It was you who gave that ring to Malcolm. And then got him to propose to Violet. Just to *fok* things up for me.'

Victor opened his mouth to speak, but Kurtz waved him away. 'It's no good trying to deny it. You must've found out I was going to propose to Violet and decided to ruin it.' Kurtz took the de Beers engagement ring from his pocket. 'I've got an engagement ring of my own. I'm going to propose to Violet at tonight's charity do.'

'You and Violet?' said Victor, slowly. He was surprised that Kurtz could hold a torch for anyone. Except maybe Lucrezia Borgia.

'So, here's the deal, Tubby *Tets*.' Kurtz prodded a finger in Victor's direction. 'Either you get Malcolm to call off his engagement to Violet – before tonight – or I tell Angel you stole her ring.'

Victor stroked his right breast as he mulled over Kurtz's words. It was pointless asking Malcolm to break off his engagement to Violet. The only time Malcolm remembered he was engaged was when he, Victor, reminded him. Even then Malcolm didn't really take it in. No, if anyone was going to break off the engagement it would have to be Violet. The problem was, asking Violet to return an engagement ring was a bit like asking the British Museum to return the Elgin Marbles.

He moved to his left breast. With Kurtz on the matrimonial substitute's bench Violet might play ball. The problem there was, Kurtz always played the man. Even if he managed to split Malcolm and Violet up and Violet and Kurtz became engaged, Kurtz would still tell Angel he'd stolen the ring.

Stalemate as usual.

Before he could say anything, Kurtz started up again.

'Violet's what I call a real *choty goty* – a real beautiful girl. What I want to do is take her back to South Africa and set up a pumpkin farm. Maybe have a couple of kids…'

Victor didn't hear the rest of the sentence. He was trying to

imagine what the offspring of Kurtz and Violet would be like.
A Viking wrestler, probably. If it was a girl.

'So, we've got a deal then?'

'What?' said Victor, his mind still on brawling Norsemen.

'Get Malcolm to call off the engagement and I won't say
anything about Angel's ring.'

Victor decided to bluff it out. Adopting as swashbuckling
a pose as someone with oversized breasts can, he gazed
heroically into the far distance. 'Only a bounder and a cad
bandies a lady's ring about in public,' he said. 'I challenge
you, sir, to do your worst.'

Kurtz's pale blue eyes narrowed and right cheek started to
twitch. 'So that's how you want to play it, is it? Very well.' He
moved closer so he could whisper into Victor's ear. 'You've
got until tonight, my old *chommie*. Then I'm going to tell
Angel. And we both know what that means.' He flicked one
of Victor's breasts. 'She's going to *donner* you to death.'

Victor's musketeer-like pose began to crumble.

'Oh, and one last thing,' said Kurtz, turning to go. 'I'll be
keeping a close eye on that charity tin. We don't want the
money to go missing like it did last year.'

Victor opened his mouth to protest. But by then Kurtz had
disappeared back into the bushes. Now that Kurtz knew about
Angel's ring, Victor knew he would have to act fast. After all,
the last thing he needed was to be *donnered* to death. Forgetting
all about the DVD, he ran back into the store.

III

WOBBLING AT TOP speed through the back area, Victor made
his way to the men's changing room. Opening his locker, he

threw the DVD inside. He was about to do the same with the suggestion slips when he heard what sounded like a mule with emphysema wheezing in the corridor. Only Violet laughed like that. Victor stuffed the suggestion slips back into his pocket and ran out to catch her.

She was standing by the clocking-in machine showing other members of staff her engagement ring. 'It's a bit on the small side,' Victor heard her say. To him, it was manna from heaven. He could use it to get the ring back by telling her that Malcolm wanted to get it enlarged.

He waved over at her.

'We're going to have a black and white chequerboard floor in the marquee,' Violet was saying. 'The whole reception is going to be *Love Island* meets *Alice in Wonderland*.'

Victor tried again.

'Excuse me, girls, Peeping Tits wants a word.' Violet walked over to talk to Victor. 'And don't give me any more pathetic excuses about poetry performance evenings.'

But Victor's mind wasn't on poetry performance evenings. It was on Viking maidens with ginger goatees rolling around in the mud. '"No battle's won in bed",' he said.

Violet stood with her arms folded.

'It's an old Scandinavian saying.'

'I haven't got time to listen to Scandinavian sayings, old or new. I've got a wedding to arrange. I've only got until next week.'

'I thought the wedding was tomorrow?'

'Yes, but I can't arrange an *Alice in Wonderland* reception in one day. The wedding will be tomorrow and the reception next week. So, time is pressing.'

'It's about the ring.'

'What about the ring?' said Violet, clutching it to her chest.

'Malcolm knows it's too small and wants to get it altered.

He's asked me to get it off you.'

'He didn't mention anything to me.'

'Well, you know how he is,' said Victor, trying to sound relaxed. 'He'd forget his name if people didn't keep reminding him.'

He watched as Violet twisted the ring round her finger. When it came to body sizes Violet was definitely Godzuki to Angel's Godzilla. But oddly it was Violet who had the bigger fingers. A bit like uncooked sausages or Mickey Mouse's oversized digits, there was no point putting her name down for Tarquin Travers-Booth's piano lessons.

'It's bad luck to return an engagement ring,' said Godzuki. 'When Bella Delaware returned hers for a bigger diamond in Amy Lovelace's *Bad Luck Bride*, she was run over outside the church by her own Cinderella carriage.' Violet stopped her ring-twisting. 'I'm going to have a giant teacup for my carriage. But the principle's the same. Once it's on your finger, you should never give it back. A ring on the finger is worth two in the -'

Victor made a lunge for the ring.

'- bush,' said Violet, pulling her hand away.

'I was putting my name down for the poetry performance evening!'

Violet set off like a greyhound to the ladies' changing room.

'Alright, alright, alright,' said Victor, running after her. Violet stopped in the doorway of the changing room. 'I was looking through the crack in the door. But only because… because…' He had one last card to play. He would tell Violet about Kurtz wanting to marry her and hope true love ran its course. He resented having to play Mercutio to Kurtz and Violet's Romeo and Juliet. But if it meant getting Angel's ring back and saving Malcolm from a fate worse than death, then, love be rough, he would do it.

'Because…I wanted to tell you, you have another admirer. No, don't speak. There's someone close by whose heart aches for you with a burning intensity. Someone whose whole being trembles every time he sets eyes on that…that…flaming hair. Someone who…who…who…'

Victor's mind went blank. Despite having enough purple prose to outgun Mr Roget, it always ran dry when he was trying to speak the language of love. Especially when the object of it was so lacking in muse-like inspiration. He felt like a landscape painter looking out upon a barren wasteland.

'Oh, Victor,' said Violet, sadly. 'I thought Malcolm was supposed to be a friend of yours?'

'He *is* my friend,' said Victor, puzzled by the turn the conversation was taking. Violet's 'Oh, Victor' had started it off. Said in an accusatory rather than an amatory way, there was nothing of the honeying or making love about it and a lot more of the nasty sty.

'And that's how you treat your friends, is it?' said Violet, in the same I-put-it-to-you-courtroom-voice.

Victor half expected her to demand he give a yes or no answer. Had she done so, he wouldn't have been able to oblige. There he was expressing a wooing mind on behalf of someone else and all Violet wanted to do was talk about his friendship with Malcolm.

'Friends,' said Violet, continuing her theme, 'don't try to steal other people's fiancées.'

'Steal other people's what?'

'There I was hoping you were just after the charity money. But declaring your love to your best friend's intended…Really, Victor, can you sink any lower?'

Had he been in a real courtroom, Victor would've shouted 'Objection, your honour' by this point. Instead, all he managed was a spluttered, 'N-N-No, you've got it all wrong.'

But for Violet the verdict seemed to be in. 'Trying to steal my ring because you can't bear to see me married to someone else!'

She flounced into the changing room and slammed shut the door.

'You've got it wrong,' said Victor, putting his mouth to the crack. 'Your ring's too tight. I was just going to loosen it for you.'

'He doesn't give up, does he?'

When Victor looked up it was to find Kevin grinning down at him. 'I was talking about her engagement ring.' He noticed Derek and Frank watching him from the office opposite. 'I was talking about her engagement ring!'

Frank slammed shut the office door.

'You're not very good at this?' said Kevin, taking his mobile phone from his pocket. Victor leaned against the wall and let out a long sigh. 'Say cheese.'

CHAPTER SEVEN

RETURNING TO THE back area, Victor found Malcolm by the sink filling up a watering can.

'Going to help me water the plants?' said Malcolm, ignoring the pool of water from the overfilled watering can sloshing about his feet.

'You don't water plants with hot water,' said Victor, turning off the hot water tap.

'I was going to put in some *Plant Grow* as well.'

Victor emptied the watering can and filled it with cold water. 'Kurtz is in love with Violet,' he said.

'Well, he better hurry up and tell her,' said Malcolm, taking hold of the watering can. 'From what I hear she's already engaged.'

'To you, you idiot.'

Spilling even more water on the floor, Malcolm lifted the watering can on to the Produce desk. 'When did I get married to Violet?'

'This morning. If you want my advice, keep away from car parks.'

'That's when cars are at their safest. When they're parked.'

'I wonder if the Great Leader is still in the boss's office?'

'Frank? He's in the car park. Funny, he's always out there. Must be helping collect trolleys or getting engaged to Violets.'

'Malcolm, how many trolleys have you ever seen him collect? He stands out there smoking all day like some self-immolating Tibetan monk. That trolley shed should be fitted with a smoke alarm, the amount of time he spends in it.'

Malcolm took out his little black book and a pen. 'Smoke alarms for trolley sheds,' he said, writing down the words. 'I'll bring it up at the next Colleague Council.'

'In the highly unlikely event that the Great Leader asks where I am, just cover for me, or something, will you?'

'Are you sick?' said Malcolm, opening the Produce desk drawer and taking out a bottle of *Plant Grow*.

'I've got to sneak into Personnel…'

'Human Resources.'

'…and steal the locker master key.'

Malcolm unscrewed the top off the *Plant Grow* and poured the whole lot into the watering can. 'What do you need that for?' he said.

'Oh, death where is thy sting,' said Victor, covering his eyes with his hands.

'And you should've gone to Human Resources at lunchtime.' Malcolm picked up the watering can. 'If you're stealing locker master keys you should really be doing it in your own time.'

Victor grabbed hold of Malcolm's shirt, causing even more water to spill out of the can. 'I'm doing this for you, you ingrate.'

'I haven't lost my locker key.'

Victor let go of Malcolm's shirt. 'I couldn't do it at lunchtime,' he said, trying to remain calm, 'because there were too many people about.'

'All these people losing their locker keys.' Malcolm shook his head. 'They should do what I do and keep it on their key ring. That's funny…' Malcolm checked his pockets. 'Must've dropped it somewhere. Get a master locker key for me when you go upstairs, will you?'

Victor turned to go.

'Wait a minute,' said Malcolm, grabbing Victor's arm. 'Look at all this water on the floor! There should be a wet-floor warning sign or something.'

'Ever heard of a midlife crisis, Malcolm?'

'I've heard you go on about it a lot. Something to do with a book, isn't it? That doesn't help us with this spilt water. I remember the last pre-Covid Lunestone Marathon. It'd been raining for about a week before the race and -'

'Listen, Malcolm, I've more on my mind than a bit of spilt water!'

'Be alert! Accidents hurt!' Malcolm took a small booklet from his pocket. 'The Nineteen Seventy-Four *Health and Safety at Work Act.*' He flicked through the booklet. 'Spillages, spillages, spillages…'

'Just cover for me.'

'Hmmm?' said Malcolm, looking up from the booklet.

'If Frank asks where I am, cover for me.'

'What shall I say?'

'I don't know, tell him I'm helping a customer.'

'He won't believe that.'

Victor knew Malcolm was right. Telling Frank that he was helping a customer was a bit like telling Doubting Thomas that Jesus had just made a comeback. 'Well, tell him whatever you like. Just don't tell him, or anyone else, I'm in Personnel…'

'Human Resources.'

Victor walked off.

'You can rely on me,' Malcolm shouted after him.

II

Victor locked the cubicle door and took out the bottle of whisky. It was going to require nerves of steel to infiltrate Personnel. Dutch courage restored, he tiptoed to the changing room door and opened it just wide enough to see the door to Personnel opposite. Knowing it would be unlocked he was about to make a dash across the corridor when he heard the sound of metal-heeled footsteps and jangling keys.

Kurtz!

Victor ducked back into the changing room and started frantically looking for a place to hide. If Kurtz found him in the changing room just after lunchtime it would send that policeman's mind of his into overdrive. Kurtz would never be off his back.

Instead of running into one of the cubicles Victor hid himself among all the coats and jackets hung up behind the door. Covering every part of his body except for his ankles and feet, he had just wedged himself into position when he felt the door being pushed open. He moved with the door so Kurtz wouldn't feel the extra weight. By the time the door swung back Victor found himself staring at Kurtz's enormous rear. Unable to move so much as a muscle in case Kurtz heard him, he felt a collar jacket tickling the end of his nose. With one eye on Kurtz, he tried to move the collar by gently blowing on it upwards.

After checking all the cubicles to make sure they were empty, Kurtz went over to the sink to wash his hands. '*My Sarie Marais is so ver van mij af,*' he sang. '*Ek hoop haar weer te sien…*'

Behind the coats, Victor could feel a sneeze beginning to build.

Kurtz pulled a handful of paper towels from the dispenser

and dried his hands. '*Sy het in die wijk van die Mooririvier gewoon…*' He threw the paper towels into the bin. '*Nog vor fi oorlog het begin.*' After checking his beard and moustache in the mirror, he walked over to his locker. '*O, bring my terug na die ou Transvaal.*'

With his nose ready to explode, Victor watched as Kurtz opened the locker and took out the charity tin. Kurtz unscrewed the top of the tin, took some money out and put it in his pocket. Victor forgot about his twitching nose for a moment and remembered instead the line about the terrorist and the policeman coming from the same basket.

'*O bring my terug na die ou Transvaal.*' Kurtz screwed the top back on the charity tin. '*Daar waar my Sarie woon.*'

Having seen the gamekeeper turn well and truly into the poacher, Victor turned his attention once more to his twitching nose.

'*Daar onder in die mielies…*'

Just when Victor thought he couldn't hold on any longer, he felt the door swing open again.

'There you are,' said Kevin's voice.

'So?' said Kurtz.

'There's some drunk downstairs making trouble.'

'Not Victor, is it?'

Kurtz and Kevin broke into laughter. Behind the door Victor scowled.

'You know they caught him perving into the woman's changing room again,' said Kevin.

'Man, he's just the sort to steal *broekies* off the washing line.'

'What's a *broekie*?'

'Ladies' pants, what do you think? Though I guess it's bras he really needs.'

'What are you doing with the charity tin?' said Kevin,

opening the door wider.

'I told Violet I'd look after it over lunch,' said Kurtz, pushing Kevin out of the door. 'You know what happened last year. Bet that was Tubby *Tets* as well. I was just about to return it to her. I'll tell you this about Victor. During lockdown…'

As Kurtz and Kevin made their way down the corridor, Victor fought his way out from under the coats and ran into a cubicle. 'ACHOOO!!!' Leaving the cubicle he took a paper towel from the dispenser to blow his nose. So, now he knew. It was Kurtz stealing the charity money.

'"It's the oldest question of all, George,"' he said, coming over all John le Carré. '"Who can spy on the spies?"'

Victor screwed up the paper towel and threw it into the bin. 'I bloody well can.'

III

KURTZ AND KEVIN arrived at the Customer Service desk to find Violet talking to a man with dark glasses and a white stick.

'I thought you said he was drunk?' said Kurtz.

'He was all over the place before,' said Kevin.

'That's because he's blind, you *domkop*.' Kurtz went behind the Customer Service desk. 'Is there a problem?'

'This gentleman is looking for a Helping Hand,' said Violet. 'I can't do it. I'm not supposed to leave the desk unattended.'

'I'm the security guard,' said Kurtz, 'I can't do it either.'

'There's no one else.'

'What about Kevin?' But when Kurtz turned around, Kevin had scarpered. Over by the floral display Malcolm was watering the plants. Kurtz beckoned him over.

Malcolm strolled over with his watering can. 'He's not here.'

'What?' said Kurtz.

'My, you've got a big one, Malc,' said Violet, pointing at the watering can. 'You can water my bush anytime. Hee-haw. Hee-haw. Hee-haw…!'

Malcolm smiled. 'The bigger the capacity, the less you have to refill it,' he said. 'It's interesting with watering cans…'

'Who's not here?' said Kurtz.

'Hmmm? Oh. Victor. He's not here. I'm covering for him.'

'I wasn't going to ask you about Victor, I was going to ask you to do a Helping Hand.'

Malcolm took a sudden step back, spilling water from the can. 'I don't know where he is,' he said, blushing. 'But he definitely isn't upstairs in Personnel, I mean, Human Resources. I think he's having a midlife crisis, or something.'

Kurtz shot out from behind the Customer service desk and raced past a stunned Malcolm. 'I'll *fokking* kill him,' he said.

IV

VICTOR HAD BEEN in Personnel a million times. Usually for disciplinary reasons or to help Malcolm get whatever piece of safety equipment he needed that week. What Victor *hadn't* done was go into Personnel when it was pitch black to steal something. The reason it was pitch black was because the blinds were still closed from Saturday night. He decided to leave them closed and not switch on any lights in case it attracted attention.

Lights on, blinds up, the distance from the door to the gun-grey metal key box at the far end of the office was but a few short steps. In the dark, those few short steps became more like the Royal Marines Commando assault course.

Feeling his way along the wall, the first obstacle he came to was what felt like a picture frame. Victor knew what it really was. A Personnel slogan – MAKING THE IMPOSSIBLE POSSIBLE – that someone from the department had hung up for propaganda purposes. Many times during his numerous disciplinaries he'd had it pointed out to him. Usually after he'd made some comment about the amount of work he was expected to do exceeding the daily quota for your average British POW on the Thai-Burma railway during World War Two. Or after comparing the work targets he was expected to meet with the Nazi concept of *Vernichtung durch Arbeit* – annihilation through labour.

After touching the frame with his hand, he moved a few inches from the wall so as not to knock it off. What he'd not calculated for were his breasts, the left of which knocked against the frame and made it fall from the wall. He just managed to catch it before it hit the floor.

'Betrayed by my own knockers,' he said in a low voice. 'I bet Jack "Superthief" MacLean never had this problem.'

He hung the slogan back on the wall.

'Now, pull yourself together,' he said, slapping one of his tits. 'Silence is golden.'

There followed a loud crash as Victor's foot kicked a metal wastepaper basket. Acting as if the foot belonged to someone else, he put a finger to his lips and said 'Sssshhh!'

He listened out for anyone coming. All he could hear was a whistling sound. It was Baz, who was mopping the floor outside.

Victor wiped a bead of sweat from his forehead and continued his journey along the wall. He was just thinking how in length it was starting to resemble the one in China when his knee hit a solid object. It was the Personnel desk. On it, rocking this way and that and threatening to topple over at any moment was a small bottle of ink. Worried it would fall on the floor and smash, he scooped it up and – working purely on instinct – put it in his pocket. Continuing on his way, his hand knocked against something metallic. Using both hands to explore further he realised he'd reached his target.

'No Plan B,' he said, triumphantly, reaching for the clasp that opened the key box door. He unhooked the clasp and opened the door.

'Oh, shit!'

KURTZ MOVED THROUGH the back area at top speed. Pushing other members of staff to one side with a hard shove or a growled, 'Out of the way, *domkop*,' he flung open the door that led upstairs and climbed the steps two at a time.

Stealing engagement rings off Neanderthals was one thing. But being in Human Resources on a Sunday with no HR staff present was something else altogether. He'd lost count of the number of times he'd gone on about security being too lax. And for the door to be permanently locked. Paranoid they'd called him. The ones who were out to get him. But now everything he'd said had come true. For an unauthorized person to be in there unsupervised – especially when that unauthorized person was Tubby *Tets*…It was like giving a jihadi the keys to a nuclear power station.

The whole place could go up.

#

VICTOR STARED AT all the keys hanging up inside the box. Expecting to find maybe half a dozen, there were exactly forty-nine. All were numbered and attached to each was a plastic fob with an abbreviated description of what the key was for.

There was only one thing to do. Starting from the top, he picked up key number one. On the fob was written the words MAN-OFF. Victor rubbed one of his breasts. 'Man-Off?' he said, trying to figure out the strange hieroglyphic. 'Man-Off? Manager's office!' He was about to put the key back when a thought came to him. Maybe he could use it to sneak into Derek's office and steal the sunglasses? That would get Kevin off his back at least.

He hung the key back up. The more keys he stole the greater the chance of them being missed. Besides, with the locker master key he could open Kevin's locker, steal his mobile phone and wipe clean the incriminating photograph. Without any hard evidence of his peeping Tom antics he could tell any future biographer that it was all a vicious rumour put about by a jealous Tarquin Travers-Booth to smear him.

After replacing key number one, he moved on to the others. Two, three, four, five – they all had strange abbreviations like 'Plan Ro' (Plant Room?), 'Pharm K' (Pharmacy key?) and Ar-Ses' (??). Six, seven, eight, nine, ten. Victor's hands were starting to sweat. He'd already been in Personnel longer than he'd expected. Eleven, twelve, thirteen, fourteen. At this rate it was going to be Monday before he'd finished. Fifteen, sixteen, seventeen, eighteen, nineteen, twenty. But as Victor reminded himself, when you're up to no good and running the risk of being caught in your perfidy, time always seems to creep with leaden foot. Twenty-one, twenty-two, twenty-three, twenty-four, twenty-five. The image of someone – Kurtz probably – flinging open the door and catching him in the act, made Victor feel even more plumbiferous.

Twenty-six, twenty-seven, twenty-eight, twenty-nine, thirty. With the sweat on his hands making them slippery, Victor was finding it harder to pick up the keys. Thirty-one, thirty-two, thirty-three, thirty-four, thirty-five.

A sixth sense came over him, telling him that he was in danger and needed to hurry. But it only seemed to have the opposite effect and make everything happen in slow motion.

Thirty-six, thirty-seven, thirty-eight, thirty-nine, forty.

The closer he got to the end, the more the panic started to build. Maybe someone from Personnel had forgotten to hang the locker master key back up? Or had taken it home by mistake?

Forty-one, forty-two, forty-three, forty-four, forty-five – forty-five – 'Mast Lock K'.

Master locker key!

Overcome with excitement, Victor dropped the key on the floor. He was on his hands and knees looking for it when he heard a loud crash from the corridor. Picking up the key, he ran to the door and poked his head out. On his back, covered in water and with a bucket on his head was Kurtz. Baz was next to him, bobbing up and down and repeating the line, 'The *Eagle* has fucking landed!'

With Baz too busy laughing at Kurtz to see him, Victor nipped across to the men's changing room. Locking himself into one of the cubicles, he sat down on the toilet to catch his breath. Seconds later there was a loud banging on the cubicle door.

'Open this *fokking* door right now!' said a voice.

VII

THE POUNDING ON the door continued, but louder and with greater force. What else continued – also louder and with greater force – were the threats, 'Get your fat *tets* outta there right now, you *bladdy mompie*', being the latest.

Inside the cubicle, Victor decided to adopt a haughty *sangfroid*. 'Can't a man go to the toilet in peace anymore,' he said.

'You *soeking* with me, you *muggie*?' came the response. Followed by even more door-pounding. Victor had to think fast on his seat. A flash of inspiration hit him.

'I'm having complications,' he said, making a straining sound.

'Complications? I'll give you *fokking* complications if you're not outta that *fokking* shitter in five *fokking* seconds!'

Victor was about to open the door when another flash of inspiration came over him. Reaching behind, he flushed the toilet. Hiding the locker master key in his shoe, he opened the door. On the other side – stinking of bleach, and his hair and beard saturated with mop-bucket water – was Kurtz. Looking like some rain-soaked old English sheepdog who's lost his flock, he was hopping from one water-drenched foot to the other in anger. Affecting a nonchalant air, Victor walked casually over to the sink to wash his hands. As he did, he came out with another gem. 'Touch of constipation.'

Kurtz pointed a dripping finger at Victor. 'By the time I've finished with you, *mampara*, the *kak*'s going to be leaking from you like water from a busted radiator.'

The irony of a man soaked from head to toe in mop-bucket water deploying such a simile was not lost on Victor. 'I do not care to be spoken to in that manner,' he said. 'Especially by someone masquerading as a human sponge.'

Kurtz stormed over to the sink with his fists clenched.

And it was here that Victor came out with his best line yet. Cupping his breasts, he took a step back and – playing the gender reassignment card – said, 'You wouldn't hit a woman, would you?'

It created enough confusion for Kurtz to be rendered temporarily mute. Victor knew Kurtz didn't really think he'd undergone gender reassignment. After all you don't go to the trouble of having bits taken off and bits added and then forget to shave off your beard. Even Eddie Izzard picked up the Gillette Fusion before donning the dresses. No, Victor was just doing what generals down the ages – from Alexander the Great to 'Stormin' Norman Schwarzkopf – have done when faced with a vicious foe: sown confusion in the ranks. And it had worked. Confused *and* confounded, Kurtz – all droopy moustache and soggy beard – took a step backwards.

'You've just been in Human Resources,' he said.

'Personnel,' said Victor, finishing off his handwashing. 'No, I haven't.'

'Oh, yes you have.'

'Oh, no I haven't.'

'Oh, yes you have.'

Victor was just wondering when this pantomimic back-and-forth was going to end when an announcement came over the Tannoy. 'Security guard to the front door, please. Security guard to the front door. Code nine.'

Code nine. Potential shoplifter. Victor could see the conflicted look on Kurtz's face: stay and beat him to a pulp or answer the code nine.

'This isn't over,' said Kurtz, turning to go. 'If I find out you've been in HR I'll gut you like a freshly-caught stumpnose.'

Victor watched as Kurtz squelched his way out of the changing room. 'Masquerading as a human sponge,' he said, taking the bottle of whisky from his pocket. More convinced than ever that he could write that book, he lifted the bottle to his mouth. He was about to take a swig when he realised that it wasn't the bottle of whisky he was holding but the bottle of ink. He looked at the label. *Glow-Cop Security Ink.* The type of ink that businesses, churches, and the once-burgled brigade slapped all over their laptops, chalices, and family heirlooms to deter future thieves, the ink showed up under infrared light and would cling to the hands of anyone touching it.

Screwing the top back on, Victor's mind went into overdrive. Every Whiting's do involved a set of coloured infrared lights. If he could somehow coat the money left in the charity tin with the *Glow-Cop* then he could catch Kurtz red-handed. Blue-handed, actually, according to the label. The best part about it was that Violet would know Kurtz had been up to no good. As Whiting's in-house security liaison officer – Kurtz was contracted in from an outside company – only she was supposed to use the *Glow-Cop*. Victor had seen her splash the stuff about like she was painting the Forth Bridge. Or putting nail polish on her oversized fingernails.

But first he had to get Angel's ring back. And with Kurtz on the warpath, the sooner he did that the better. Taking the master locker key from his shoe, he took off for the ladies' changing room with a cry of 'No Plan B.'

CHAPTER EIGHT

HAVING CHANGED INTO a dry set of clothes, Kurtz stood glowering by the checkouts. Replaying the events of the last half hour over in his mind, he felt his blood starting to rise.

'Was that it?' he asked himself. 'The start of the culture wars? Wokery rising? Trans-activism? Or was it just a man shoving a big pair of *tets* in my face?' Any of the first three and he'd failed miserably. Let his own side down. To be bested by a man who hid behind a huge set of *tets*…He'd read online about the wave of trans-terrorism sweeping the world. And watched with horror the stories on GB News about ten-year old's being primed for gender reassignment, sometimes against the wishes of their parents, but sometimes *with*. But to have it literally thrust in his face…It was South Africa, 1994, all over again, after the *kaffers* took over and ruined the place.

Why didn't he listen more to Laurence Fox. And Katie Hopkins. And Nigel Farage. All they ever did was speak common-*bladdy*-sense. The only person who spoke more was Jacob Rees-Mogg. Even if he did look like a wet fart dribbling down the hindleg of a spaniel. But then so did that other guy who looked like Rees-Mogg and who Kurtz used to watch in those *Carry On* documentaries back when he was living in South Africa. Charles – Huntley? Hartley? Hawtrey? Charles Hawtrey, that was it. And he was a man's man. Look at all those sailors he wrestled down at the docks every night.

That was the country Kurtz thought he was coming to when he first arrived in the UK back in '97. The world of the *Carry On* documentaries. Instead, what he'd got was Tony *bladdy* Blair, Cool Britannia and Graham Norton. For the next twenty years everything seemed to get worse. Until Boris Johnson took over. Big, bouncing, Aryan-blonde Boris. He was right about everything. He was right about Trump. About Brexit. About the number of *bladdy* foreigners invading the country from God-*bladdy*-knows-where, who couldn't even *praat* speak – *bladdy* English. He was right about piccaninnies with watermelon smiles and Muslim women looking like letterboxes. And he was right about Jacob Rees-Mogg, Sir Jacob, if there was any justice and the PC-brigade and left-wing rags like *The Daily Mail* and *The Telegraph* stopped picking on him. Look at how he was attacked for tweeting a video from AfD, the Alternative for Germany Party. To Kurtz, it proved what a true patriot Rees-Mogg was. As for being a true man of God…Hadn't Rees-Mogg voted against same-sex marriage, state benefits for the poor *and* human rights? The man was a *bladdy* saint. And the one to take over once that coconut who'd snatched the throne from Johnson was shaken from the tree.

The little man in his stomach was grumbling worse than ever. 'Don't worry yourself, Jacob' he said, patting his belly, 'if fat *tets* wants a trans war, he'll get a trans war.'

Over by the tinned vegetable aisle Angel was lifting the shelving with one hand while searching underneath with the other for her ring. *She* was the weapon Kurtz would use to win the war. Fight fire with fire. Trans with trans. Biologically female, she was bigger and butchier than any dyke he'd ever seen. Come to think of it, she was bigger and bulkier than any *dike* he'd ever seen. Anyone trying to put a finger into *that* would lose their entire *bladdy* body. She'd go through them like Covid through an old folk's home. All he had to do was tell her about the engagement ring and Victor would be transitioning from a living, breathing, walking bag of *tets* into a rotting, stinking, maggot-ridden corpse faster than you could say LGBTQ+. Man, she'd lay him flatter than a punctured sex doll. The question was whether to deploy her now or wait until the charity do?

He placed a soothing hand on his stomach. The sooner Angel found out the better. That was his first thought. Nothing would give him more pleasure than to see her rip Victor's fat *tets* from his fat body. Especially after what had just happened in the men's changing room. Alright, it was Baz's mop bucket that had caused the mess. But it wouldn't have happened in the first place had Victor not been up to no good. And he'd definitely been up to no good. There was no strong physical evidence that could prove it. But Kurtz's little man and policeman's nose told him something was up.

But there was one big, fat, problem. If Victor was busy getting split apart by the Angel of Death, he wouldn't be able to split up Malcolm and Violet. And right then – with the wedding due to take place the next day – *that* was the most important thing.

Kurtz adjusted his tie and smoothed down his shirt. The best thing to do was to wait. As Akila, his Swahili maid, always used to say, 'A patient person never misses a thing'. He shifted his weight from one foot to the other. 'Never marry a woman who has bigger feet than you.' That was Akila's other favourite saying. He glanced down at his own feet. Despite his huge frame, they were only a size six and looked a bit feminine.

He looked over at Violet behind the Customer Service desk. Her feet were like her hands, clownishly big. Like enormous pieces of gammon, they gave her a walk a little bit like a top-heavy penguin. Kurtz pictured her waddling up the church aisle.

Pulling himself together – 'You don't look at the *bladdy* hearth when you're poking the *bladdy* mantelpiece, or whatever the *bladdy* phrase is' – his thoughts turned to the charity do. As compere he would have complete control over what happened on the stage. His plan was to wait until Victor had split Malcolm and Violet up, make his own proposal of marriage to Violet, then finish off the evening by telling Angel that it was Victor who had stolen her ring. What better way to end proceedings, him engaged to Violet, and Victor smashed to smithereens by Angel.

Kurtz let out a chortle as he imagined the part where Angel fell upon Victor like her avenging namesake. At the checkout nearest to him, Malcolm appeared with the blind man. Kurtz watched as they fought over who would put the shopping on the conveyor belt. Amazed that anyone could think of marrying such a *domkop*, he looked over again at the Customer Service desk. This time Violet saw him and waved. Kurtz waved back. Her feet couldn't be more than size eleven. Twelve, at the most. He let out a sigh. Angel finding out about the ring would spoil Violet's big night. The night she has spent so much time organising and looking forward to. That, and the fact that finding out her engagement ring really belonged to Angel, would really knock the *pap* out of her. Still, as Akila used to say before he sacked her for talking too much, 'You can't make the bread rise without pounding the dough'. And anyway, he'd be there – good old Captain Kurtz – to save the evening by giving her another engagement ring. Violet would be saying 'I do' before the ring was even on her finger.

Over at the checkout Malcolm was putting the blind man's debit card in the machine the wrong way. Putting it the right way, the blind man gestured angrily for Malcolm to start packing. Kurtz let out another chortle as he watched Malcolm put all the light groceries at the bottom and the heavy ones on top. But then a thought hit him that made him stop chortling. He knew that Victor would turn up to the charity do. Malcolm never missed a work's night out. And wherever Malcolm went, Victor was sure to follow, usually with his hand out. But would Victor stay until the very end?

Kurtz's plans depended upon Victor doing so. And as he watched Malcolm and the blind man fight over who would carry the bags of shopping to the taxi rank, he came up with a solution. Whistling loudly and swinging his bunch of keys he went off in search of Derek.

II

Near to the ladies' changing rooms, Victor was waiting for the corridor to clear. Every time he thought it had someone would come careering out of nowhere. He couldn't hang around for much longer. It would look too suspicious. Especially as by now the whole store would know about his crack-peeping. If he was to get inside Violet's locker, he would have to act quickly. There was only thing to do. Throw caution to the wind and storm the room.

He was just psyching himself up when he saw Violet heading towards him. Ducking for cover, he could see that she was wearing a pair of earphones and repeating out loud, 'I, Violet Melissa Dungworth, take thee, Malcolm Vernon Legg, to be my wedded husband, to have and to hold from this day on…'

Pushing open the changing room door, Violet disappeared inside. From his hiding place, Victor let out a silent curse.

With Violet inside the changing room, his moment had surely passed. Instinctively he reached inside his pocket for the bottle of whisky. Instead he pulled out one of the suggestion slips Malcolm had given him earlier.

BURN DOWN THE SUPERMARKET!!!

Such a thought had run through Victor's own mind a million times. Usually at Christmas after having to listen to seasonal songs on a loop for eight hours a day. He glanced down at the slip and then at the fire alarm on the wall.

'Maybe, just maybe…'

III

KURTZ FOUND DEREK on the shopfloor chewing on a toothpick. 'Got a minute, boss?' he said.

'What's on your mind, deputy?'

'It's about the charity do this evening.'

Derek spat into a nearby bin. 'What about it?'

'I need someone to help me tidy up afterwards.'

Derek put the toothpick back in his mouth. 'Well, here's what you do, deputy. You mosey on round this here shop floor and raise yourself a posse. Anyone complains, you tell them that the head honcho here's laying down the law.'

'I only need one man.'

'Then go get him and stop wasting my time.'

'Problem is, boss, he won't want to do it.'

Derek looked up at Kurtz. 'Who won't?'

'Victor.'

At the mention of Victor's name a pained expression fell across Derek's face. 'Why the hell do you want that yellow-livered piece of trash to help you?' he said.

'Because I know he'll hate it.'

Derek stopped chewing on his toothpick and thought for a moment. 'Then he sounds just like the man we're after,' he said, breaking out into a wide grin. 'You tell him I said that.'

'And if he cuts up rough?'

Derek removed his Ray-Bans. 'Then you tell him to come and see me and I'll tear him a new a-hole. You got that?'

'*Ja*, boss.'

'By the time I've finished with him he'll be shaking like a rattlesnake in a canvas bag. They don't call me Derek "the Destroyer" Braithwaite for nothing, you know…'

RRRRRRRRRRRRRRRRRRING!!!!!!!!!!!!!!

'Sweet child of mine!' said Derek. 'What in the name of Miss Nancy is that?'

'It's the fire alarm, boss.'

The colour drained from Derek's face.

'We better start evacuating the building,' said Kurtz, moving over to the checkouts.

But Derek ''the Destroyer' Braithwaite had other ideas. Moving as fast as a man in four-inch heels can, he ran out of the building screaming 'FIREEEEEEEEE!!!!!!!!!!!'

IV

WITH THE HEAD Honcho running around the car park like a demented Yosemite Sam, Kurtz took charge. Ushering terrified customers out the front door, he grabbed hold of Malcolm. 'Open the fire doors.'

'Don't panic!' said a hysterical Malcolm, running up and down the checkouts. 'Don't panic! Don't panic!! DON'T PANIC!!!'

Baz ambled past with a lit cigarette in his mouth. 'C'mon, baby, light my fucking fire,' he said, making his way into the car park. Coming the other way was Frank.

'What's going on?' he said.

'London's fucking burning,' said a cackling Baz. 'Here, fetch the fucking engines, fire fucking fire. Go on you bastard, burn yourself to the fucking ground.'

'Open the fire doors,' said Kurtz to Frank.

'What, with my back?' said Frank, turning back around and heading in the direction of the car park. 'I'm retiring in twelve months.'

Angel appeared carrying an axe in one hand and a fire extinguisher in the other. She set the fire extinguisher down on the ground and proceeded to smash the axe into the fire door. Kurtz ran over. 'What're you doing?' he shouted over the din of the alarm.

'Breaking down the door,' said Angel.

Kurtz held up a hand. Angel froze in mid-swing and watched as he pressed down the handle on the fire door and opened it. Angel stared blankly at him for a few seconds before smashing the axe repeatedly into the open door. Giving up on her, Kurtz shepherded out the last few remaining customers. He ran over to Malcolm, who was still running around waving the 1974 *Work Act* in the air. 'What're you doing?'

'Don't panic!' said Malcolm. He read from the booklet he was holding. 'According to the Nineteen seventy-four *Health and Safety at Work Act*, make your way to the fire safety point quietly and in an orderly manner. Do *not* stop to pick up your belongings…!'

Kurtz grabbed hold of Malcolm and shook him. 'Everyone's out!' he said.

'Yes,' said Malcolm. 'Everyone out!'

Kurtz pushed Malcolm out into the car park where the noise from the fire alarm didn't drown out what he was trying to say. 'I said, everyone *is* out.'

Jackie walked over carrying a clipboard. 'There you are,' she said, ticking Kurtz's and Malcolm's name off the list. 'Three still missing...'

Distracted momentarily by Derek running around the car park screaming 'FIREEEEEEEEEEE!!!!!!!!', Kurtz turned to Jackie and said, 'You can cross Angel's name off as well.'

'She's out, is she?' said Jackie, ticking off Angel's name.

'Out of her *fokking* mind.' Jackie looked up from the clipboard. 'She's turning one of the fire doors into matchsticks.' Kurtz nodded in the direction of the store. 'Who's left?'

Jackie looked down her list. 'Erm, just Violet and Victor.'

'What?' Kurtz turned to Malcolm. 'Have you seen them?' he asked.

'Don't panic!' said Malcolm.

'Go on, Malc,' said Baz, lighting another roll-up. 'Stand by your fucking beds.'

Kurtz set off back in the direction of the building.

Jackie pulled on his sleeve. 'We can't go in until the fire service gets here,' she said.

Kurtz shrugged off Jackie's hand and ran into the store.

'Fetch the fucking engines,' said Baz, bobbing up and down.

THE FIRST THING to hit Victor as he charged into the ladies' changing room was just how tidy and fragrant it was. He paused for a moment to take it in. *Maybe gender reassignment was the way to go?* he thought. Better facilities. And if there was ever a *Titanic Part II*, at least he'd be in the lifeboats with the women and children instead of clinging to the side of a barrel freezing his tits off.

Snapping to, he went to work. Taking the master key out of his shoe, he found Violet's locker and opened it. Inside was the charity tin, some makeup, some old face masks, a purse and a book.

No ring.

Dismayed, Victor opened the purse. All it contained was some small change and a picture of George Clooney. He picked up the book, *Love Me Twice, Shame on Me!* by Amy Lovelace, and in desperation flicked through the pages.

Nothing.

Victor was just thinking over the many ways of committing suicide – a car exhaust and six feet of plastic piping was this week's favourite – when he saw something glinting on the top of the charity tin. At first he thought it was a coin that hadn't been properly pushed through the slit. He looked closer at it.

Angel's ring!

Like he was handling some antique Grecian urn, Victor carefully lifted the tin down. All the humiliations he'd had to go through to get hold of the ring! The threats! The heartache! The being labelled a pervert! Finally, it would all be over. And finally things had worked out just as he'd planned. Usually, everything he touched turned into a disaster. But not this time.

With trembling fingers, he reached out for the ring.

'Violet!'

There was no mistaking it. Even above the fire alarm Victor could tell that it was Kurtz's voice. He turned sharply. As he did, the ring slid through the slit and into the tin. 'No!' he cried, trying to force his fingers through after it.

'Violet!'

Victor just had time to shut Violet's locker and shove the tin down the back of his trousers when the door flew open and in ran Kurtz.

VI

THE SHOCKED LOOK on Kurtz's face told Victor one thing. He better have a good explanation for his presence in the ladies' changing rooms. And it better not be one based on gender politics. Not if he wanted to keep all his teeth in his head. Fortunately, he had an obvious one at hand.

'I was just making sure everyone was out,' he said.

'What?' said Kurtz, cupping a hairy ear.

'I said, I was just making sure everyone was out.'

Before Kurtz could reply one of the cubicle doors swung open. Out of it stepped Violet. Still wearing her earphones and practising her wedding vows, she screamed when she saw Victor and Kurtz. 'No,' she said, backing away. 'There is no lawful impediment why Malcolm and I can't be joined in holy matrimony.'

Victor gestured for her to remove the earphones. Whether it was the shock of there possibly *being* a lawful impediment as to why she couldn't be joined in holy matrimony to Malcolm. Or the sound of the fire alarm sounded to her like church bells chiming and she thought she was about to be thwarted at the last minute. Whatever, Violet flung herself on the ground and in a pleading tone said, 'I do, I do, I do, I do, I do…!'

'Violet!'

Kurtz's peremptory tone shut Violet up. Until…

'Nothing to worry about,' said Victor. 'It's just the fire alarm.'

NO PLAN B, MALCOLM!'

Violet picked herself up from the floor and started running around the room screaming. Victor looked on as Kurtz – no doubt falling back on his police training – caught hold of her and slapped her hard across the face. Victor expected Kurtz to follow this up with a kick to the nether regions and a, 'Now are you going to tell us where it is, sambo?' Instead, Kurtz grabbed hold of Violet and shook her.

'Pull yourself together, *bokkie*,' he said.

'It's alright,' said Victor, playing the part of good cop and taking a gentle hold of Violet's arm. 'I've come to escort you downstairs.'

Holding the slapped side of her face, Violet turned to Victor with tears of gratitude in her eyes. 'Oh, my knight in shining armour,' she said.

'*We've* come to escort you downstairs,' said a scowling Kurtz, taking hold of Violet's other arm.

'My two knights in shining armour,' said Violet.

'I don't remember Lancelot socking Guinevere in the mouth,' said Victor, leading a limp Violet towards the changing room door.

With Kurtz's scowl growing more scowly, Victor realised he'd said the wrong thing. He also realised that with thirty-odd quid in loose change half-stuck up his jacksie he was walking like a cowboy with the trots. Or rather, because of the clinking sound the coins were making, a cowboy with the trots wearing an enormous pair of spurs. For now, the clinking sound couldn't be heard over the noise of the fire alarm. But if the fire alarm was to stop ringing…

'No Plan B,' he said weakly, pushing open the changing room door.

VII

Outside in the car park the fire engine had arrived. 'Right, where's the fire?' said the first fireman to Baz.

'Up me fucking ring,' said Baz, bending over.

The fireman paused for a second. 'If you can just stand back, sir, and let us deal with it.'

Baz stuck his arm in the air. '*Heil* fucking Hitler!'

'How's it looking?' said a second fireman.

The first fireman looked across at Baz, who was goose-stepping around the car park. 'He's just told me his arse is on fire and now it looks like he's off to invade Poland.'

'I bloody hate Sundays,' said the second fireman, putting on his helmet.

VIII

With Violet threatening to fall over every few steps, progress down the corridor was painfully slow. It gave Victor time to think. What he needed to do was to go back to the changing room, fish the ring out of the charity tin, then return the tin to Violet's locker.

But how?

Whatever plan he came up with it had to be soon. Given the odd way he was walking, Kurtz was already giving him sideways looks. What was required was some kind of holding action.

'I've soiled myself,' he said to Kurtz, above the din. 'Always happens when I'm excited. Like the time I saw David Starkey. Poured out of me like larva from a volcano.'

'Your constipation's cured, then,' said Kurtz.

Victor let out a silent curse. He forgot he was supposed to be bunged up. His lies were beginning to catch up with him. Which was more than what Violet was doing. Dragging her size twelve feet, he and Kurtz were practically having to carry her. They came to the door at the top of the stairs.

'That's it, *bokkie*,' said Kurtz, leading Violet down the steps one at a time. 'We'll be down on the shop floor soon and then out into the car park where it's safe.'

Safe? Resembling a real safe with the amount of money he had shoved up his rear end, Victor couldn't help but see the irony of the word. Doubly ironic, given how *un*-safe he was about to be once he reached the car park and his bottom started paying out in silver dollars in front of everyone. He needed a reason to abandon the rescue party and go back upstairs to the ladies' changing room. The trouble was, he couldn't think of one.

'I've just remembered, I've left my engagement ring in my locker,' said Violet.

'We can't go back for it now, *bokkie*,' said Kurtz. 'We've got to get you outside.' Violet appeared to faint. Kurtz reached down and gently slapped her face. 'Are you still with us, *bokkie*?'

'Leave me,' said Violet, with a limp flick of her hand. 'Save yourselves.'

Kurtz looked over at Victor. 'What did she say?'

'She said we should save ourselves,' said Victor. Had there been a real fire he would've considered this sound advice. But Violet had given him a way out. Before he could take it, however, Kurtz bent down and shouted into Violet's ear.

'It's alright, *bokkie*,' he said, 'I'll go and get your ring.'

Victor let go of Violet's arm and rushed over to the door that led back upstairs. 'I'll go,' he said.

Kurtz let go of Violet's other arm and raced across to the door. 'I said, I'll go.'

The two began to scuffle. Still prostrate on the floor, Violet opened her eyes and smiled. 'Oh, having two men fight over me,' she said. 'It's like Peaches Melba in Amy Lovelace's *Love Rivals in Paradise.*'

Victor and Kurtz were still tussling when the alarm suddenly stopped. They stood there, frozen to the spot, hands all over each other like lovers. It was Violet who broke the silence. 'It's stopped.' Kurtz ran over and helped her up from the floor.

'We still need to get you out, *bokkie*,' he said. 'Just because the alarm's stopped doesn't mean the fire's out.'

Victor saw his chance. 'I'll go and get the ring.'

'You heard what Kurtz said,' said Violet. 'The fire might not be out.'

'Then I'll see you in hell.' Having heard this line spoken in many a dramatic moment in many a dramatic film, Victor had always wanted to use it. Pleased to finally have got the chance, he then proceeded to walk into the frame of the door and bang his nose.

'Oh, Victor!' said Violet, clasping her hands together.

'It's nothing,' said Victor, rubbing his sore nose and gripping the tin with his buttocks to lessen the sound of the coins rattling. He turned to go.

'Haven't you forgotten something?'

Victor shuddered to think what that something might be. Despite being in a wrestling match with a hairy Boer at the time, he'd heard Violet's Peaches Melba comment. And seen the simpering smile she had plastered all over her face. Any more pretend gallantry on his part and she'd go full-on Amy Lovelace. 'What?' he said, hardly daring to turn around.

'My locker key, silly.' Violet unhooked it from her key ring and held it out for Victor to take. 'And remember, this isn't goodbye, it's just *adieu*.'

'*Adieu*,' said Victor, taking possession of the key and ignoring both Violet's syrupy smile and Kurtz's granite glare. 'I mean, see you later.'

The last thing he heard as he disappeared up the stairs was the sound of a kiss being blown in his direction.

IX

THE FIRST FIREMAN walked over to where Frank was standing smoking a cigarette. 'Are you in charge?' he asked him.

Frank looked behind him at Derek cowering in the far corner of the car park. 'I suppose so,' he said with a sigh. 'Although I'm supposed to be retiring in twelve months' time.'

'Lucky you,' said the fireman. 'We've had a look around and can't see any fire. The alarm was set off outside the men's changing room. Someone must've set it off by accident. Either that or it was a prank. We've switched it off now. But the fire doors will need closing and the alarm resetting before anyone's allowed back in.'

Frank glanced up at the dark clouds above him. *Another job for him to do.*

'Oh, one more thing,' said the fireman. 'There's one of your lot in there smashing the place to pieces with an axe. Big lad with long hair. We tried to stop him, but he took no notice. I'll leave him to you.'

After watching the fire engine drive off, Frank lit another cigarette. It was pointless him rushing. Everyone needed some time to calm down. He took a couple of mediative puffs and began prioritizing. First, he would finish his cigarette. Then he would ring his wife and find out what he was having for tea. After that he would reset the fire alarm and close all the fire doors. Unless someone else had already done it.

VICTOR RAN UP the stairs as quickly as his breasts would allow him. He knew from his fire training that once the alarm had been switched off and the all-clear given there would be a five-or-so minute break before staff and customers were allowed back in. Just enough time to do what was needed.

He rushed into the ladies' changing room, retrieved the tin from his trousers, unscrewed the top and took out the ring. Using Violet's own key, he opened her locker and put the tin inside. He was about to shut the door when a thought came to him. Taking the *Glow-Cop* from his pocket, he poured half a dozen drops through the slit of the tin and then gave the tin a good shake.

'Thief break through and steal if you dare,' he said, slamming shut the locker door.

WITH VIOLET HALF-SLUMPED against him, Kurtz steered the two of them into the car park where they were met by a loud round of applause from the other members of staff. With little royal waves along the way, Violet insisted on walking the last few steps unaided. She made it to the fire assembly point, and in a voice trembling with emotion, presented herself to Jackie. 'Violet Melissa Dungworth, Customer Service, reporting for duty.'

As the assembled throng clapped and cheered, Baz let rip with a joyous, 'Go on, Violet, you fucking bitch!'

Jackie looked over at Kurtz. 'Victor?'

'Still inside,' said Kurtz.

'Oh, my brave hero,' said Violet, clutching a hand to her breast.

'Good job there's no fire,' said Jackie.

'What?' said Kurtz and Violet in unison.

'Fire engine's been and gone. They reckon someone set the alarm off by accident.'

'Oh,' said Violet, her shoulders slumped in disappointment. 'I thought I might make the local news.'

Kurtz had other things on his mind. For one thing Jacob had started gurgling again. 'Accident?' he said, holding his stomach.

'Either that or a prank,' said Jackie. 'But who on our staff would do something like that?'

'How do you know it was a member of staff?'

'Apparently it was the alarm outside the men's changing room that was set off.'

'The men's changing room…?' Kurtz listened to Jacob rumbling even louder. 'I'm with you, Jacob,' he said under his breath, setting off towards the store.

Jackie ran after him. 'No one's allowed in until Frank's given the all-clear.'

'We could be out here until the middle of next *bladdy* week.'

Jackie shrugged her shoulders. 'It's a sackable offense.'

Kurtz stared in the direction of the store while rubbing his gurgling stomach. 'Don't worry, Jacob,' he said. 'We'll get him, we'll get him.'

XII

VICTOR OPENED HIS locker and put the ring inside. His plan was to tell Violet he dropped it when he was running out of the store. He knew she'd be angry. But anything was better than the stewing, storming, homicidal wrath of Angel. As for Kurtz telling Angel…Without any physical proof there would be nothing to tie Victor to the ring. He was in the clear. All he had to do now was delete the picture on Kevin's mobile phone and posterity wouldn't be able to lay a hand on him either.

Plastered as it was with pictures of ex-dart's player Phil 'The Power' Taylor, working out which locker was Kevin's was easy. When Victor opened it using the master key it was like opening a Pandora's box of porn. Inside were piles of specialist magazines – *Schindler's Fist, Tricophilia-Times, Foot Fetish for Amputees* – DVDs, sex toys and a small blow-up doll. The latter came with a Barbie-style body – naked – and the head of *Coronation Street* legend Bill Roache. One thing there wasn't was a mobile phone.

Thwarted, Victor was about to close the locker door when he noticed a piece of paper stuck to the inside of it. Written across the top were the words PEEPHOLE PARADE, followed by a list of the names of every female employee in the store. Each name had a score of ten next to it.

'Seven!' said Victor, when he saw Angel's score. He continued down the list. 'Mandy – five, Catherine – eight, Jackie – seven, Amy – seven, Violet – six, Victor – six, Linda – nine…'

Victor?!

Victor grabbed his breasts in horror. The thought of Kevin spying on him was bad enough. But then to be only given a six…Feeling twice violated he punched the Bill Roache doll in the face and slammed shut the locker door. Flinging open the changing room door, he stomped his way downstairs.

XIII

VICTOR MADE HIS way on to the shop floor. With the customers and staff still not let back in, and the fire alarm and checkouts switched off, everything seemed deserted. And except for the mantra-like hum from the fridges, there was an eerie silence. As he moved through the empty aisles he felt like he was in some post-apocalyptic movie, where a natural disaster, or maybe a new Covid variant of concern, had left him the only survivor. Having dreamed of such a scenario all his life – in Victor's perfect world the population of the Earth would be kept to well below a hundred – he knew exactly what to do next.

Making his way to the Beers, Wines and Spirits aisle he helped himself to a third quarter bottle of whisky. Had it really been a *The Omega Man/I Am Legend* situation, then his next move would've been to break into the local police station, arm himself to the teeth with fifteen pump action shotguns, find himself a stray dog, and then save what was left of mankind. Instead, he stuffed a cream cake in his mouth and made his way leisurely to the front entrance. As he passed General Merchandise, he heard a loud thudding sound.

Darkseekers?

Victor ducked down behind a shelf. As the thudding continued, he crept towards where it was coming from.

Thud!

Zombies?

Thud!

Dementors?

Thud!

Orcs?

Thud!

Victor peeped over the top of one of the cabinets.

Angel! Smashing chunks of masonry from the wall with an axe.

Thud! Thud! Thud!

Victor hit the palm of his hand against his forehead. If only he hadn't left the ring in his locker. He could've handed it back to Angel and said that he found it whilst the store was being evacuated.

Thud! Thud! Thud!

Given how worked up she was it was best to let sleeping dogs – 'rhinos' was probably the more accurate zoomorphism – lie. One thing he couldn't do was use the locker master key to put the ring back in Angel's locker.

Thud! Thud! Thud!

Angel had had hers taken off her after she'd put two members of the Food-to-Go counter in it after they'd burnt her pizza.

Thud! Thud! Thud!

Victor took evasive action as pieces of debris flew over his head. His next thought was to run back upstairs, get the ring, and drop it somewhere for Angel to find. But the plan was too risky. Knowing his luck Malcolm would probably find it again and end up getting engaged to Violet for a second time. Then they'd be right back where they'd started.

With bits of concrete raining down on him, he came up with what he thought was the best solution. He would sneak it back to Angel at the charity do. Usually, a small changing room was provided for those doing a turn. He would slip it into her bag there.

Thud! Thud! Thud!

Problem solved; Victor started his retreat. As he did so he noticed a rack of women's jewellery across from him. Ducking over, he sorted through the rings. Made from cheap metal alloys with plastic stones, they were the sort you'd find in a Christmas cracker or a grab machine on Blackpool seafront. He searched through them until he found one that looked like Angel's ring. The nearest he could find was silver in colour with a single diamond-like stone in the centre. Shoving it into his pocket, he made his way to the front entrance.

Frank was there, talking on his mobile phone. Surprised to find his department manager anywhere near the epicentre of the action, a startled Victor took a step back. 'What're you doing here?' he said.

'Hold the line, please,' said Frank to whoever was on the other end of the phone. He looked over at Victor. 'I'm not retiring for another twelve months.'

'I mean, here in the building? Aren't you supposed to be at the fire assembly point?'

Frank let out a deep sigh. 'You know me,' he said, 'first in, last out.'

Victor *did* know Frank. Which was why he was so surprised to see him. And which was why Frank's 'First in, last out' only worked if they were standing in the car park. But with an unopened bottle of whisky soon to be burning a hole in his oesophagus, Victor didn't have it in him to argue. 'Well, don't forget about Angel,' he said, prising open the front doors.

But Frank was back on his phone. 'Chicken? We had that on Friday. Can't we have lamb chops?'

XIV

VICTOR EXITED THE store. Ahead of him the rest of the staff had formed into a semi-circle. As he approached, they started clapping and cheering. He moved slowly, milking the moment for all it was worth. It wasn't every day he got to play the hero and he planned to enjoy every second of it. Even the odd shout of 'Go on, big boobs!' and 'Well done Mr Man-Tits', wasn't going to spoil it. With his reputation as the branch pervert receding, and his reputation as the saviour of Violets and engagement rings growing, he marched up to Jackie and in a clear steady voice said, 'Porter. Victor. Produce.'

The clapping and cheering reached a crescendo. Victor held up his hand for silence. There was a long pause as he let the drama build. He then walked up to Violet, took the cheap ring from his pocket, and said with a bow, 'Yours, I believe.'

With tears streaming down her cheeks, Violet clasped the ring to her breast and whispered breathlessly, 'I do.'

The clapping and cheering resumed. All except for a glum-looking Tarquin Travers-Booth and a stony-faced Kurtz. Kevin nudged the latter and said, 'I wouldn't be surprised if those two ended up in the broom cupboard again.'

But Kurtz's mind was on something else. Moving closer to where Victor was having his back slapped and hand shaken, he bent down and pretended to tie his shoelace. What he was really doing was picking up the piece of paper that had fallen out of Victor's pocket, the same pocket that Victor had so theatrically produced the ring from. As Kurtz made his way to his original spot he realised that it was actually two pieces of paper.

'Here,' said Kevin, 'I wonder if there are any cracks in the broom cupboard door. With Victor's tits it'd be like watching a pair of lezzers!'

Ignoring Kevin, Kurtz unfolded the first piece of paper. BURN DOWN THE SUPERMARKET!!!! As if he'd been hit by electricity, all the hairs on Kurtz's body lifted So, Victor was planning on setting fire to the store? *He* must've had set the alarm off. Kurtz looked around at the rest of the staff. This was probably a dry run. To see how everyone would react.

He unfolded the second piece of paper.

KILL FRANK!!!

Kurtz's eyes seemed to lose focus and he reeled as he reread the words. He always thought Victor was a *mompie*, a real *mampara*, but a murderer…?! Kurtz folded up the slips and put them back in his pocket. So, this was how far the rot had set in, was it? Burning down supermarkets. Killing department managers. Trans-terrorism on a global scale. *Ag sies*, man, not even Laurence Fox could've seen this coming! LGBTQ+ was on the warpath. And it was obviously not going to stop until everyone was either dead or gender reassigned.

Over my dead body, thought Kurtz. *Over my dead* male *body*.

He watched Frank exit the store and disappear into one of the trolley sheds. Within seconds puffs of cigarette smoke wafted across the car park. Angry that Frank hadn't given the all-clear, Kurtz set off towards the building thinking that – in Frank's case at least – Victor might have got it right.

'We haven't had the all-clear,' Jackie shouted after him.

'Hiawatha's sent us a smoke signal,' said Kurtz, aiming a thumb at the fumes coming from the trolley shed.

'Alright, children,' said Jackie, sighing, playtime's over. Everyone back to work.'

There was a collective groan and the shuffling of feet as people slowly made their way back into the building. Disappointed that his moment in the sun hadn't last a little longer, Victor was one of the last to set off. He was joined by

Malcolm, who said, 'Do you think we should be going back in when one of the trolley sheds is on fire?'

An exasperated Victor raised an eyebrow. 'That's Frank.'

'Frank's on fire?' Malcolm pulled out the *Work Act* and started rifling through it. 'There's nothing in here about what to do when a department manager's on fire,' he said.

'Malcolm.'

'L-Learn not to b-burn,' said Malcolm, crumpling up the *Work Act*. 'F-Fire catches, so don't p-play with matches. Don't panic, Frank!'

Victor grabbed hold of Malcolm. 'Pull yourself together, sir!' he said, slapping him lightly across both cheeks with one hand. 'He's only having a cigarette.'

'A cigarette?' said Malcolm, wide-eyed. 'In the car park? Frank?'

Victor was about to inform Malcolm that Frank having a cigarette in the car park was about as rare an occurrence as Baz using the F-word when he was interrupted by Violet. 'See how it sparkles,' she said, flashing the ring on her finger.

'It matches your eyes,' said Victor, taken slightly off-guard. '"They sparkle still the right Promethean fire".'

'I thought you couldn't have smoke without fire?' said Malcolm, peering over at the trolley shed.

'And to think that I ever called you Harvey Weinstein,' said Violet, ignoring Malcolm. 'Can you ever find it in your heart to forgive me.'

This time Victor hesitated. He'd laid it on a bit thick with the eyes sparkling and Promethean fire lines. Partly because Violet had ambushed him and he wasn't really thinking about what he was saying. And partly in the hope that it would deflect Violet's attention from the fact that the ring had been switched. The problem was the soppy look she was giving him. It was similar to the one she had given him right before their tussle in the broom cupboard. And it told Victor one thing. He'd gone too far. With just a few ill-judged words the love-genie was out of the bottle.

'I will never forget what you did for me today,' said Violet, uncorking the bottle even further.

Victor opened his mouth to protest.

'No, don't speak,' said Violet, pressing a sausage finger to Victor's lips.

'Umh-wa-mhha-wrily,' he said. Translation: 'It was nothing really.'

With her finger still covering Victor's mouth, Violet turned to Malcolm. 'Sorry, Malc,' she said, 'the wedding's off.'

'Oh, fine,' said Malcolm, uncrumpling the *Work Act.* 'Whose wedding?' But Violet was too busy gazing adoringly into Victor's increasingly bulging eyes to hear.

'My heart belongs to another,' she said.

'Nw-hld-en-frgs-saak!' Or: 'Now, hold on for God's sake!'

Violet adjusted her hand to grip his entire mouth and chin. Leaning in, she whispered into Victor's ear. 'I know you switched the ring.' Victor's eyes stopped bulging and started darting from left to right in panic. 'You couldn't bear to see me with another man.'

Here, Victor made a fatal error. Despite being held in a Mark 'the Undertaker' Calaway-type death grip, he still managed to nod his head up and down. It was his way of saying, 'Yes, he *could* bear to see her with another man'. But then he realised his mistake. All that he'd done was signify his agreement with what Violet had just said.

'Oh, Victor! Look at you. Boring into my soul with those come-to-bed eyes!'

Behind the shovel-like grip of Violet's hand, Victor was

amazed at how badly she was reading the situation. The only come-to-bed eyes he was giving her were come-to-deathbed ones.

'But we must wait.'

Victor nodded his head once more. Except this time more vigorously. For once he and Violet agreed. After all, the wait could be a year. Ten. Or until hell freezes over.

'Until tonight,' she said, 'when we will announce our love – and engagement – at the charity do.'

Had he been free to do so, Victor would've let out an ear-piercing scream. However, with Violet's hand gripped even tighter over his mouth, all he could manage was a kind of strangulated hiss.

'I know how disappointed you are that we have to wait,' said Violet. She put her mouth to Victor's ear again. 'But patience, *mon cherry*; it won't be long now.' She removed her hand from Victor's mouth and walked off.

A gasping Victor fell to his knees. 'I'm engaged,' he said, when he finally got his voice back. 'Congratulations!' said Malcolm, holding out his hand.

CHAPTER NINE

BY THE TIME he'd rushed around the supermarket, re-sealed the fire exits, collected the fire extinguishers and stopped Angel from demolishing any more of the shop floor, Kurtz was ready to join Victor in murdering Frank. Until, stopping to catch his breath, he took the two slips from his pocket and – for the hundredth time – reread them. They were nothing short of a declaration of trans-warfare. A call to arms for the intersex brigade. He couldn't just sit on them. Or use them at a later date. They required action now. Before things got really out of hand. As he saw it, he had two choices. Either he used them to blackmail Victor into splitting up Malcolm and Violet or he reported them to the powers-that-be.

He was making his deliberations when a news story he'd read online the night before flashed into his head. The story was about a group of trans activists – with the assistance of Bill Gates and George Soros, of course – putting special chemicals into cleaning products that shrank the testes and sperm count of men and gave them *tets*. Within a generation the male sex was going to be wiped out. *The Great Gender Replacement Theory*, the story was headed. Kurtz looked down at his crotch. With that kind of battle raging he couldn't just hang around on the side lines. The entire male sex was at risk. No more nob jokes, punch-ups or farting competitions.

No more arse-pinching, arm-wrestling or Jeremy Clarkson. No more Jeremy Clarkson...!!! What were his own needs compared to that?

There's was no choice. He had to use the slips of paper for a bigger cause and report Victor straightaway. It would almost certainly mean Victor getting the sack. Which in turn would mean he couldn't use Victor to split up Malcolm and Violet. Or give him – Kurtz – the chance to tell Angel about the ring and let her rip his – Victor's – head to pieces. Unless he told Angel about the ring now, *before* he reported Victor. But if he did that when Violet still had possession of the ring, she'd be caught up in the mayhem too.

Kurtz let out a long sigh. Everything seemed so difficult in the United Kingdom. Back home, in the good old days, at least, it would be much easier. Victor would be breaking rocks by now or pushing up – 'What's the *bladdy* saying? Dandelions? Daisies?' As for Malcolm, he'd have fallen down a steep set of stairs a long, LONG time ago.

Mind made up, he put the slips into his pocket. He would report Victor to the boss and then try and split up Malcolm and Violet himself. Malcolm's memory was so bad the *domkop* would probably forget to turn up to the church anyway. The male sex came first. Consoling himself with this thought, he made his way to Derek's office with a jaunty jog. He was finally going to get rid of Victor for good. Maybe not in the number thirteen, resisting arrest way. But the two hundred and one arrests and two hundred and one convictions way was good enough. And at least Jeremy Clarkson would still be on his screen.

He knocked loudly on the boss's door.

'Come.'

Kurtz found a Ray-Ban-less Derek at his desk along with a glum-looking Frank.

'Sorry, boss,' said Kurtz, glancing at Frank. 'I didn't know you were in a meeting.'

'Well, someone's got to get this show back on the road,' said Derek. He put a toothpick into his mouth. 'I mean, Jesus H. Christ, one little fire drill and everyone starts running around like headless chickens, screaming blue murder. Fortunately, the head rooster's here to whip 'em back into line.'

Kurtz hesitated. The last time he looked Derek was acting more like a headless chicken than a head rooster. In fact had he been pushed he would've said that Derek was more head headless chicken than head rooster. Derek's mention of blue murder, however, brought Kurtz nicely to the point he had come to make. He put the BURN DOWN THE SUPERMARKET!!! slip down on the desk. 'The fire was an inside job,' he said.

'Inside job?' said Derek slowly, picking up the slip. 'You mean some cocksucker did this on purpose?'

'*Ja,* boss.'

'Derek's knuckles turned white as he gripped the slip of paper. 'Who?' he asked through gritted teeth.

'Victor.'

'Victor!' Derek shoved a fist in his mouth to stifle a scream.

'But there was no fire,' said Frank.

'That boy's trying to bring the temple down from within,' said Derek, ignoring Frank. 'Just like Delilah.'

'He'd be Samson, wouldn't he boss?' said Kurtz.

'You think Samson had bazookas like Dolly Parton?' said Derek.

'I don't think so, boss.'

'Alright, then. Let's see if we can stay on the ball. I mean Delilah.'

'*Ja,* boss.'

Derek flung the slip across the desk. 'Burning down

supermarkets…bad for business. I don't know what the folks down in Milton Keynes are going to say.'

'Milton Keynes, boss?'

'Managers' conference. They find out we've got a pyromaniac on the Produce department and we're gonna slide down that league table faster than a greased monkey down a drainpipe.'

'But there was no fire,' said Frank.

'You're sticking up for him?'

'No, I'm just saying…'

'That dirty, double-dealing, no-good, son-of-a-bitch…'

'No, but…'

'That two-bit, fat-titted, privy-peeping, Mystery-Shopper-stuffing, whisky-swilling, pantry pervert.'

'I'm just saying we don't know if it was Victor who set off the alarm.' Frank nodded at the slip on the desk. '*That* was probably a joke. You know what an unusual sense of humour he's got.'

'Maybe you think this is just a joke, too,' said Kurtz, laying the second slip on the desk.

Frank picked it up and read it. '"KILL FRANK!!!"' He looked up, stunned. 'But I'm retiring in twelve months.'

'If we don't watch our backs, Tubby Tits is gonna retire us all,' said Derek. 'The man – or whatever the hell pronoun he, she, it, them, their, we is – is obviously a psychopath.'

'It's all part of the *Great Gender Replacement Theory*, said Kurtz. 'Trans-terrorism.'

Derek let out a long whistle. 'So, ol' Ezekiel had it right after all.'

'Boss?'

'*Book of Ezekiel*. The Four Horsemen – Horse-*persons*, I suppose you gotta say now – of the Apocalypse. War: the Russkies and the Ukrainians. Famine: cost of living. Plague:

Covid. And now the wild beasts.'

'Wild beasts? What wild beasts, boss?'

'Men with coozes putting on dresses. Women riding shotgun with twelve-bore John Thomases between their legs. Homos knocking back hat-full's of hormones…That wild enough for you, son? Hell, there's everything out there from bi to cisgender to transvestitism. It's like Mother Carney's Freakshow. Without the popcorn. We now live in a world where tits on a boar are not only useful, they're also goddam *desirable*.'

The word 'boar' made Kurtz put a hand to his chest. Maybe the cleaning products were working already? 'I wouldn't go that far, boss,' he said.

'I mean, Jesus H. Christ! A prime minister with a tan browner than David Dickinson's. *Just Stop Oil. Extinction Rebellion. Black Lives Matter. Me, Too!*. What the hell happened to this thing?'

'You work your fingers to the bone and this is how you end up,' said Frank. 'Murdered by a man with big boobs!' He took off his steamed-up glasses and wiped them on his shirt. 'Why *me*, that's what I want to know?'

'I'd have thought that was obvious,' said Derek. 'He's starting with the low-hanging fruit. The easy pickin's. First, a department manager, then the store, then…'

'Jeremy Clarkson,' said Kurtz.

'Clarkson?! They're trying to take Clarkson down, too?'

'He's their number one target. The wild beasts.'

'He's a goddam national treasure, for Christ's sake. The greatest Englishman since Winston-goddam-Churchill! That piece he wrote on *Duchess* Meghan Markle deserved a goddam Pulitzer Prize. And that's who they're targeting!' Derek let out another long whistle. 'We're a long way from Kansas, alright, that's for sure. Question is, what're we gonna do next?'

Kurtz stepped forward. 'Want me to bring him in for interrogation, boss? Give me a damp rag and a bucket of water and I'll have him singing like a Rudd's lark in no time.'

Derek moved his head from side to side. 'Interrogation? Hmm, not sure how well that'd go down in Milton Keynes. Don't think any of our competitors are torturing their staff. I heard some rough stories about how Ninety-Nine Pence Land across the river treat their workers, but…' He shifted his chair. 'What would John Wayne do in a situation like this? That's what we should be asking ourselves. Broke the mould when the Duke died. Maybe we could do a George W. Bush and call it enhanced interrogation techniques…?' He gathered the two slips together. 'No, we'll wait.'

'Wait?' said Frank, jumping up from his seat. 'Wait for what? For me to be bludgeoned to death by an unripe pineapple?'

'Alright, deputy, there's no need to panic.'

'It's alright for you,' said Frank, wild-eyed, 'it doesn't say "Kill Derek" …'

'Sheriff,' said Derek, pointing to his five-pointed star.

'…it says "Kill Frank".'

'If he burns down the supermarket we're all gonna end up there on Boot Hill.'

'So, why not phone the police?'

'And say what? That one of my department managers is filling his breeches because of a little bitty piece of paper. We're gonna need more than that, deputy.'

'You're going to get more than that if we don't do something. My head for a start. How'd you think that's going to go down at your managers' conference?'

'He's got a point, boss,' said Kurtz. 'And if Jeremy Clarkson's taken off our screens…'

Derek thought for a moment. 'Alright,' he said, eventually,

'here's what we do.' He pointed at Kurtz. 'I want you to stick to Victor closer than drawers on a vicar's wife. If that boy breaks wind I wanna know for how long. Round the clock surveillance until his shift finishes.'

'Right, boss.'

'And while we're at it, let's have some kind of locker search. Say it's the annual security spot-check, or something.'

'*Ja*, boss.'

'Find out what kinda heat this boy's packing.'

'Good idea, boss.'

'Okay, let's roll.'

'Wait a minute,' said Frank. 'Maybe I should keep a low profile? Hide in the car park or something until all this blows over?'

'Hide in the car park, deputy, and he'll find you faster than a famished flea finds a fat dog. Best thing you can do is hide in plain sight. And whatever you do, don't let yourself get trapped alone with him.'

II

FRANK MADE HIS way to the men's changing room. He wanted to get his mobile phone from his locker. With a madman with large boobs on the prowl, he needed to call his wife. She would know what to do about Victor's death threat. Working for the BBC's TV licensing company, she received threats all the time. He also wanted to get his cigarettes and lighter. How a man was expected to do any work after what he'd just discovered was beyond him. Really, what should be happening was that he should be given some compassionate leave. Or they should bring his retirement forward twelve months. Then he could take his caravan up to Scarborough and duck out of sight for a while. Maybe by then Victor would've found another department manager to murder. Someone who wasn't about to retire in a year's time and hadn't put in thirty years loyal service.

Weighed down by such thoughts, Frank was oblivious to everything that was going on around him and all the people coming and going. He reached out for the handle of the changing room. As he did he felt another hand on top of his. When he looked up it was to find Victor standing right next to him. On Victor's face was a wild, thousand-yard stare.

'A-A-After you,' said Frank, trying to step to one side.

'Hmm?' said Victor, looking right through him. 'Oh. No. After you.'

Frank felt his entire body go cold as he pushed open the door and walked unsteadily into the changing room. Behind him – breathing heavily – followed Victor. The door creaked shut leaving the two of them alone. 'What was that?' said Frank, turning around.

'Hmm?' said Victor, in a distracted voice.

The glazed look on Victor's face reminded Frank of someone who was about to slaughter someone else and serve them up with some fava beans and a nice bottle of Chianti. Unable to speak because of the fear coursing through him, an awkward silence ensued.

'Erm, nice weather we're having for the time of year,' said Frank, eventually.

'Weather?' said Victor, repeating the word in a pre-occupied voice.

'Yes,' said Frank, alarmed by the faraway look in Victor's eyes and the hushed tone of his voice. 'Quite sunny, I mean. For the time of – erm – for the time of year.'

'Sunny?' The blank look on Victor's face gave way to a

strange, sinister smile. 'Sunny. Yes, it's sunny. Everything's sunny. Life's…sunny. Sunny, sunny, sunny. It'll probably be sunny tomorrow when I get, I get…oh, it's bound to be sunny.' Victor broke out into a bitter, sardonic, laugh. Building in intensity until it reached a kind of deranged hysteria, his whole body seemed consumed by some diabolical design. 'Yes, it's sunny.'

Frank darted across to one of the urinals. Given the situation, nature wasn't just calling, she was screaming. He thought that by answering her, he could buy himself some time. After all, no self-respecting psychopath was supposed to slay their victim from behind. They were supposed to wait until they could see the whites of their eyes before doing their thing.

To Frank's horror Victor joined him at the urinals. Frank tried to affect a nonchalant air by staring up at the ceiling and whistling the theme tune to *Top Gear*. Unable do his thing because of Victor standing next to him, he zipped up his trousers, and with a loud 'That's better' made his way to one of the sinks. Victor followed him a split second later at the adjoining sink. Frank watched with growing panic as Victor washed his hands. Slowly and methodically, it reminded Frank of a surgeon washing their hands before an operation. Shaking all over, Frank reached for the tap. His plan was to get the water scalding hot so he could throw it in Victor's face and run.

A thin stream of lukewarm water drizzled out.

Switching from *Top Gear* to *The Dam Busters*, Frank's whistling and hopes of leaving the changing room alive began to falter. In the mirror above the sink he could see right into the vacuum of Victor's glazed eyes. And his own pale face staring back at him in fear. There was only one thing he could do. Meet his fate head on like a man by throwing himself on the ground and begging for mercy. He was just thinking about what to say after falling to his knees when the changing room door was flung open and in burst Kurtz.

'This is a locker search,' said Kurtz. 'Nobody move.'

III

EVER SINCE FINDING himself engaged to Violet, Victor had fallen into a kind of stunned stupor. Oblivious to everyone and everything around him, he had wandered around the store like a man lost in his own nightmare. Shaken from it by Kurtz's dramatic entrance, he looked down at his wet hands. Why they were wet, why he was in the men's changing room and how he got there, he had no recollection. Trying to gather his thoughts, he watched as Frank – whom he was seeing for the first time – ran over to Kurtz.

'Where the hell have you been?' said Frank. 'You know I'm not supposed to be left alone with...' He nodded his head in Victor's direction.

'Trying to find the master locker key,' said Kurtz. He glanced over at Victor. 'It's gone missing.'

'You're supposed to be keeping a close eye on things,' said Frank, nodding once more in Victor's direction.

'Alright, keep your wig on.'

The changing room door swung open and in walked Kevin. 'Probably finding out whose got the biggest,' he said. 'If I had to guess, I'd say Victor. Sorry, Frank, but he's got bigger feet than you.'

'That's an old wives tale,' said Kurtz, glancing down at his size six feet.

'I don't know,' said Kevin, 'I've got this magazine...'

'Shall we make a start?' said Kurtz, staring over at Victor.

Victor licked his lips nervously. The words 'locker search' had shaken him from one nightmare and plunged him straight into another. Inside his locker were half a dozen empty bottles of whisky, a copy of *A History of Western Philosophy*, a DVD full of midget porn, and, of course, one platinum engagement ring. None of this would've been a problem if his locker had belonged to Caligula. Or Charlie Sheen. But as it belonged to him he knew that questions were bound to be asked. Given that he didn't have any answers, he decided to come out swinging. 'Have you got a warrant?'

'Warrant?' said Kurtz, sounding nonplussed. 'What's a warrant?'

'In this country you need a warrant to search a man's locker.'

'Says who?'

'Magna Carta.'

'Well, you tell this Magna Carta, whoever the *bladdy* hell she is, that I've got regulations on my side.'

'What regulations?'

'Company regulations. There's supposed to be a spot-check every twelve months.'

'It's never happened before and I've been here seven years.'

'Don't know why you're getting your *broekies* in a twist.' Kurtz thrust a thumb at Kevin. 'He's here to make sure the proper procedures are followed.'

'Make sure he doesn't plant anything,' said Kevin, grinning. 'Wouldn't be the first time, right Kurtz, me old mucker?'

Kurtz ignored Kevin. 'Start with yours, Frank, shall we?'

Frank rushed over to his locker and opened it. Kurtz felt inside. Among all the caravanning magazines and lighters was something stuffed at the back. 'What's this for?' said Kurtz, pulling out what looked like a dead rat from the locker.

'It's a wig!' said Kevin.

'It's a special cloth to clean the inside of caravans,' said Frank. He grabbed the wig and one of the cigarette lighters and ran from the changing room. 'There's some paperwork I need to finish downstairs.'

'Right,' said Kurtz to Victor, 'your turn.'

Victor pointed at Kevin. 'What about him?'

'The order is random,' said Kurtz. 'Your number came up.'

'Don't say you never win anything,' said Kevin, patting Victor on the shoulder.

'It's discrimination,' said Victor, stonewalling. 'I'm being victimised because of my medical condition.'

'What medical condition?' said Kurtz with a smirk.

'He means his hairy coconuts,' said Kevin, cupping a hand to an imaginary breast.

'What if I refuse?' said Victor.

'Refuse?' said Kurtz. 'I'll tell you what'll happen if you refuse. First, you'll be suspended and escorted from the premises. Then Kevin here will go down the road to the fire station to get a crowbar…'

'I'm barred, don't forget, because of those nuisance calls,' said Kevin.

'…and then your locker will be opened anyway. So, it's up to you.'

Victor looked from Kurtz to Kevin and then back again. 'Oppressors of men,' he said. 'Well, remember this: "you can't hold a man down without staying down with him."' He patted his pockets. 'I've lost my key.'

'What's that on your keyring, then?' said Kevin, pointing to the single key attached to the belt hoop of Victor's trousers.

'Oh, I forgot to look there,' said Victor. 'Thanks Kevin.'

Victor knew he was trapped. The only thing he could do was open the locker and hope Kurtz didn't see the ring. The only problem was Kurtz saw everything. He'd even found Frank's secret hairpiece. It was like being examined by the Eye of Providence.

'We're waiting,' said the all-seeing one.

Victor put the key in the locker door. 'It's jammed,' he said, pretending to turn the key.

'You turn it the other way,' said Kevin.

'Do you? Oh, yes, thanks again, Kevin.' Victor opened the door and before either Kurtz or Kevin could react, palmed the ring while grabbing the DVD with the same hand. 'This is private,' he said, holding the DVD to his chest.

'We're all friends here,' said Kurtz, grabbing hold of the DVD.

Victor's decoy seemed to have worked. While Kurtz and Kevin looked over the DVD, he had time to put the ring into his pocket.

'Want to explain yourself?' said Kurtz.

Victor froze. He thought for a second that Kurtz had seen him put the ring in his pocket after all. 'Erm…'

'*Backdoor Boys*? *Fathers and Daughters*…?

'*Midget Mayhem*,' said Kevin.

'*Midget Mayhem*.' Kurtz raised himself to his full height. 'You do know that it's against company policy to bring pornography to work?'

Victor was so relieved they were talking about *Midget Mayhem* and not the ring that he said, 'To you it's pornography, to me it's art.'

'Art?' said Kurtz. 'Midgets getting screwed on camera and you're calling it art? *Ag sies*, man, Ezekiel was right about your sort.'

'Why shouldn't little people get screwed – make love – on camera? Or are you saying that only those above a certain height should be allowed to do it? Because if you are, that's discrimination. Little people have as much right as the next man to...to...to...' Victor could see that he was losing his audience. To be fair, he never really had them. Turning midget porn into a human rights issue had been a tactical error. But there was no turning back now. 'I have a dream,' he said, 'that I will live in a nation where a man and, indeed, a woman, and of course anything in between, will not be judged by the size of their... of their...by their size, but by the content of their character...'

'First, he tries to peep inside the ladies' changing room and now this!' said Kurtz. 'Wait a minute.' He reread the titles on the DVD. 'Didn't that *mompie* Malcolm read these out over the Tannoy this morning?'

'Erm, that was a different *Backdoor Boys, Fathers and Daughters* and *Midget Mayhem*,' said Victor.

'Peddling filth to retards! Have you no *bladdy* shame?'

'Malcolm is *not* a retard, he's just a bit forgetful.' Victor was angry now. He didn't like it when his pal was called names.

'He's not likely to forget *Midget Mayhem*.'

'They'd have to go on top,' said Kevin.

'What?' said Kurtz.

'The midgets. Well, you can't have them underneath. They'd get crushed.'

'What do you know about what midgets can and can't do in the bedroom?'

'Simple physics,' said Kevin. 'P equals F over A, where F is the normal force and A is the area of the surface on contact.'

'Wrong,' said Victor. One hand holding his work shirt as if it was the lapel of a robe, he started pacing up and down the men's changing room like a barrister in a courtroom. Having remembered where the DVD had originally come from, it was time to go on the attack. 'I put it to you, Kevin Duncan

NO PLAN B, MALCOLM!'

Snodgrass, that the reason you know so much about the sexual behaviour of midgets is because of your intimate and expert knowledge of midget pornography…'

'I thought you said it was art?' said Kevin.

'…indeed, because of your intimate and expert knowledge of *all* types of pornography.'

'Eh?'

'I further allege,' said Victor, snatching the DVD from Kurtz, 'that it was you who supplied Malcolm with this DVD, and that your locker is so crammed with others of a similar kind, and full of magazines of the same sort, *and* contains a Bill Roache sex doll, that you could open your own adult emporium in Soho. How does the defendant plead?'

'He's gone potty,' said Kevin, laughing nervously.

'One way to find out,' said Victor.

'Find out what?' said Kevin, backing away.

'Open it,' said Kurtz.

'My number didn't come up.'

'Open it.'

'I'm going to put in an official complaint about this.' Kevin unlocked his locker.

'Exhibit A,' said Victor, pulling the door open. But the locker was completely empty. Gone were the DVDs and magazines, and the Bill Roache sex doll. Gone, too, was the peephole parade on the inside of the door. It had been replaced by a picture of Pope Francis.

Doing a double-take, Victor checked the front of the door to make sure it was the right locker. The pictures of Phil 'The Power' Taylor confirmed that it was. In desperation Victor felt inside the locker with his hand. 'It's all been moved.'

'Alright, that's enough,' said Kurtz, snatching back the DVD and taking hold of Victor's arm.

'It was full before! There was a peephole parade – members of staff he'd spied on. He marked them out of ten. I got a six.'

'He really has gone potty,' said Kevin, shaking his head. 'And I'd be grateful if you didn't molest the Pope like that.'

'You a Catholic?' said Kurtz.

'In the name of the Father and of the Son and of the Holy Spirit,' said Kevin, crossing himself.

'Calvinist,' said Kurtz, pointing to himself.

'I don't understand it,' said a shocked Victor, craning his neck so he could see inside Kevin's locker again.

'Of course you don't understand it,' said Kurtz. 'Degenerates like you can never understand religion.'

'Amen,' said Kevin.

As he was pushed over to the door by Kurtz, Victor just had time for one last look over his shoulder. With one thumb in the air and the boss's Ray-Bans covering his eyes stood a grinning Kevin. In his hand was his mobile phone. The picture of Victor peeping into the ladies' changing room was its screensaver.

IV

DEREK THREW THE DVD on the desk and looked Victor up and down. 'You been keeping up with our TV adverts?'

'Oh, yes,' said Victor. 'Never miss them.' That was a lie. Victor didn't have a television set. He had got rid of it after having fallen behind with his TV license payments and reading an article about how Jacques Derrida never watched television.

'So, you know what our new slogan is?'

Victor fixed his eyes on Frank, who was standing behind Derek aiming a staple gun at him. 'Erm, "Whiting's is number one for price"?'

'That was last year's, goddam it!' said Derek, banging his fist on the table.

Victor gasped. 'You mean we're not number one anymore?'

'Of course we're number one. In everything. But "We've just got even better because…"?'

'Erm…'

'Brilliant!' said Derek. 'We've just got even better because "Erm…" That's gonna get 'em filling the aisles, ain't it, boy? Jesus H. Christ, I should have you horsewhipped from here to Kentucky!'

'I don't think that's a very catchy slogan, boss.'

Derek's knuckles went white as he grabbed the sides of the desk. 'You laughing at me, boy?'

'No, boss.'

'You're already in a world of pain. Don't make it worse is my advice.'

Victor tried to think of something worse than a world of pain. *A galaxy of pain? A universe of pain?*

'Now. Let's start again. "We've just got even better because…"?'

Victor folded his arms and pretended to think. 'Erm…'

'Goddam it!' Derek threw a pen across the room. 'If the folks in Milton Keynes could see this! Tell him, Frank.'

Frank shook his head. '"We've just got even better",' he said, '"because now there's something for the whole family".'

'You hear that, boy?' said Derek. '"Something for the whole family".'

'Oh, *that* new slogan,' said Victor.

'You mind telling me which member of the family…' Derek picked up the DVD from the desk. '…*Midget Mayhem* is for?'

Victor felt the sweat running down his forehead. He knew that Derek had a point. The only family who might possibly watch *Midget Mayhem* was the Manson family. The problem was families like that only made up about half of Lunestone Whiting's clientele. There was only one thing to do. Take a chance. 'All the family?'

Derek jumped up and banged both fists on the desk. 'All the family?! This ain't the Pickle Family Circus we're talking about, boy! This is midgets screwing the shit out of each other!'

'"Think 25", of course.'

The door to the office opened and Kurtz came in wheeling a TV-DVD combo.

'"Think 25"?' said Derek, sitting back down. '"Think 25"? I'll tell you what I'm thinking, boy. I'm thinking that you're about the sickest, kinkiest, most depraved son-of-a-bitch I've ever had the misfortune to meet. I try to run a nice clean store and what do you do? Try and catch yourself a snatch of the old crinkum crankum under the ladies' changing room door while peddling filth to innocent folk downstairs. Well, not on my watch!'

He held out a hand. 'Frank.' Frank handed Derek a file. 'This here's your rap sheet, boy,' said Derek, opening the file, 'And let me tell you, it makes lamentable reading. Lateness. Drunkenness. Being rude to customers…'

'Insubordination…' said Frank, aiming the staple gun at Victor. Victor stuck his tongue out at him.

'…insubordination. Hell, there's even something in here about flashing your piece at customers. I've seen men hung for less, let me tell you.'

Victor rubbed his left breast nervously.

'You've got nothing to say?' said Derek.

'I wasn't flashing,' said Victor. 'I was out in the car park collecting trolleys and my belt broke. It just so happened that I hadn't put on any underpants that day. We've all done it.'

Derek snapped shut the file. 'Hell, you've had more lives

than a barrelful of cats. Well, it ends here.' He looked across to Kurtz. 'Plug her in.'

'*Ja*, boss.' Kurtz plugged in the TV-DVD combo. 'Ready, boss.'

Derek put the DVD into the machine and pressed play. 'If this is porn, boy, then you're in for the high jump, let me tell you. You'll be outta that door faster than a midget from a cannon.'

Victor was about to ask why it was okay to shoot midgets from cannons but not okay to watch them having sex, when the TV screen turned from black to a grainy, slightly-out-of-focus grey. This was followed by a blurred image of a man with large glasses and a smile playing the guitar.

'Turn it up,' said Derek. Kurtz turned up the volume.

Surrounded by children, the man with the guitar was playing an instrumental version of the song *Heartbeat*.

'It's Hank Marvin,' said Frank, lowering the staple gun and moving closer to the screen. He looked over at Derek. 'What's Hank Marvin doing surrounded by a load of midgets?'

'They're not midgets, they're children,' said Kurtz.

'Two words,' said Derek. 'Operation Yewtree.' He shook his head. 'And to think I've got that man's autobiography at home. No wonder we're going to hell in a handcart.'

The words 'Hank Marvin's Christmas Special' flashed up on the screen. 'Something tells me this isn't *Midget Mayhem*, boss,' said Kurtz.

'Or Operation Yewtree,' said Frank.

Derek pressed the fast forward button. 'I'm gonna find me a midget if it harelips the governor.' He pressed play. It was still Hank Marvin surrounded by children. 'Goddam it!' Fast-forward. Play. Hank Marvin giving a rendition of *White Christmas* while the children dressed the tree. 'Goddam it!' Fast-forward. Play. Hank Marvin handing out presents. 'Goddam it!' Fast-forward. Play. Etc. Etc. Etc. Eventually – frazzled and fried – Derek put his arms around the TV and started to sob.

Ding-dong! 'We have another great offer for you here today at Whiting's,' said Malcolm's voice. 'New for 2023…' In the office time seemed to stand still. 'Orange juice. New for 2023…ugh!'

Ding-dong! 'Good afternoon, ladies and gentlemen…' Malcolm had been ousted by Violet. 'With the time approaching five o'clock, the supermarket is now closing. Will all customers make their final selections and make their way to the checkouts.'

Derek unglued himself from the TV and sat down. 'Saved by the bell,' he said, looking over at Victor. 'Well, boy, looks like you've dodged another bullet.' Kurtz bent down and whispered in Derek's ear.

Victor saw the look on Derek's face change from someone who'd just lost the Alamo to looking like someone who'd just found it again. His store manager motioned for him to sit.

'So, Victor,' said Derek, tapping his teeth with a pencil, 'you going to this shindig tonight?'

Discombobulated by the change in Derek's demeanour and the aggressive way Frank was aiming the staple gun at him, Victor said tentatively, 'If you mean the charity do, then, yes, I'm going.'

'You doing a turn?'

'Malcolm and I are doing Punch and Judy.'

'Excellent choice. You'll make a swell Judy.'

Victor bristled. 'Actually, I'm playing Punch.'

'Well, ain't that a kick in the paps.' Derek glanced up at Kurtz, smiled, then turned his attention back to Victor. 'I thought with your…your…excuse my French, mammary glands, you'd be playing Judy.' He point up at Kurtz. 'Say, I almost forgot. My deputy here's looking for someone to help him clean up afterwards. How're you fixed?'

'Sorry,' said Victor, 'I won't be staying until the end. You see, I have this book to write…' Victor wasn't lying. When it came to not doing any writing, he always did it late at night.

'Well, butter my butt and call me Biscuit, looks like we've got a writer in our midst. What's the book about, son?'

'Have you ever heard of a subject called philosophy?'

'Philosophy, you say. Only philosophy I know is the one that says never trust a cowboy who can't lie to his horse.' Derek turned to Kurtz. 'How about you, deputy, you got yourself a philosophy?'

'Don't leave your host's house and throw mud in his well,' said Kurtz.

'Well, ain't that fine and dandy,' said Derek. 'Looks like you boys are gonna have a whole lotta fun when you're sweeping up together. I just hope you don't get up to any of that *Brokeback Mountain* stuff. You leave all that nonsense to the wild beasts.' He fixed Victor with a steely look. 'Any objections?'

'Well, as I say…' began Victor.

'Or,' said Derek, smirking at Kurtz and Frank, 'I can send your ass to Tills.'

Victor felt his mouth go dry and his head spin. 'T-T-Tills?!' The Tills. The point of no return. The dead zone. The ninth circle of Hell. The endless queues of moronic customers. The screaming babies. The pointless small talk. The plastered on smile. A stunned Victor rose to his feet.

'"Would you like some help with your packing?"' said Kurtz.

'"Do you need some extra bags?"' said Derek.

'"Have you got you Club card?"' said Kurtz.

'"Going anywhere nice on your holiday this year?"' said Derek.

Derek and Kurtz fell about in a fit of hysterical laughter. Victor gave a strained smile. 'We've all got to do our bit, I suppose,' he said.

V

VICTOR PUT ON his coat and clocked out.

'See you tomorrow,' said Malcolm, pushing past wearing his pink florescent tracksuit.

'You mean tonight.'

'Tonight?'

'You're coming to the charity do, remember. Don't forget the costumes.'

'Costumes?'

'Malcolm, why is that every time I have a conversation with you I feel like I'm talking to a deaf person?'

'Pardon?'

'The Punch and Judy costumes for tonight. Don't forget them. And the fake breasts.'

But Malcolm had disappeared into the changing room.

'Fake breasts?' It was Violet.

'They're for tonight,' said Victor. 'Malcolm and I are doing a Punch and Judy piece.'

'That's perfect, Victor. Oh, I can't wait to see you in a dress.'

'I'm playing Punch.'

'And then afterwards we can declare our love to the world. Who knows, it might even make tomorrow's newspapers.'

Victor could see the front page now: 'Man With Boobs Butchers Fiancée in Charity Gala Gore-fest!' 'I'm glad you brought that up,' he said, putting on his flying hat. 'I've been thinking things over…'

'I hope you haven't changed your mind?'

No, Victor hadn't changed his mind. He *still* didn't want to get married to Violet. 'Well…'

'Because if you have, I will have to tell Angel a certain somebody stole her ring.'

Victor reeled backwards. 'You know – about the ring – the other ring, I mean – you know it was Angel's?'

'Of course I know, silly. She's smashed up half the store looking for it.'

Victor wasn't about to point out to Violet that she would have been in danger of being smashed to pieces had Angel found out she had the ring. Having been tied to his mother's knee for nearly his whole life, Victor had learned the basic rule for dealing with the fairer sex at an early age. And that rule was to be obedient to those who are your masters with fear and trembling.

Violet flashed the cheap ring on her finger. 'At the moment I'm too busy planning our wedding to worry about such things. Still,' she said, fixing her hair, 'if it was called off I'd have a lot more time on my hands. Who knows what I might do then?'

Victor feared and trembled.

'I'd like to stick to the Alice in Wonderland theme if it's okay by you?' She tied the flap on Victor's flying hat. 'I can't wait to see you dressed up as the Mad Hatter. You're going to look so smart in your top hat and tails.'

Victor looked like a man who'd just hit his finger with a hammer. Not only was he being blackmailed into marrying a woman who could swallow a whole bagel in one mouthful. He was being made to do it while dressed up as Vivienne Westwood's brother.

Violet looked down at Victor's breasts and shook her head. 'What we're going to do with those I do not know. Oh, well, I suppose every girl has her cross to bear. And breasts on men are very fashionable these days. Look at Simon Cowell.' She kissed Victor lightly on the cheek. 'Oh, Victor, we're going to be so happy! To think, we could be together for the next fifty years. It'll seem like…forever.' She walked off down the corridor.

Feeling like he was going to faint, Victor propped himself up against the wall. Fifty years! He did some quick calculations. That was eighteen thousand, two hundred and fifty days. One million and ninety-five thousand minutes. Sixty-five million and seven hundred thousand seconds. If after each one of those seconds he was to die a thousand deaths, it'd become like one of those numbers physicists use in their equations. The how-many-atoms-can-you-fit-in-the-universe kind of number. That's what his life was going to be reduced to. A mathematical equation. A few squiggly lines. A hieroglyphic chalk mark on the blackboard of life. And then what? Wiped out. Erased. Nothing left but a few specks of dust.

'What're you hanging around here for? You're normally first out of the door.'

It was Kevin. Victor look up at him and said with ten-to-the-plus sarcasm, 'Counting my blessings.'

'Well, here, take one of these.' Kevin handed him a flyer. On it was printed the picture of Victor peeping through the crack of the ladies' changing room. At the top of the flyer were the words 'Peep Show Special: Guess the Pervert', and underneath 'One pound a go. All proceeds (excl. costs) to Monster-Hausen by P.'

'After finding the boss's sunglasses in the car park during the fire alarm I was going to delete the picture. Then I thought, hang on a minute, he's a chance for me to put something back.

That's when I got the idea. I got them run up on the photocopier. One hundred and fifty of them. Not bad, eh?'

'You can see that it's me,' said Victor.

'I know. Funny thing is it hasn't stopped people buying them. I've nearly sold out. I was thinking of getting some T-shirts made. What do you think?'

'You want to know what I think about you putting a picture of me peeping into the ladies' changing room on a T-shirt?'

'Anyway,' said Kevin, nodding at the flyer Victor was holding, 'that's a quid.'

'If you think I'm going to give you a pound for that...' Victor screwed up the flyer and threw it on the floor.

'It's for charity!' said Kevin, picking up the flyer.

'I don't care if it's the answer to the meaning of life,' said Victor. 'I'm not a pervert.' Malcolm came running out of the men's changing room. 'Don't forget the false breasts,' said Victor, as Malcolm raced past. He turned his head to find Kevin looking at him with a raised eyebrow. 'Come on! It's for the Punch and Judy sketch we're doing tonight!'

'I don't think someone with your reputation should be putting on dresses,' said Kevin.

'I'm playing Punch!'

'Playing Punch? You'll be getting punched if you haven't done what I asked you to do.'

It was Kurtz.

'Want one of these?' said Kevin, offering Kurtz one of the flyers.

'I've already bought three,' said Kurtz. 'One for my locker, one for the shed at home and one to put behind the bar in my local.'

'Oh, yeah, I forgot. I've sold so many I've lost count.'

'Give me five minutes with Tubby *Tets*, will you?'

'No problem.' Kevin jangled a pocketful of coins. 'If you want any more flyers let me know.' He disappeared into the men's changing room, leaving behind Kurtz and a petrified Victor.

'Alright, *chommie*,' said Kurtz, grabbing hold of Victor's collar. 'Have you had any thoughts about our conversation earlier?'

'About helping you tidy up after the charity do? Yes.' Victor felt like he was going to have another David Starkey moment.

'Not that.' Kurtz tightened his grip. 'About getting that *mompie* Malcolm to call off his engagement to Violet.'

'Ah. Yes. That.'

'*Ja*, that.'

'Since we last spoke on the matter there have been one or two developments.'

'Developments? What developments?'

'Well, I guess you could say we're in a good-news-bad-news type of situation,' said Victor, straightening his collar.

Kurtz raised a fist. 'Bad news?'

'The *good* news,' said Victor emphatically, 'is that Malcolm is no longer engaged to Violet.'

Victor could see Kurtz's demeanour change in an instant. Gone was the knuckle-cracking, bone-crushing, bottle-chewing Mamlambo from just a few seconds earlier. To be replaced by a Kurtz rarely seen by Victor. Soppy of eye, rosy of cheek and brimming over with *bonhomie*, it was as if his nemesis had been hit by a quiver-full of Cupid's arrows.

'You know, Vic,' said Kurtz, putting a friendly arm around Victor's shoulders, 'there's this place just outside Pretoria called Bushman's Rock. Beautiful place. Looks right out across the Moreletta River. You can get married there and then afterwards go for a swim or watch the zebras and the antelope…No longer engaged, you say.' He slapped Victor on the back. It was a friendly slap, but it still felt to Victor like he'd been hit by a sledgehammer. And this was the good news.

'I know we've had our ups and downs in the past,' said Kurtz, holding out a hand. 'But how about we let bygones be bygones?'

Victor noticed Kurtz's vice-like grip as he shook his hand.

'South Africa is a beautiful country, Vic. You should come over and stay with us after we're married. Better still, come to the wedding.'

Victor had never seen anyone as happy as Kurtz was at that moment. Any happier and he'd burst into song.

'"*Oh, lang ik om terug te gaan naar de Zuid-Afrikaansche Republiek, waar mijn lieve Sarie woont/ Darar, tussen her koren en het groene doorn boom, daar woont mijn lieve Sarie Marais.*"'

'Nicely put,' said Victor, who hadn't understood a single word. For all he knew Kurtz could be singing about the ultimate mastery of the white race.

'See you tonight, Vic… "*daar woont mijn lieve Sarie Marais…*"'

Victor began to tiptoe away.

'Oh, by the way, what was the bad news?'

Victor froze. 'The bad news?' He inched slowly back around.

'*Ja*. You said there was good news and bad news. You've given me the good news.'

'The bad news,' said Victor slowly, 'is that I won't be able to come to South Africa.'

'Pity.'

'Yes,' said Victor, warming to his theme. 'I suffer from air sickness.'

'You could always come by boat.'

'And sea sickness.'

'Oh, well, we'll just have to WhatsApp you the photos of the wedding.'

'Good idea.' Victor turned to go. As he did Malcolm came racing up the corridor in the opposite direction.

'Forgot my pedometer,' he said, rushing past Victor and Kurtz.

'Forget his head if it wasn't screwed on,' said Kurtz, before breaking into a whistle.

Victor gave out a polite laugh and started tiptoeing away again. He'd just reached the end of the corridor when he heard Malcolm shout from the changing room door, 'Congratulations on your engagement again, Victor! You and Violet are going to be very happy together!' He disappeared into the changing room.

Over his shoulder Victor could see Kurtz – lips half-pursed beneath his moustache – grow redder and redder. There was only one thing to do.

Run!

With tits and flaps a-flying, Victor set off down the stairs as fast as his bulk could carry him. Jumping down the steps three at a time, he tore into the back area. Behind him came the cry of '*Usuthu!*' and the sound of metal-heeled boots in pursuit.

Usually, too slow to catch a pig in a corridor, Victor surprised himself by how quickly he could run when he was being chased by a bloodthirsty Boer. Flat-out when he reached the shop floor, he headed for the front entrance. Just ahead of him, going through the de-activated electric front doors, was Violet.

'Wait!' said Victor, as Violet pulled the doors shut. She opened them again and Victor rushed through.

'Aw!' said Violet. 'You couldn't let me go without saying goodbye properly.'

Gasping for breath, Victor was more concerned about where

Kurtz was than saying goodbye properly to Violet. Nowhere was the answer. At least, nowhere that Victor could see.

'You're just going to have to hold on a little longer, pumpkin,' said Violet. 'I know it's difficult, but after tonight we can tell the whole world. Until then…' She blew Victor a kiss and walked out into the car park. Victor was about to follow when he felt a burly arm coil around his neck and drag him from the foyer.

'Gotcha, you *bliksem* snake,' said Kurtz, dragging Victor out into the car park.

'How did you…?'

'How did I get out? I took a short cut through the fire door.'

Had he not been turning blue at this point, Victor could've pointed out that it was a disciplinary offence to use the fire doors when there wasn't a fire. Instead, he just kept on turning bluer.

'So,' said Kurtz, relaxing his grip a little. 'The bad news is you're engaged to Violet?'

'I can explain,' said Victor.

'I'm not interested in your explanations.' Kurtz spun Victor around. 'You see over there?' In the far corner of the car park Angel was lifting up cars looking for her ring. 'Look at that. She's lifting those cars up with one hand. Imagine what one of those hands could do to someone's neck.' At the word 'neck' he gave Victor's a hard twist to emphasise his point. 'Either you break off your engagement to Violet or I get Angel to go to work on you. And believe me, when I tell her you stole her ring…man, she'll boil you alive and feed you to the crocodiles!'

Again, Victor wasn't in a position to point out that there were no crocodiles in Lunestone. Not with his neck still firmly attached to Kurtz's arm. Kurtz gave it one last twist and let go. Victor fell gasping to his knees.

'You've got until the end of the charity do,' said Kurtz. He bent down so he could whisper into Victor's ear. 'And don't think setting off fire alarms or poisoning cleaning products is going to save you.'

Still fighting for breath, Victor watched as Kurtz climbed into his Range Rover and drove off. With Violet threatening to tell Angel about the ring if he called off the engagement and Kurtz threatening to tell Angel about the ring if he didn't, Victor was trapped. He looked up at the darkening skies. 'If you're there, mum,' he said, imploringly, 'I need your help. If you can. Please.' Getting nothing back except for a few spots of winter rain, he lifted up his arms and cried, 'Give me a sign, mum!'

'What are you doing down there?' It was Malcolm. 'You'll catch your death kneeling on the ground like that.' He helped Victor to his feet.

'Wouldn't matter if I did,' said Victor.

'It would to me,' said Malcolm, brushing the dirt off Victor's knees. 'I'd have no one to talk to. And besides, who would I get to play Judy?'

'I'm playing Punch!'

'Who am I playing, then?'

Victor looked up at the sky and smiled.

'I suppose we could always do something else?' said Malcolm.

'No, Malcolm,' said Victor. 'No Plan B.'

VI

VICTOR STEPPED ON to the bus. 'You're not a Jehovah's Witness, by any chance?'

'No,' said the driver.

Victor got off the bus and started walking up the street.

CHAPTER TEN

WITH HIS DOG, Rosie, trotting along after him, Baz made his way to the Dog and Whistle pub. Located at the very edge of Lunestone, it was the last spit-and-sawdust establishment in the town. Not for Baz the trendy wine bars selling continental beers for seven pounds a bottle and fries in miniature metal buckets. For seven pounds at the Dog and Whistle you could get two pints of real ale and a plate of pie and peas. You could also get served, it's busiest night – DJ Gordon 'The Flash' Trotter's Friday Night Dance Night – attracting about twenty regulars.

Climbing the rickety, beer-splattered wooden steps that led upstairs to the function room, Baz stopped halfway up to light a freshly rolled cigarette. Sixteen years ago the smoking ban had been introduced. And for sixteen years Baz – and most of the other regulars – had been ignoring it. Plenty of other things Baz had been ignoring in those sixteen years. Men getting fannies. Digital cash. Brexit (despite being a passionate leaver). Covid. *The X Factor*. Harry bastard Potter…A thirty-gram bag of Old Holborn and *Mortimer and Whitehouse: Gone Fishing*. That's all Baz needed. As for the rest…

'They can shove it up their fucking arses,' said Baz under his breath. He reached down and patted Rosie on the head. A brown lurcher with half her tail missing, she was fat-bellied, bow-legged and covered in scars – war wounds from her constant battles with rubbish bins. 'Eh, Mrs Doo?' said Baz, scratching Rosie's ear. 'Shove it right up their fucking arses.'

He continued up the stairs to the function room. Every bit as spit-and-sawdust as the rest of the pub, it smelled of stale beer, cigarette smoke and damp. In one corner there was a one-armed bandit which paid out in tokens, while in another there was a broken black and white television set. Dotted about the room were a dozen tables. As rickety and beer stained as the stairs, they sat atop an old Axminster carpet worn so thin you could see more of the floorboards than the pattern. The main feature of the room was a small proscenium stage running along the back wall. With its floorboards sagging like the galley of an old herring-drifter, and shabby red velvet curtains hanging limply down like a pair of storm-wrecked sails, it reminded Baz of his old fishing boat, *The 'Effing 'Ell*. The only sign of the modern world were the eight infrared disco lights arranged in two groups of four at either side of the stage. Hired specially for the evening by Violet at great expense, they were too powerful for the ancient electrics at the pub and could only be switched on at the end.

'Waste of bastard money,' said Baz, making his way to the bar. He sat down on one of the stools. 'Right. Time to get this fucking show on the road, Rosie.' The barmaid came over. 'Half a pint of Abbot's, luv.'

While he was waiting for his drink, Baz did a keep recce of the room. Dotted about in twos and threes were about fifteen or so other members of staff. Talking quietly among themselves or standing on their own looking bored, they represented what Baz called 'The sad, the bad and the bastard-all-else-to-do brigade'. All Whiting's dos were the same. Anyone with any sense had made up their excuses weeks ago.

Baz watched as Kurtz walked up to the microphone on the

stage. 'Testing, testing, one, two, three…'

'Come in, number seven,' said Baz, through hands shaped like a foghorn. 'Your time is fucking up. Hear that, Rosie,' he said, cackling through his few remaining teeth. '"You're time is fucking up"' But Rosie was no longer next to him. She had made her way to the buffet in the corner and was busy tucking into a plate of pork pies.

Baz lit another roll-up.

'How many time have I told you,' said the barmaid, 'you can't smoke in here.'

'Can't smoke in a fucking pub?' said Baz, stubbing out his cigarette. 'What next? Not being able to take a piss in the bog?'

'You usually do it in the sink.' The barmaid put Baz's half pint on the bar. At the buffet, Rosie had finished off the pork pies and had moved on to a plate of paste sandwiches. 'And get that bloody dog away from the food,' said the barmaid, throwing a dishcloth in Rosie's direction. Rosie grabbed a couple of sandwiches and went and hid underneath Baz's stool. 'I wish you'd feed her before bringing her in here.'

'Feed her five fucking times a day,' said Baz. He picked up his glass. 'Bastard eats me out of house and fucking home. Don't you, Mrs Doo?' he said, affectionately. 'Eat me out of house and fucking home?'

The double doors to the function room opened and in walked Kevin wearing a T-shirt with the picture of peeping Victor printed on it. With Kevin was a short, middle-aged, pot-bellied man who seemed familiar to Baz, but whom he couldn't quite place. Sporting a mop of suspiciously lush ginger hair, a pair of glasses with coloured lenses and a Mexican-style moustache, the man looked to Baz like a cross between Elton John and Pancho Villa. Baz watched open-mouthed as Kevin and El Tonio walked up to the bar.

'Like the T-shirt, Baz?' said Kevin, showing it off.

'Eh?' said Baz, his attention fixed firmly on El Tonio.

'Nine ninety-nine,' said Kevin. 'Two quid to Monster by P.'

But Baz wasn't listening. He had moved closer to El Tonio so he could get a better look.

'Och aye the noo,' said El Tonio in a thick Scottish accent. 'Hou's it gaun?'

Baz jerked his head back. He'd met many Scots in his time. Not a single one had ever said 'Och aye the noo'. 'Wae the fuck you ganning at?' yes. But never 'Och aye the noo'.

The barmaid came over. 'Eenin, lassie,' said McEltonio. He pointed at Kevin. 'A pint for me man 'ere and a wee dram for meself.' Baz watched closely as McEltonio raised the glass of whisky the barmaid had put in front of him and said, 'Guid health, laddie.' As he knocked the whisky back in one, McEltonio's ginger hair began to slip off his head. 'Juist a wee – a bittie – foo muckle's this,' he said, trying to adjust the hairpiece.

'Frank?' said Baz.

'Blast it!' Frank threw the hairpiece on to the bar.

'I told you it wouldn't work,' said Kevin.

'The makeup glue was supposed to keep it on.'

'I used all that on the moustache.'

'All of it?' Frank tugged on his moustache.

'What's he dressed like that for?' said Baz.

'He thinks someone's trying to kill him,' said Kevin.

'Who?'

'I'm not allowed to say,' said Kevin, before mouthing the word 'Victor'.

'Old Tubby Tits?' Baz nodded over at Frank. 'What did he do, shove a cucumber up his jacksie.'

'Ssshhh!' said Kevin. 'It's top secret.'

'I won't say now't,' said Baz. 'You can count on me.' He turned to the rest of the room. 'Old Tubby Tits is on the warpath again, so watch your fucking backs!'

'It won't come off,' said Frank, pulling harder on the moustache. 'How long's it supposed to last?' Kevin took the used tube of glue from his pocket and showed it to Frank. 'Superglue?' said Frank, reading the label. 'I told you to get makeup glue.'

'Superglue, makeup glue, what's the difference said Kevin.

'That's the difference,' said Frank, pointing to the words printed on the tube.

'"Warning! Do not place near skin",' said Kevin, reading the words. 'I wouldn't take any notice of that.' He gave the tube a sniff. 'It'll probably peel off by next week.'

'My daughter's getting married on Wednesday. I can't give her away looking like one of the Marx Brothers!'

The doors opened again and in came Victor and Malcolm. The former was dressed in a tight blue miniskirt, women's apron and a pair of green wellington boots. Round his head was wound a yellow tea-towel. Plastered across both cheeks was white foundation. With blue eyeliner around both eyes and bright red lipstick smeared around his mouth. At the bar, Frank did a double-take and put on his hairpiece back to front. Kevin gave a goofy grin and switched to video mode on his mobile phone. Meanwhile, Baz, who just moments earlier had taken a long swig of ale, spat it out along with the words, 'Fuck-a-duck on Friday!'

'I told you not to forget the fake breasts, didn't I?' said Victor, as he and Malcolm headed for the bar.

'My mum's using them to keep her pegs in,' said Malcolm, who was wearing a pointed red hat, false nose, cream scarf, red pullover and pair of yellow tights with blue boxer shorts over the top. In his hand he carried a large rolling pin.

'*I* was meant to be Punch?' said Victor.

'But I'm flat-chested,' said Malcolm.

'You could at least have got me a costume that fits. I look like Arnold Schwarzenegger's mother in this.'

'I wonder where she keeps her pegs?'

'Fuck me, Rosie,' said Baz, looking Victor and Malcolm up and down. 'Don't like the look of yours.' But with all eyes on the newcomers, Rosie had made her way back to the buffet.

'A double whisky and a lemonade,' said Victor to the barmaid.

'What the fucking hell have you come as?' said Baz. 'The bearded fucking lady?'

'Ant and Dec,' said Victor. 'Who do you think we've come as?'

'I thought we were supposed to be Punch and Judy?' said Malcolm, paying for the drinks. 'Do Ant and Dec even use rolling pins?'

Dressed now in black tie and tails and a pair of white gloves, a laughing Kurtz shouted down from the stage, 'Hey, Victor, the dressing room's back here when you want to get changed.'

'I knew I should've come as Wat Tyler again,' said Victor. He looked over at Frank, who seemed to shrink to about two feet when he saw Victor staring at him. 'I see Freddie Mercury's been taken. Although, I'm not sure his hair was ever that colour.' Victor drained his glass in one. 'Same again, barmaid.'

KEVIN PULLED OUT his notebook and started looking down the list of names inside. Mandy. Catherine. Jackie. Amy. Victor. He crossed out the six next to Victor's name and put in an eight. Looking over at Victor again, at the way he bulged and protruded and swelled out of his miniskirt and apron, Kevin chewed on his pencil thoughtfully. Still in two minds, he scribbled out the eight and wrote in '9?'.

11

VIOLET SQUEEZED HERSELF carefully into the back seat of the taxi. Wearing a gold lamé bodysuit with a seven-pointed, tinsel-covered, papier mâché gold star fitted over the top, she found herself unable to fasten her seatbelt.

'No faster than five miles an hour,' she said to the taxi driver. 'I don't want to damage my points.'

As the taxi trundled along at walking speed, Violet gave regal waves to bewildered pedestrians passing by. Her big night had finally arrived. And she was going to make sure that she enjoyed every second. A charity gala *and* an engagement party. Not even Elton John could top that. The big question now was, how many of the newspapers that she'd invited to cover the evening's proceedings would turn up? She had invited them all, national as well as local. And except for the man at *The Daily Mail* who'd accused her of harassment, they'd all been very nice. As had the television stations she'd written to. And although she hadn't received any RSVPs from Broadcasting House or News International, she still expected them to be there. The only thing nagging her was her insistence that the BBC send Graham Norton to interview her. After a great deal of thought she'd realised that Vernon Kaye, or even Paddy McGuinness, would've done.

She straightened the tiara on her head and checked that every bauble and piece of tinsel was in place. Yes, tonight was about her, but it was also about sufferers of Munchausen by thingy. It was important not to forget that. She only hoped there wasn't a member of the paparazzi outside the Dog and Whistle waiting to upskirt – or more accurately, up-star – her. That would ruin everything for everyone. As would Johnny Depp turning up and punching someone in the face. But if it happened it happened. She would just have to deal with it.

The taxi pulled up outside the pub. Violet waited for the driver to open the door and help her out.

'Twenty-six pounds ninety,' said the driver. 'I'd walk next time if I were you, love. It was only five minutes away.' Violet placed her gold glitter wand on the roof of the taxi so she could get some money from her gold purse. The driver pushed one of the points from his face. 'Watch you don't have someone's eyes out with those things.'

After paying the fare, Violet adjusted her tiara and tottered off in her gold high heels.

'Don't forget your wand, love,' said the driver. Violet tottered back and picked up the wand from the roof of the taxi. 'Haven't you forgotten something else?' Violet checked her costume to make sure all the gold glitter balls and gold tinsel were still properly attached. 'My three wishes.'

Violet gave a coquettish smile and waved her wand.

'I'll pick you later for the first of them, then?'

'I'm already taken, I'm afraid,' said Violet, flashing her engagement ring.

'What's the point of having three wishes if they don't come true?'

Violet shrugged her shoulders. With all her dreams coming true at the same time, she wasn't in the mood to discuss broken ones with taxi drivers or anyone else for that matter. Staggering across to the pub's side entrance, she slowly made her way up the stairs to stardom.

III

INSIDE THE PIG and Whistle's changing room, Kurtz was fixing his tie in the mirror. Over his shoulder he could see Frank's glum face reflecting back at him. 'Cheer up, you miserable *muggie*,' he said.

'What have I got to be cheerful about?' said Frank, fiddling with his ginger hairpiece. 'I've got a sixteen-stone psychopath with knockers like a pregnant woman who wants to kill me, a false moustache on my top lip that makes me look like one of the village people…'

'Thought you were supposed to be one of the Marx Brothers?' said Kevin, joining them.

'…and a comedy partner' – Frank pointed at Kevin, who was sniffing more glue – 'who's about as funny as a caravan on the motorway with a flat tyre.'

'Comedy partner?' said Kurtz.

'We're doing a double-act,' said Kevin. 'I'll give you a sneak preview.' He stood on top of a nearby crate of beer and, taking on both roles, said in an exaggerated comic voice, '"Where've you been, Kevin? You're late." "Talking to Kurtz." "Talking to Kurtz?" "Yeah, talking to Kurtz. He's South African, you know? "Did he have anything interesting to say?" "No, not really." "He never does." "No, you could say he's a real Boer."'

'With lines like that I won't need to worry about Victor killing me,' said Frank, twisting on the false moustache. 'I'll die a death out there before he gets his hands on me. And only twelve months to go…'

'Then it's a good job you've got old Kurtz here to look after you,' said Kurtz, combing his moustache and beard.

'Why, have you got some good gags we can use?' said Kevin.

'I'm talking about Victor. You don't need to worry about old Tubby *Tets*. Kurtzy here's got it covered.'

'Easy for you to say,' said Frank.

Kurtz halted his grooming. 'Have I ever let you down in

the past?'

'No,' said Frank slowly. 'I can honestly say that when it comes to stopping sixteen-stone men with large knockers from killing me, you've never let me down. But maybe that's because I've never had a sixteen-stone man with large knockers trying to kill me before.'

'How'd you know?' said Kevin, sniffing some more glue. 'Maybe you've had dozens and Kurtz has stopped them every time. I'd be a little more grateful if I was you.'

'Take a look at this.' Kurtz took the engagement ring from his pocket.

'Whee!' said Kevin

'Nice, eh?'

'Where'd you get it? Marks and Spencer's?'

Kurtz cuffed Kevin around the ear. 'That's a genuine one-carat De Beers diamond. Cost me a fortune.'

'How did you afford that, Kurtzy?' said Kevin. 'You rob a till or something?'

'Never you mind,' said Kurtz, tapping the side of his nose.

'How's that going to help me with Victor?' said Frank. 'Are you going to marry him?'

'You could do worse,' said Kevin.

Kurtz cuffed him around the other ear. 'I'm going to wait until the end of the show and then ask Violet to marry me.'

'I thought she was engaged to Victor?' said Kevin.

'*Bladdy* hell, you don't miss a trick, do you?'

'I like to know what's going on,' said Kevin, pushing the notebook further down into his pocket.

'Well, it's off.' Kurtz brushed some hairs off the front of his tuxedo. 'At least, it will be by the time I propose. And then...'

'What?' said Frank, throwing his hairpiece on to the floor. 'Victor's going to die of a broken heart?' He started stomping on the hairpiece. 'Twelve sodding months!'

Kurtz adjusted the belt on his trousers. 'Oh, Victor's going to die alright,' he said. 'But not of a broken heart.' The door that led out on to the stage was open and Kurtz could see Angel jumping up and down on the boards. 'Look,' he said, pointing at her. Kevin and Frank followed Kurtz's finger.

'What's she doing?' said Kevin.

'Probably seeing if the stage will take her weight,' said Kurtz, combing his hair. 'She's doing some *bladdy* ballet dance later.'

'Ballet?' said Kevin. 'Jesus, it'll be like watching an elephant trying to ice skate. That stage was only built to hold a dozen people, you know.'

'So, your plan is to get Angel to fall on top of Victor?' said Frank.

Kurtz threw his comb into the sink. '*Mompie*. What has Angel been looking for all day?'

'Has she been looking for something?'

'*Bladdy* hell! You can't have been in the *bladdy* car park all *bladdy* day?'

'Her engagement ring,' said Kevin.

'*Presies*,' said Kurtz. 'And guess who stole it?' Kevin and Frank looked wide-eyed at each other as the answer dawned on them. 'Now do you see?'

'She'll tear him limb from limb,' said Kevin.

'*Ja*. All it will take is for someone to say the word.'

Frank's eyes lit up. 'Well, what're we waiting for,' he said, heading towards the stage door.

Kurtz pulled Frank back. 'Not yet. First I've got to make sure Tubby *Tets* has called off his engagement to Violet.'

'She's getting through them, isn't she?' said Kevin. 'Maybe if I wait long enough I'll get my chance, too.' He ducked to avoid Kurtz's fist.

'Why do you have wait until Victor's called off the engagement?' said Frank. 'Violet can't marry him if he's dead.'

'Ask for her hand in marriage when she's grieving for another man?' said Kurtz. 'Can't take that risk. She might turn me down. Besides,' he said, smoothing down the front of his shirt. 'I'm not a cold-hearted barbarian.'

'Warmest hearted barbarian I've ever met, Kurtzy,' said Kevin, this time forgetting to duck.

'And don't you say anything either.' Kurtz checked himself in the mirror. 'I don't want my big moment ruined by you two *bladdy mompies*. It's a delicate situation. Timing is everything. If I find out you've said something I'll tell Angel you helped Victor steal the ring.'

'It might be too late by then,' said Frank. 'He might already have killed me.' He crossed his legs. 'And I need to use the facilities.'

'Relax,' said Kurtz. 'I told you I had it all covered. The boss only told me to keep an eye on you until the end of your shift. But with this trans-warfare going on you've got to be on your guard twenty-four seven. Ask Laurence Fox. So…' He opened the door that led out into the bar. Standing to attention just outside was a frosty-looking fellow of about fifty. Cross-eyed and sporting a toothbrush moustache and bushy sideburns, he had dyed black hair and a suit to match. 'Boys,' said Kurtz, leading the man into the room by the shoulder, 'I'd like you to meet Inspector Mould, one of Lunestone's finest.'

'A policeman?' said Kevin, backing into the corner. 'A real-life policeman?'

'Arthur's agreed to help us out on his night off,' said Kurtz. 'Well, we old coppers have to stick together. Especially with the LGBTQ+ brigade throwing their pronouns about. Right, Mouldy?'

'That's right, Kurtz,' said Mould, looking at Frank.

'While I'm out there being the compere I won't be able to see what's going on off-stage. Mouldy's going to be my other set of eyes.'

'He'll keep a watch on Victor?' said Frank.

'Like a hawk. Right, Mouldy?'

'Right,' said Mould, looking at the wall.

'Wait a minute…' Frank waved a hand in front of Mould's face. Getting not such much as a blink of the eye back in return, Frank took Kurtz to one side. 'He's as blind as a bat!'

'Shut your *mond*!' said Kurtz. 'He's very sensitive about his eyes.'

'And I'm very sensitive about being murdered by men with big tits,' said Frank. 'How's he going to keep an eye on things when he can't even see what's two inches in front of him?'

'He's been a policeman for thirty years, hasn't he?'

'What department?'

'Braille division.'

'Braille division…?' Frank leaned against a stack of crates and covered his face with his hands. 'Twelve months to go and this happens…You can say goodbye to those caravan holidays, Frank. And to that pension. You can say goodbye to everything.' He let out a sarcastic chuckle. 'Murdered by a man with boobs!'

'Look,' said Kurtz, taking out the engagement ring. 'Do you think I'd trust him with this if I didn't think he was up to the job?'

Kurtz dragged Frank back over to where Kevin and Mould were standing.

'…and they said he had the mobile phone *and* the charger up there,' Kevin was saying. Kurtz pushed him out of the way.

'Here, Mouldy.' Kurtz held up the engagement ring. 'Guard

this with your life. I don't trust the pockets in this suit.'

'Sure thing, Kurtz.' Mould grabbed at thin air. Kurtz took hold of his hand and put the ring into it.

'Are you going to give him the charity tin to look after as well?' said Kevin, pointing to under the sink.

'No, I'm keeping an eye on that.' Kurtz retrieved the tin from under the sink. 'I'm going to give it back to Violet when she gets here.' He noticed how clammy his hands felt inside the gloves. Sticky almost. Passing it off as nerves, he grabbed hold of Mould. 'Right, Mouldy, back to your station. And if you see any men with big *tets* acting suspiciously you know what to do.'

Mould turned and walked straight into the door. 'You're under arrest!' he said, pulling out his warrant card. 'Obstructing the police is a very serious offence!' Kurtz guided Mould out of the dressing room and into the bar.

'Stand here, Mouldy,' said Kurtz. 'And don't let anyone in unless I say so.' Kurtz went back inside the dressing room and closed the door. 'Told you I had everything covered. Victor tries to pull any of his cleaning products shit or attempts to murder any department managers then he'll get what for.'

'I'll be lucky to make curtains up,' said Frank. 'Oh, well, if I'm about to meet my maker I might as well do it with an empty bladder.' He pulled open the dressing room door. 'And just twelve months to go…'

IV

VIOLET STOOD AT the top of the stairs and prepared herself for her grand entrance. Fluffing her hair and adjusting her glitter balls, she straightened the tiara on her head. Now she knew what supermodel Melissa Millicent had felt like while waiting to go on at the Carrousel du Louvre for the first time. The hero of Amy Lovelace's *See, Dreams Can Come True!*, Melissa had worked her way up from a lollipop lady to become the world's highest-paid supermodel. Waiting in the wings at her first Paris Fashion Show, she was ready to take on the world. And how the world had loved her. Especially after she had saved the show following a mix-up with the choreography and music. With the catwalk a confused mess of meandering models, Melissa had grabbed one of the huge paper flowers on sticks that were part of the show and – falling back on her lollipop lady skills – restored order.

Now Violet was ready to take on the world. And although she didn't possess Melissa's lollipop ladies' skills if the music and choreography messed up, she was sure the world was going to love her just the same. All it would take was a big entrance on her part.

With every bauble and piece of tinsel in place, she threw open the double doors and stood with her arms in the air. She just had time to shout, 'Ta da!' before the double doors, fitted as they were with spring hinges, flew back and catapulted her halfway down the stairs. Airborne like a real shooting star for part of her journey she landed with a heavy thud amidst a blizzard of glitter and gold paint.

Undaunted, Violet picked up her tiara and broken wand and climbed the stairs once more. After straightening out her points and putting the dented tiara on her head, she eased herself through the double doors. This time when she said 'Ta da!', it wasn't a set of double doors that attacked her, but a set of dog's teeth. Perhaps sensing a rival for the buffet, a snarling Rosie grabbed hold of one of the points and began to pull.

'Get off!' said Violet, twirling around to try and shake herself free.

'That's it,' said Baz from his stool, 'tear the fucking thing to pieces.

ONCE AGAIN VICTOR was forced into the role of knight in shining armour. Picking up a sausage roll from the buffet table he held it out for Rosie to take. Torn between the sausage roll and Violet's star, Rosie snapped at one and then the other before greed finally got the better of her. Snatching the sausage roll she disappeared with it under Baz's stool.

'Thank you...' Violet put her hands to her face in shock. 'Victor...?'

'There's not many that can resist the succulent taste of mechanically recovered gristle,' said Victor.

With tears in her eyes, Violet took hold of one of Victor's hands and said, 'I understand, Victor.'

'Understand what?'

'I want you to know that I love you and I'm prepared to accept you for who you are.'

'Eh?'

'But if you want to go out dressed in women's clothes at least let me find you some that fit.'

'No, no...' began Victor, who, although he would've preferred it if Violet *didn't* love him and *wasn't* prepared to accept him for who he was, didn't want her to think he was a transvestite or kinky cross-dresser. He had nothing against transvestites or kinky cross-dressers, he just didn't want to be thought of in that way.

'No, Victor, I'm here to support you. Now, I've plenty of old dresses that will probably fit you. Shoes might be a bit of a problem, I'm only a size eleven. I wonder what Caitlyn Jenner does...?'

'No, you don't understand...'

Violet clicked her fingers. 'The internet. I bet we can find you some shoes on there. But, oh, Victor...' She put her face closer to his. 'Who put that makeup on for you? You look like a beaten up panda. And that beard! Do you really want to go about looking like Garry Bushell in drag?'

'No,' said Victor, firmly. 'I do not want to go about looking like Garry Bushell, in or out of drag, thank you very much. I told you Malcolm and I are doing Punch and Judy.' He pointed to Malcolm. 'I was supposed to be playing Punch but he forgot the fake breasts...'

'My mum's using them to keep her pegs in,' said Malcolm.

'...so now I'm playing Judy.'

Violet put her hands to her face again. 'And here's me thinking I was marrying a transvestite! Hee-haw! Hee-haw! Hee-haw!' She stopped laughing. 'Not that I'd have minded. Lily Savage looked so glamorous in her gowns. And she looked like that Paul O'Grady with his glasses off. God rest his soul.'

'I need a drink,' said Victor.

'Don't forget about our announcement later.'

Victor looked across at Angel. She was still busy bouncing up and down on the stage. Imagining it was him she was jumping on he gave Violet a forced smile and clomped over to the bar. Violet was about to join him, but Rosie growling at her from under the stool halted her in her tracks. Gathering up her points she said no one in particular, 'I'll go and check everything's ready backstage.'

VICTOR SAT DOWN at the bar full of regret. Regret that he'd rescued Violet from Rosie's jaws, regret that Malcolm had forgotten the fake breasts, regret that he'd involved himself with Angel's ring, regret that he hadn't made any progress on the book, regret about his upcoming engagement, regret that he hadn't paid more attention at school, regret about the size of his breasts, regret, regret, regret. A few stools down sat Tarquin Travers-Booth. Freshly shaved, spikey-haired and wearing the costume of a Nineteenth Century symbolist poet, he was sipping a glass of emerald-green absinthe.

'Ever wondered where we're heading, Malcolm?' said Victor, after knocking back his glass of whisky.

'Thought we were in the Dog and Whistle?' said Malcolm, paying for another round. 'Or is that tomorrow?'

'You always go around town dressed like that, do you?' said Victor, looking pointedly at Malcolm's red hat, false nose and yellow tights. Malcolm looked down at himself in surprise. 'I'm talking existentially. Where are we heading existentially? Wasn't it Jean-Paul Sartre who said, "Everything's been worked out, except how to live"?'

'Probably,' said Malcolm. 'Unless it was someone else.'

'I mean look, at me. I look like one of Jack the Ripper's victims *after* he's done the rounds. And in a couple of hours' time I'll either be crushed to death by Mammoth Fonteyn over there or engaged to Ursa Major and *then* crushed to death by Mammoth Fonteyn.'

'Who's Ursula Major?' said Malcolm, handing Victor another glass of whisky.

'Ursa Major. Ursa. It's a constellation. The Great Bear.'

'I wouldn't advise getting engaged to a bear,' said Malcolm. 'They've got these massive claws that'll ruin all your soft furnishings. Or am I thinking of anteaters? Anyway, they hibernate for half the year – bears, not anteaters. You'd have no one to watch TV with or go out for a meal.'

'I haven't got a television. And it's Violet I'm engaged to, not a bear.'

'Still, it could be worse,' said Malcolm, not listening. 'You could be engaged to a shark or a crocodile or even a skunk. Imagine taking that down to your local eatery. And even a shark or a crocodile or a skunk's better than not being engaged at all. At least you've got someone to enjoy *The Chase* or go fishing with. When you're on your own, all you've got is the cold empty void of loneliness.' A shivering Malcolm tied his scarf tighter around his neck. 'Give me a shark or a crocodile or a skunk over that any day.'

As he listened to Malcolm's soliloquy, Victor felt his mood switch from despair to something more sunlit and hopeful. To say that he was brimming over with joy at the prospect of being engaged to Violet was pushing it. But as he drained his glass for a second time and thought over Malcolm's take on love and marriage, there was definitely more of a silver lining casting a gleam over his tufted grove. Taking possession of another whisky, his thoughts turned to Socrates and what he had to say about wives. Get a good one, the Athenian sage famously said, and you'll be happy. Get a bad one and it'll turn you into a philosopher. To Victor, it was a win-win situation. Either Violet tows the line vis-à-vis all that love, honour and obey guff and it was all Sunday morning outings and never a cross word spoken; or, more likely, she turns into a regular Xanthippe and pours chamber pots over his head and nags him all day, and he becomes what he's always wanted to be. A philosopher.

Victor banged a fist on the bar. If he was serious about becoming a philosopher he would have to make sacrifices. 'Thank you, Malcolm,' he said, slapping his friend on the back.

'You're welcome.' Malcolm put down his glass of lemonade. 'Thank you for what?'

'For talking some sense into me.'

'My pleasure,' said Malcolm, beaming. 'Maybe we should celebrate? Go to the zoo, or something? I don't know if they have skunks, but they definitely have crocodiles and bears.'

But for Victor his tufted grove had become overcast once more. 'I'm forgetting about Angel.'

'She can come with us, but only if she promises not to quarrel with the elephants again.'

After making sure no one was watching, Victor took Angel's ring from his apron pocket. With a Frodo Baggins battle raging inside him, he was torn between throwing the damn thing away or fulfilling was seemed to be his destiny by returning it to Angel. ""'Tis all a Chequer-board of Nights and Days, Where Destiny with Men for Pieces play…"' He put the ring back in his pocket. ""Hither and thither, moves and mates and slays…"' Victor shuddered at the thought of being slain or mated by Angel. 'What we've got to do is put her in a good mood.'

'Who?'

'Angel.'

Malcolm frowned. 'It's going to be difficult. Last time she was in a good mood was when Joe from Food-to-Go had that accident with the meat cleaver.'

'That was no accident,' said Victor. He turned his stool so he was facing Malcolm. 'Listen, all we need to do is make sure she gets a really good foot-stomping, cheering-to-the-rafters round of applause when she does her bit.'

'That's going to be even more difficult. You saw her warming up before.'

'Difficult to miss with all that plaster falling from the ceiling.'

'She looked like a rhinoceros in cement boots trying to tap dance.'

'Well put, Malcolm, I noticed the resemblance myself. But

if we make sure she gets a standing ovation, it'll put her in such a good mood she won't want to tear the place apart when she gets her ring back.'

'How're we going to make sure she gets a standing ovation?'

'Only one way.'

'What's that?'

'Bribery.'

'Bribery?'

'Let's have a look at the running order.' Victor took a piece of paper out of his pocket. On it was printed:

WHITING'S CHARITY GALA

FOR: A GOOD CAUSE
(Brought to you by V.M. Dungworth Productions)

Compere: Kurtz Grobler

Act I. Violet Melissa Dungworth – Yvaine's monologue
from *Stardust*

Act II. Malcolm and Victor – Punch and Judy

ACT III. Angel R.S.E. Hole – *Swan Lake*

Act IV. Kevin and Frank – Crosstalk

Act V. Tarquin Travers-Booth – Rimbaud's *Le Bateau Ivre*
(in French)

Act VI. Baz and Rosie – One Man and His 'Effing Dog

Special announcement: Kurtz Grobler

FINALE

'Good,' said Victor. 'We're on before Angel.'

'I wonder what the special announcement is going to be?' said Malcolm, pointing to the bottom of the page.'

For Victor, the penny, like his jaw, had dropped. Now he knew why Derek and Kurtz were so keen to keep him there until the end. 'I don't know,' he said. 'But I bet it's got something to do with yours truly here. And not in a thank-you-Victor-for-all-your-hard-work way, either.'

'That's because you don't do any hard work.' Malcolm pointed again at the sheet. 'You could always leave after One Man and His 'Effing Dog.'

The beep-beep of items being scanned at a checkout filled Victor's head. 'No,' he said, driving the sound from his mind. He put the sheet of paper back in his pocket. 'Here's the plan. We go around the room and tell people that whoever claps the longest and loudest when Angel does her bit gets free drinks for the rest of the evening.'

'For as long as funds last, you mean,' said Malcolm, checking his wallet.

'It won't matter. Because after we've done our bit, *you'll* be in the audience and you can make sure that it's *you* who claps the loudest.'

'And the longest. But isn't that cheating?'

'This is not time for scruples, Malcolm. We're fighting for our lives.'

'So, you want me to clap?'

'And cheer.'

'*And* cheer?'

'And stamp your feet and raise the roof.'

'That's against health and safety.'

'Not literally raise the roof, Malcolm. Anyway, isn't being crushed by one of your workmates a health and safety issue?'

'I'll check,' said Malcolm, reaching inside his tights for the 1974 *Health and Safety at Work Act*.

'Just keep it going for as long as you can.'

'Where will you be?'

'In the dressing room putting the ring back in Angel's bag.'

'Right. What ring?'

'So the longer you clap…'

'And cheer.'

'…and cheer, the more time I'll have.'

'And if it doesn't work?'

'There's no Plan B, Malcolm.' Victor watched as Angel – a feral look on her face – stomped across the stage towards the dressing room. Perhaps something had gone wrong with her warmup? Or Kurtz had already broken the news about the ring? Whatever it was, *something* had put her in a bad mood. 'At least there's one thing,' he said, lifting up his drink.

'What?'

'Things can't get any worse.'

The words had barely left Victor's lips when the double doors swung open and in swaggered Derek. Wearing a blue denim shirt covered in rhinestones and a yellow silk bandana slung around his neck, he had on a pair of canvas trousers with imitation sheepskin chaps and snakeskin boots with four-inch heels. On his head was a high-crowned, wide-brimmed cowboy hat and a pair of huge sunglasses. Unable to see properly through their dark lenses, he had to feel his way to the bar.

Derek sat down next to Victor just as someone in the dressing room – Kurtz probably – was checking the house lights by dimming them. 'Evenin', mam,' he said, flicking the brim of his cowboy hat.' He looked over at the barmaid. 'Whisky straight up. And one for the little lady.'

'Quadruple whisky,' said Victor in a high-pitched voice. He felt Malcolm tug on his sleeve. When he turned he could see his friend mouthing the word 'No!'.

'What?' Victor mouthed back.

'Well, I'll be damned!' said Derek. 'Work hard, play hard, eh, little lady?' The barmaid put his drink in front of him. 'Here's to you.' Derek raised his glass to Victor, before taking a small sip. 'Dang!' he said, almost choking. 'That's got a kick like a whole stable of mules.'

Victor knocked his quadruple whisky back in one.

'Jesus H. Christ!' said Derek. 'Last time I saw a dame drink like that was back in 09 down in Milton Keynes. She ended up in the car park of the Grand Hotel with her drawers on her head singing the national anthem. Ever been to Milton Keynes?'

Victor felt a hand on his leg. 'No,' he said, in a strangulated voice.

'It's got the biggest roundabout in the country. You should let me show you it some time.'

Victor was more concerned with Derek's hand, which was heading towards his own 'roundabout' at sixty miles an hour. 'I'll have to check my diary,' he said in a falsetto voice. He felt Derek's hand disappear up his miniskirt.

'Afterwards,' said Derek, 'we can go to a hotel and roll about like a couple of hogs in heat. How'd you like the sound of them apples?'

'Great!' Victor's voice now sounded like someone who had just inhaled a balloon full of helium.

'Then we can…' Derek's hand paused. 'What the hell…? Are you packing a piece, young lady?' Derek whipped off his sunglasses. Just then the house lights were turned back up. 'Victor?'

'Glad you could make it, boss. Thanks for the drink.'

They both looked down at Derek's hand, which still had hold of Victor's 'piece'.

'Thundering hootenannies…!' Derek let go.

'I think you'll find the biggest roundabout in the country is in Swindon,' said Malcolm, adjusting his fake nose.

The look of disgust on Derek's face grew stronger. 'The wild beasts,' he said, pointing a finger at Victor and Malcolm. '"For she lusted after lovers with genitals as large as a donkey and emissions like those of a horse…"' He started to back away. '"You revisited the indecency of your youth, when the Egyptians caressed your bosom and pressed your young breasts". Agh!...'

When Derek looked down, it was to find Rosie tugging on his chaps. As his trousers started to slide down a crowd gathered and began clapping and cheering.

'I doubt Angel will get a bigger round of applause than that,' said Malcolm, joining in.

Having sold his manhood for thirty millilitres of whisky, Victor climbed down from his stool. 'I need to pee,' he said.

'Use the gender appropriate toilets this time,' said Malcolm. 'Remember, gender reassignment isn't a lifestyle choice, it's a state of being.'

'I'll tell you what state of being *I've* been in for the past twenty-five years,' said Victor, pointing a finger at each breast. 'School sport's day was a mental health nightmare. Getting changed on my own. Being laughed at by all the other kids.'

'No one should be laughed at for being different. But it's time to show others the respect you want shown to you.'

'Respect? Huh! Look what happened to me this morning.

First, I couldn't blag my way on to the bus because the driver recognised me from my tits. Then the Visigoths ambushed me again with that *Swing low, sweet chesticles* song of theirs. Then I had that misunderstanding with that old woman…All because I'm built differently.'

'Not quite all. If you'd paid the bus fare like you're supposed to then the driver wouldn't have said anything to you about your breasts. If you hadn't been late for work then you wouldn't have needed to go through the park and the Visigoths wouldn't have been able to ambush you. As for that misunderstanding with the old woman…It was your fault, not hers. You put two and two together and got thirty-six double-d.'

'To perceive is to suffer. You try walking around like a Bactrian camel all your adult life. It's bound to give you the hump.'

'Doesn't stop you from using them to get a free drink from the boss.'

'Sometimes you've got to use what you've got,' said Victor, setting off for the toilets.

'Happiness depends on yourself, Victor,' Malcolm shouted after him. 'You should remember that.'

VI

DESPITE MALCOLM'S SERMON, Victor decided to chance his arm with the ladies' toilets. He'd served his time as a (close) member of the opposite sex. Now it was time to reap the rewards. He'd seen for himself at Whiting's how cleaner, more private and pleasanter they were compared to the men's. And in the ladies' he didn't have to worry about faces appearing under and over the door trying to find out if he'd undergone a vaginoplasty. If he was challenged he could always play the gender reassignment card again. It was starting to become something of a get-out-of-jail pass. No wonder JK Rowling was wary of such things. It had greater magical powers than Harry Potter. Of course in the wrong hands – like Kevin's for example – it could cause untold damage. But for someone who used it sensibly, the opportunities were endless.

When Victor entered the toilets he discovered that he wasn't the only one to have played the gender reassignment card. Frank had also dealt himself in. He was just leaving one of the cubicles – and the seat up! – when Victor burst in. Upon seeing him, Frank turned a deathly white and backed himself up against the wall. Victor was just about to allay Frank's fears by telling him that his Freddie Mercury costume gave him a free pass to the ladies' – sort of – when, to his amazement, Frank, hairpiece in place, started talking in Scottish.

'Aye, wifie,' he said, 'nice tae meit ye.'

Puzzled as to why Frank was talking in this way when he was supposed to be playing Freddie Mercury, Victor began throwing out the names of all the Queen songs he knew. '*All Dead, All Dead*. Hey, *Another One Bites the Dust*.' He clenched his fist and made a stabbing motion with it. '*And another one bites, another one bites, another one bites the dust…*'

Frank turned even paler and started to sob. 'Goad a'michty,' he said, holding up his hands as if he was praying.

Victor, whose mother had been a Queen fan (she liked the dresses and Brian May's hair), still had plenty of ammunition. '*Chinese Torture. Don't Lose Your Head. Hammer to Fall. I Go Crazy*' – here Victor widened his eyes to look like a crazed psycho – '*I'm Going Slightly Mad.*'

Frank fell to his knees. 'Ma dampt hoovercraft's breemin' ower wi biuddy eyls, man,' he said in a pleading tone.

'Well,' said Victor, wondering what the hell Frank was talking about, '*Keep Yourself Alive*, or *Man on the Prowl*, *Pain is so Close to Pleasure*. Anyway, *Who Wants to Live Forever*?' He watched in amazement as Frank ran out of the toilets screaming. '*Stone Cold Crazy*,' said Victor, hitching up his miniskirt.

CHAPTER ELEVEN

IN THE DRESSING room an anxious Kurtz was pacing up and down. There was only a few minutes to go before curtains up, and Victor and Violet were both missing. He still didn't know if he was I-doing or I-don't-ing. Holding his gurgling stomach, he turned to Kevin who was sitting on a nearby crate sniffing what was left of the glue. 'Where the *bladdy* hell is everyone?'

A glazed-eye Kevin shrugged his shoulders. 'How do I know? Dead, probably, or going at it like rabbits in the broom cupboard.' Kurtz grabbed the tube of glue and threw it out of the window. 'What did you do that for?'

'One more *bladdy* word about broom cupboards and you'll be following it!' To release the stress and soothe Jacob, Kurtz decided to practise his opening speech. Removing his white gloves, he took a card from his pocket. He turned to face the mirror. Staring back at him was a face loaded with terror. 'Good evening, ladies and gentlemen, and welcome to tonight's charity evening…to this evening's charity night…' Trying to adjust the card in his hand, he noticed it was sticking to his palm.

'Nervous?' said Kevin.

'Don't be so *bladdy* stupid,' said Kurtz, peeling the card from his hand. But he knew Kevin was right. He was nervous. Not about being compere. Any *mompie* could do that. No, what he was worried about was the getting down on one knee and proposing bit. What if Violet said no? Or even worse decided to marry Victor instead? It was this last bit that was really gnawing away at him. To be bested by any man was bad enough. But by a man who read *bladdy* books and had women's *tets*…He would never be able to take part in a GB News poll again. Or go to a Jeremy Clarkson book-signing and look the great man in the face.

He glanced over at Angel, who was getting changed behind a screen. *Tell her about the ring.* That was what Jacob was saying to him. Kurtz took hold of his stomach. If he did, it would almost certainly mean sacrificing his walk up the aisle with Violet. But at least it would guarantee Victor being unable to walk anywhere. As he mulled it over, he put his gloves back on. Outside, in the bar, there were raised voices. Opening the door, he found Violet and Mould wrestling on the floor.

'Intruders!' said Mould, with a star point in each hand. 'Three of them, at least.'

'It's alright, Mouldy,' said Kurtz, dragging Violet into the dressing room by her high-heels. 'She's one of us.'

What with her tussle with the double doors, Rosie's teeth and now a blind policeman, Violet's costume was starting to look a bit battered. Covered in dents, creases and dog teeth, much of the gold paint on the papier mâché star had chipped off to reveal the newspaper underlay. The points, meanwhile, drooped to floor and hung twisted and broken like snapped branches on a dead tree.

'Up you get, *bokkie*,' said Kurtz, helping Violet to her feet.

'Thank you,' said Violet, one hand holding on to her tiara. 'Oh, it all happened so quickly! One minute I was walking along without a care in the world and the next…I thought I'd been attacked by that dog again.'

'Dog?' Kurtz barred his teeth. He didn't see eye to eye with dogs. Not since one of the police dogs back in Pretoria had turned on him and bitten him on the backside.

'Then I realised there was a man's claws on my points.' Violet held one of the broken points in her hand. 'At first I thought it might be Johnny Depp, but then…Who is he, anyway?'

'He's a policeman,' said Kevin. 'A real policeman. So keep your mouth shut about that cannabis *someone* put in the bread mix.'

'He's a blind policeman,' said Frank, entering the dressing room from the stage.

'I can't say I'm surprised,' said Violet, trying to straighten the point she was holding. 'There can't be too many criminals who go out dressed as gold stars.'

'He's just making sure our things don't get stolen,' said Kurtz. He took the charity tin from under the sink and handed it to Violet. 'Like this.'

'Thank you,' said Violet.

Kurtz looked at his watch. 'Nearly show time. We could move you down the order until you get yourself looking pretty again, if you like?'

'No, no, I'm fine.' Violet fanned herself with the broken wand. 'After all, the show must go on.' She tried to see out past the stage and into the audience. 'Even if Johnny Depp hasn't turned up. Or Graham Norton.'

'Why must the show go on?' said Frank, slumping against a stack of crates. 'Why must anything go on? It only leads to the same thing. Death.' He collapsed to the floor. 'We're all doomed, I tell you. Doomed!'

'Take no notice of him, *bokkie*.' Kurtz put a hand on each of Violet's shoulders. 'Have you spoken to Victor?'

'Oh, yes,' said Violet, brightening. 'It was Victor who rescued me from that dog. Armed with just a sausage roll. Such courage.'

Frank rolled around on the floor. 'Dear God!'

Kurtz's cheek began to twitch. Victor rescuing Violet instead of rebuffing her made his own will-you-do-me-the-honour bit even more of a gamble.

'Are you all right, Kurtz?' said Violet. 'You've gone white.'

'I'm fine,' said Kurtz, trying to clear the dizziness in his head. He was just weighing up whether he could appear before the Truth and Reconciliation Commission and settle back in South Africa to mend his broken heart, when salvation arrived in the shape of Angel. Appearing from behind the screen dressed in a black platter tutu, she looked like a gorilla who had just swallowed a dining table. The thought of Victor trying to defend himself with a sausage roll against *that* cheered Kurtz up. The colour returned to his cheeks and the dizziness cleared. He smoothed down the front of his shirt and shot his cuffs. 'Alright, everyone,' he said, 'let's roll!'

'Good luck everyone,' said Violet. 'And don't forget, we're doing this for a good cause.'

Kurtz pulled his gloves tighter over his hands. Then in classic Hollywood director's style, he pointed at Frank and said 'Lights!' Gently squeezing Violet's chin, he jumped on the stage with a huge leap.

'Break a leg,' said Violet. Kurtz glanced over his shoulder and winked. Not looking where he was going, he tripped over the microphone cord and crashed to the floor.

'My *fokking* leg!' he moaned.

II

KEVIN DASHED ON to the stage. 'First aider, make way!' He bent down next to Kurtz. 'Where does it hurt?'

'Where do you think it *fokking* hurts,' said Kurtz writhing in pain, 'my *fokking* ear?'

'You're in shock. He's in shock,' said Kevin, to the rest of the room. 'Stand back, give him some air.' Kevin cracked his knuckles and then pinched Kurtz's nose in readiness to give him the kiss of life. With one hand holding his busted leg, Kurtz used the other to push Kevin's head away. But with his tongue like some heat-seeking missile trying to hit the target of Kurtz's mouth, Kevin fought back.

'Get him off!' said Kurtz.

No one moved.

'Is this part of the fucking show?' said Baz, lighting another roll-up.

Rosie shot out from under Baz's stool, leapt on to the stage and started snapping at Kurtz's prostrate body. With attacks coming in from all angles and just one hand with which to fend them off, Kurtz twisted this way and that.

Victor gave Malcolm a nudge. 'Here's our chance.'

'Our chance to do what?' said Malcolm.

'To slip the ring into Angel's bag.'

'What ring?'

Victor pushed Malcolm towards the stage. 'Get over there and distract them!' He watched as Malcolm climbed up on the stage and walked over to the microphone.

'Ding-dong!' said Malcolm into the microphone. The melee on the stage carried on behind him. 'We have another great offer for you here today at Whiting's…' Violet ran on to the stage and started shooing Rosie with her broken wand. 'Hot cross buns. Buy one, get one free. Hmmmmm…Perfect hot, cold or with… erm…crosses. Free today…'

'Ow!' It was Kevin. With Violet protecting his eastern front from Rosie, Kurtz had been able to turn all his attention to his western front. He did this by smashing a fist into Kevin's face. Blood pouring down his nose, Kevin ran around the stage shouting, 'First aider! First aider!'

'Also on offer,' said Malcolm, shuffling to his left to avoid Kevin's blood, 'frozen fish. Hmmmmm…for cod's sake, eat haddock…'

UNABLE TO USE the stage door because of all the chaos going on, Victor ran around to the dressing room door. Focused fully on the ring and returning it to Angel's bag, he didn't see Mould standing guard. Until he saw a hand being held up to his face and heard the words, 'Sorry, love. No entry.'

'But I'm one of the acts,' said a surprised Victor.

'Thought this was supposed to be a charity do?' said Mould. 'No one said there'd be strippers.'

'I'm Judy, from Punch and Judy.'

'Well, I'm sorry Judy, but I've got orders. No one's allowed to go in and out of here without Kurtz's permission. You'll have to use the stage door.'

Victor decided it was time to pull rank. 'I'm a philosopher,' he said, trying to push past Mould. But Lunestone's finest stood his ground. 'Have you ever heard of a subject called philosophy?'

'You mean in the academic sense?' said Mould. 'The study of the fundamental nature of knowledge, reality and existence. Or in the general sense? A theory or attitude that acts as a guiding principle for human behaviour. Personally, I prefer Wittgenstein's definition. That philosophy is not a theory, but an activity that consists essentially of elucidations.'

Victor took a step back. Here was someone who hadn't just heard of a subject called philosophy, but actually knew what it was.

'Milton put it best, don't you think, when he said: "How charming is divine philosophy! /Not harsh and crabbed, as dull fools suppose, /But musical as is Apollo's lute, /And a perpetual feast of nectar'd sweets/ Where no crude surfeit reigns…"'

'The, erm, stage door you say?' said Victor, retreating.

'"O philosophy, life's guide! O searcher-out of virtue and expeller of vices…"'

Knowing when he was beaten, Victor hurried to the bar. He arrived back just as order was being restored on the stage. Somebody had tempted Rosie back under Baz's stool with a plate of cocktail sausages. Kevin was sitting on the edge of the stage holding a handkerchief to his nose. Kurtz, meanwhile, had pulled himself to his feet and had hobbled over to the microphone.

'Good evening, ladies and gentlemen,' said Kurtz, taking some cards from his pocket. 'Welcome to…to…' Wincing from the pain, he threw the cards over his shoulder. 'First up, it's Violet.'

There was a smattering of applause followed by a 'Go on, Violet, you fucking bitch!' from Baz.

A battered and crumpled Violet 'floated' her way to the microphone. Throwing back her head, she said in a loud whisper, '"I know a lot about love. I've seen it, centuries and centuries of it, and it was the only thing that made watching your world bearable. All those wars. Pains, lies, hate…"'

'Mission accomplished?' said Malcolm, handing Victor a glass of whisky.

'No,' said Victor.

'What happened?'

'I met someone who'd heard of a subject called philosophy.'

Malcolm picked up his glass of lemonade. 'There's always that risk,' he said. 'But even philosophers have to eat fish.'

'Fish?'

'In fact being a philosopher, you'd have thought they'd have snapped it up. It's brain food, after all.'

'Malcolm, what has fish got to do with Angel's ring?'

'Nothing. Although it is supposed to be good for the digestion.'

Victor drained his glass. 'What are you talking about?'

'I thought that's why we were here. To sell fish. "For cod's sake eat haddock".'

'That was a diversion.'

'So it's not half price?'

'What's not half price?'

'Cod? I mean, haddock?'

'I've no idea how much cod or haddock is,' said Victor, putting his empty glass on the bar. 'All I know is there's someone in here who's heard of a subject called philosophy and I've still got Angel's ring. The rest is detail.'

'Well, never mind. At least hot cross buns are buy one, get one free.'

Before he could inform Malcolm that hot cross buns were just a diversion too, Victor heard his name spoken from the stage. Having got to the part where Yvaine says, 'What I'm trying to say, Tristan, is…I think I love you', Violet changed it to, 'What I'm trying to say, Victor, is…I think I love you.' Violet paused to blow Victor a kiss. From the audience came a cacophony of ironic cheers and whistling.

Looking like a goldfish at a funfair who has just found out he's been won by a family of hungry carp, Victor's mouth opened and closed in silent horror. His horror only increased when he spotted King Carp Kurtz glaring carnivorously at him from the side of the stage. To Victor's further alarm, Malcolm stood up and started clapping and cheering like a football fan whose team has just won the Champions League for the first time.

'No, not yet, Malcolm,' said Victor, trying to reign his friend in. But it was too late. Taking their lead from Malcolm, the rest of the room rose and started clapping and cheering. Refusing to be beaten, Malcolm clapped and cheered even louder. The others clapped and cheered louder still. *Ad infinitum.* Until, reaching a crescendo, Malcolm snatched two metal dishes from the buffet table – and after jumping on to the bar – started banging them together. The rest of the room again followed his lead, and soon everyone except Victor and Kurtz were standing on tables and chairs hollering, cheering and stamping their feet.

A dumbstruck Victor glanced up at Violet. Too overcome with emotion to continue, she had rushed to the front of the stage and was blowing him yet more kisses. From the corner of his eye, Victor could see someone shuffling towards the microphone.

Kurtz!

'Quiet!' he shouted.

But Malcolm for one wouldn't be quiet. Maybe thinking that there was a new entry to the who-can-clap-and-cheer-the-loudest-(and-longest) competition – a cheat, no less, given that he was using a microphone – Malcolm upped his cheering and dish-banging and jumping-up-and-downing.

'Quiet, you *fokking mompies*!'

One by one the cheerers and clappers fell silent. All except Malcolm, who jumped down from the bar and began marching round the room with his eyes closed, cheering and banging the dishes together. Kurtz waited until Malcolm passed by the front of the stage and then painfully bent down and grabbed the dishes from Malcolm's hands. When Malcolm opened his eyes he realised he was the only one still cheering. 'Winner!'

he said, clapping and cheering himself. 'Half price fish and free drinks!'

Kurtz glowered at Victor from the stage. 'As this act has overrun – and for health and safety reasons – the Punch and Judy show has been cancelled.'

'Oh, no, it hasn't!' shouted someone from the audience.

'Next up, it's Angel.'

With a series of *grands jetés* that shook the very foundations of the building and made the plaster fall from the ceiling like confetti, Angel made her appearance. To the sound of the *Black Swan Pas de deux* playing over the speakers, she proceeded to fling herself about the stage with all the grace and elegance of a wallowing hippo. Pirouetting like Frankenstein trapped inside a suit of armour, she launched herself into the air. The room took a collective gasp. She hit the boards like an asteroid hitting the Earth. Everyone threw themselves under their tables to escape the fresh chunks of plaster raining down from the ceiling. All except Victor, who grabbed hold of a cowering Malcolm and said, 'Come on. We've got work to do.'

III

WITH MALCOLM FOLLOWING, Victor marched around to the dressing room door. Mould was still on sentry duty. 'Now, look here,' said Victor, heaving up his bosom. 'We have important business in that dressing room and demand access.'

'Is that you again, Judy?' said Mould squinting. 'I'd leave off those cigarettes if I was you. You've got a voice like sandpaper.'

'Are you going to let us in that room, or not?'

'Sorry, Judy, I can't let you in unless Kurtz says so.'

'Unless Kurtz says so? He doesn't own this establishment,

you know? Oh, never mind. Come on, Malcolm, we'll find another way.'

'As Nietzsche said, "Many are stubborn in pursuit of the path they have chosen, few in pursuit of the goal".'

Malcolm opened his mouth to speak. Knowing not to get into a philosophical discussion with Mould, Victor pulled his friend over to the double doors. 'There must be another way to get into that dressing room.'

'The only other way's the stage,' said Malcolm. And Kurtz is patrolling that. Unless, of course,' he's got Nietzsche to do it.'

'Nietzsche's a philosopher.'

'Another one? They seem to be multiplying like flies these philosophers. We might never get into that dressing room.'

Victor thought for a moment. 'No Plan B, Malcolm,' he said, pushing Malcolm through the double doors.

SEEING HIS QUARRY escape before his very eyes, Kurtz limped to the front of the stage shouting 'Stop!' Off to his left he became aware of a something large spinning out of control. It was Angel, who following her *saut de chat*, had gone straight into the *Black Swan Coda*. This consisted of no less than thirty-two *fouettés en tournant* – thirty-two spins on one foot. By the time she had finished she was whirling around the stage like an out-of-control spinning top. Banging into Kurtz, he was catapulted from the stage on to the front row of tables. Landing with a loud crash on his good leg, he just had time to cry, 'My other *fokking* leg!' when a black mass came hurtling towards him. It was Angel again, who, after slipping in a pool of Kevin's blood, followed Kurtz off the stage and onto the tables. For Kurtz, it was as if he'd been swallowed up by a black hole. Disappearing beneath a carpet of black tulle, he felt the force of a thousand dead stars weighing down upon him.

IV

VICTOR AND MALCOLM dashed through the double doors. Coming in the opposite direction was Violet.

'Oh, Victor, did you hear all the applause?' she said.

'An Oscar winning performance,' said Victor, crossing his fingers behind his back.

'They weren't just applauding my performance, silly – although it was *very* Michelle Keegan – they were applauding our love. And you...' Violet turned to Malcolm. 'You were applauding the loudest.'

'And the longest,' said a beaming Malcolm.

Violet turned back to Victor. 'Imagine the noise when we announce our engagement. Why, they'll raise the roof!' She pushed open the double doors. 'Until we meet again,' she said, blowing Victor a kiss. 'Adieu.' She disappeared back into the bar.

'How about that, then?' said Malcolm, beaming even brighter. 'Loudest *and* longest.'

'And the earth opened its mouth and swallowed them up,' said Victor, holding his head in his hands.

'Free drinks all night!'

'Followed by fifty years of Violet.' Victor pulled up his miniskirt. 'Let's go.'

'Where are we going?'

'What Violet said about raising the roof has given me an idea.'

'Another competition?'

'Sort of.'

'Oh, good. I'm on a roll.'

PROPPED UP ON a chair in front of the microphone, Kurtz was preparing to introduce the next act. Both of his legs were busted, one of his arms was in a makeshift sling and every bone in his body was aching. Even leaning forward to speak made him wince in agony. Where he should've been was in hospital. But he was determined not to leave until he'd proposed to Violet and seen Angel *fouetté en tournant* Victor.

'Next up,' he said, gritting his teeth because of the pain, 'Whiting's two funniest men – for the love of Christ! – it's… ouch…Kevin and…ouch…Frank…'

Whiting's two funniest men shuffled on to the stage. Kevin was still trying to staunch the flow of blood from his nose. Frank – his disguise completely blown now that Kurtz had introduced him by his real name – followed behind looking like a man frightened of his own shadow. The only thing that might save them was the quality of their material.

'I took a shortcut through the cemetery on my way home from the pub last night,' said Frank in a frightened whisper.

'Did you, Frank – I mean, Pat?' said Kevin through his blood-soaked handkerchief.

'I did, Mike. I stopped to read a tombstone. It said, "Here lies a politician and honest man."' There was a pause as Kevin tried to stop the blood from running down the front of his Victor T-shirt. '"Here lies a politician and honest man",' prompted Frank.

'Faith, now,' said Kevin finally. 'How did they get them both in one grave?'

Except for one or two coughs and some scraping of chairs, the room was silent.

'Begorrah, Mike, you were working mighty hard on that

building site yesterday. I watched you go up and down that ladder all day with those load of bricks. Not like you at all.'

'Don't worry yourself, Frank...'

'Pat.'

'What? Oh, yes. Don't worry yourself, Pat,' said Kevin, gingerly tapping the side of his sore nose. 'I've got them all fooled. It was the same load of bricks each time.'

'Doesn't fucking work,' said Baz. 'If it's the same load of fucking bricks he's working just as hard.'

'That's the joke,' said Kevin from behind his handkerchief.'

'Joke?'

'What do you call a big Irish spider?' said Frank, almost on the verge of tears. 'A paddy-long-legs.'

Silence. The only other time Kurtz had heard one as deafening was back in the day in Pretoria. An old black man up on a charge of sitting on a white's only bench was found not guilty by the judge. The stunned silence after the verdict was announced was followed by demonstrations in the streets and an investigation by the Judicial Conduct Committee. Any committee investigating Kevin and Frank's act would reach the same decision as the JCC did in terms of the judge: early retirement. An act of kindness in anyone's book.

'Whiting's two funniest...ouch...men,' said Kurtz.

'There's more,' said Kevin.

'No...ouch...there isn't,' said Kurtz, waving them off with his good arm.

Among the smattering of applause was the sound of a cork popping. 'Don't shoot!' said Frank, hurling himself to floor. As he did, his hairpiece fell off and tumbled down into the front row. Soon, it became a hairy Frisbee for members of the audience to toss across the room.

Kevin walked over to the microphone. 'The answer to

the Guess the Pervert competition was, of course, Victor.'
He helped Frank to his feet and Whiting's two funniest men
shuffled apologetically from the stage.

'Tarquin Travers…ouch…Jesus H. Christ…Booth. Rimbaud.'

An unlit Gauloise dangling from his mouth and carrying a
half-drunk glass of absinthe, Tarquin Travers-Booth swaggered
on to the stage.

'That's not fucking Rambo,' said Baz. 'Where's his headband
and machine gun?'

'*Comme je descendais des Fleuves impassibles*,' said
Tarquin Travers-Booth into the microphone. '*Je ne me sentis
plus guidé par les haleurs…*'

'Rambo's not fucking Spanish,' said Baz. 'Boo! Get off! We
didn't leave the bastard EU to listen to this shite! Where's John J?'

'*Des Peaux-Rouges criards les avaient pris pour cibles…*'

VI

OUTSIDE THE DOG and Whistle, Victor and Malcolm were
looking up at the half-open dressing room window.

'Looks too high to me,' said Malcolm.

'Nonsense.' Victor spat on both hands and took a firm hold
of the drainpipe that ran to the ground beside the window.

Malcolm took the *Work Act* from out of his tights. 'It says
here that proper safety equipment – including safety ropes –
should be used when climbing heights in excess of six feet.' He
looked up again at the window. 'Must be twenty feet, at least.'

'This is no time for technicalities, Malcolm.'

'It might not take the strain.'

'You see that?' Victor pointed to the words 'Made in
England' running around the bottom of the drainpipe. 'The

mark of quality. We may have lost the Empire – thank goodness – but we can still make drainpipes.'

'I thought you said Britain was crap at everything now, which is why we had to stay in the EU?'

'Everything but making drainpipes. And having fuckwits run the country. Right, ready?'

'Ready.'

'No Plan B!' said Victor, pulling himself up. What with his Wellington boots on, he struggled at first to gain any purchase. But with his miniskirt hitched up around his waist to reveal his 'I Luv Philosophy' boxer shorts, he finally managed to slip and shimmy up the drainpipe.

'That's it,' said Malcolm. 'One hand over the other.'

At the halfway point Victor decided to take a break. For one thing the drainpipe was rubbing against his breasts and making them sore. Ten feet off the ground he felt nearer to the cosmos and his mother than ever before. He glanced up at the galaxy of stars above his head. Sparkling in the clear January sky, they reminded him of the gold baubles on Violet's costume. Feeling himself slip into a poetical mood, he lifted a hand to the heavens. '"I arise from dreams of thee/ In the first sweet sleep of night,/ When the winds are breathing low,/ And the stars are shining bri…" Aargh!'

BACK DOWN ON *terra firma* Malcolm heard two small metal objects hit the ground. Thinking they were coins from Victor's pocket he bent down to pick them up. Two screws. Malcolm allowed himself a little chuckle. Victor was like the monarch in that he never carried any money on him. Looking up at Victor once more, he saw the drainpipe detach itself from the wall. Like a petrified pole-vaulter too frightened to make that final push, Victor remained upright for a brief moment before gravity took over. Malcolm watched as if in slow motion Victor fell into a large pile of rubbish.

Running over to where Victor had fallen, Malcolm was met by the stench of rotten fish and out-of-date milk. He shifted some bags from the top of the pile. Underneath he found a green Wellington boot. Attached to the boot was a hairy leg. Malcolm followed it until he came to a soiled piece of white fabric with 'I luv Phil' printed across it. He was about to delve a little deeper when the bags parted like the Red Sea and up came Victor as if from the deep. Dazed, confused and covered in rotting fish heads and putrid vegetables, he picked a banana skin from the top of his head. 'What happened?' he spluttered.

'I told you,' said Malcolm, helping Victor to his feet. 'Hard hats, they're not just for decoration.'

Victor's nostril twitched. 'What's that awful smell?'

'Yesterday's leftovers, probably.'

VICTOR LOOKED DOWN at the fish bones and rotten vegetables stuck to him. Cleaning out some cabbage from his ears, a terrible thought struck him.

The ring!

He stuck his hands into the pocket of his apron. First out was a fistful of rancid fish heads. This was followed by a melange of mashed-up potato, carrot and what looked like swede. He sorted through it all with an archaeologist's eye.

Nothing!

He shoved his hands back in the apron. This time he brough out some broken bits of cake and foul-smelling fruit. Like some myopic eater searching for a creepy-crawly in their salad, he examined every crumb and pip closely. Finally, like a shiny sixpence in a Christmas pudding, he found the ring. Cleaning it with the corner of his drooping tea towel turban, he handed it to Malcolm. 'Put this somewhere safe,' he said.

Malcolm put the ring down his tights.

Victor picked up the broken piece of drainpipe. 'Made in sodding England,' he said, hurling the drainpipe over the wall.

'Ow!'

Victor and Malcolm looked at each other, then peered over the wall. On the other side was a prostrate Derek out cold.

'What are we going to do with him?' said Malcolm. But Victor had already moved on to other things. Against the wall on Derek's side was an old wooden ladder. Victor grabbed the top and fed it over to where he and Malcolm were standing. 'Good idea,' said Malcolm. 'We can use it as a stretcher and carry the boss to A and E.'

Instead, Victor carried the ladder over to the dressing room window and planted it firmly on the ground. 'You keep hold of it round the bottom,' said Victor. 'Okay, ready?'

'Ready,' said Malcolm, gripping hold of the bottom of the ladder.

Victor climbed up to the dressing room window.

'Well?' said Malcolm, down below.

'All clear,' said Victor, giving a thumbs-up. He gathered his miniskirt in one hand and prepared to climb through the window. From inside, the drop was less than six feet. With only the top part of the window open Victor had to lower himself down a couple of feet before being able to grab the inner sill. 'Piece of cake,' he said to himself, picking some stale pieces of cake from his tea towel. His plan was to pull the top half of his body through, grab hold of the sill, bring each leg over in turn and then slowly lower himself to the floor.

The window was narrower than it had looked from the ground. And Victor's bosom added several more inches to an already full figure. To fit the top half of his body through he

219

really had to squeeze himself in. But it was when he tried to bring his leg over that he realised he was in trouble. Unable to get enough purchase on the sill to steady himself he decided to manoeuvre back out on to the ladder and try again feet first. Clutching the ladder with his legs he tried to ease himself out of the window. But his breasts got lodged in the frame.

'Who will rid me of these turbulent tits?' he gasped, fighting to free himself. But the more he struggled the more the ladder wobbled. Until the inevitable happened and his feet slipped off. 'I'fackins,' he groaned, trying to find the ladder again with his Wellington boots. But by this point there was nothing to find. Having knocked it with his flailing feet, the ladder hung suspended in the air like a piece of Made in England drainpipe. Before falling to the ground with a loud thud.

Hanging half in and half out of the window Victor could only keep himself steady by gripping the inside of the frame with his hands and the outer sill with his tiptoes. And there he dangled, twenty feet in the air, smelling of rotten fish, with a tea towel on his head, a face covered in smudged make-up, a miniskirt hitched halfway up his back and a pair of boxer shorts with the legend 'I Luv Phil' flashing like a beacon to any passing owl.

VII

DOWN BELOW MALCOLM immediately went to work. If there was one thing he was good at spotting it was a health and safety emergency. And someone hanging out of a second-storey window in Wellies and a miniskirt was definitely an emergency.

Making a mental note to ask Victor who Phil was, Malcolm retrieved the ladder which had fallen backwards and landed against the wall. Also against the wall, two large lumps on his forehead, was Derek. Malcolm let out a long whistle. It was obvious what had happened. His store manager had just recovered from his meeting with the drainpipe and had tried to climb over the wall. Just as the ladder was landing.

Malcolm picked up the ladder only to forget what he needed it for. He was having one of his moments. It was what always happened when he was in a state of excitement or panic. He stood rooted to the spot trying to work out where he was and what he was doing holding a ladder. And why his store manager was slumped unconscious over a wall. All that was coming into his head were images of being on a stage talking about hot cross buns.

'Help!'

At first Malcolm thought it was Derek who was calling. But his store manager was still slumped over the wall dead to the world.

'Malcolm!'

Malcolm looked up and saw Victor dangling from the dressing room window. 'What're you doing up there?' he said, surprised.

'Quick!' said Victor. 'The ladder!'

Malcolm looked at the ladder he was holding. He was about to prop it up underneath Victor when his plastic nose fell off. Thinking for a moment that it was his real nose and that he must've been abducted by aliens and experimented on, he fell to his knees to retrieve it.

'Malcolm!'

'It's alright,' said Malcolm, picking up the fake nose, 'it's made of plastic.' He felt for his real nose. It was still attached to his face.

'Malcolm!'

The mystery of why he was wearing a fake nose would have

to wait. His friend needed him. He placed the ladder under the dressing room window.

'I'm stuck,' said Victor. 'You'll have to give me a push.'

Malcolm started to climb the ladder. 'Why have you got a miniskirt on?' he said, stopping halfway.

'I was supposed to be playing Judy, remember?'

'Judy who?'

'Do you mind if we have this conversation another time?'

'I'll have forgotten it by then.'

'I won't have, believe me.'

'Oh, fine.' Malcolm climbed to the top of the ladder. 'Now, what is it that you want me to do?'

'Push me through this window.'

Had he been able to reach, Malcolm would've consulted the *Work Act* that was stuffed down his tights. It would've told him what the correct procedure was for pushing someone through an open window. But being twenty feet up while balanced precariously on a ladder he decided to follow Victor's instructions. Placing both hands on his friend's buttocks, he started to push.

'Heave!' he said, pushing harder.

'Ho!' said Victor, moving a couple of millimetres.

'Heave!'

'Ho!' A few millimetres more.

'Heave!'

'Ho!'

VIII

BEFORE INTRODUCING THE next act Kurtz took a bottle of painkillers from his inside pocket. They were left over from the time he'd had to attend casualty following a postprandial punch-up with a rugby team out for their Christmas party. He'd got through the backline when the number eight tackled him from behind and cracked his head open on the edge of a table. He ended up with twelve stitches and a four-hour wait in A and E.

'One of the best *bladdy* Christmases I've had,' he muttered to himself, after swallowing a handful of the tablets. 'Next up, it's Baz and his 'effing dog.' Kurtz looked up from the running order. 'What the *fok* does 'effing mean?'

'It means leave the best until fucking last,' said Baz, jumping up from his seat and heading for the stage. 'Where's that fucking dog? Rosie!' She popped her head out from under the buffet table. 'Get up here, you fucking bitch.' Even more bow-legged because of the food she'd eaten, Rosie waddled across to the stage.

'Right,' said Baz, taking two spoons from his pocket. 'One, two, three…!' He played the spoons on his knee while Rosie howled along. Then he began singing. '*Me four-legged friend, me four-legged friend, she'll never let you down* – she fucking will if there's fucking food about! – *She's honest and faithful right up to the end* – like balls she is! – *Me wonderful, wonderful, one-two-three-four* fucking *legged friend…!*'

OUTSIDE THE DRESSING room door Mould tapped his foot and hummed along. He thought that in spite of Baz's ad-libs it was Rosie who was carrying the act. His thoughts and humming were interrupted by a loud heave-ho-ing coming from the dressing room. Pushing open the door, he walked in to investigate.

CHAPTER TWELVE

MALCOLM HAD JUST fed the last of Victor through the window when Mould entered the room. Hanging down like a sixteen-stone bat in drag, Victor watched with amazement as Mould walked across the floor without so much as an 'Allo, allo, allo, what's all this, then?' Seemingly satisfied that the room was empty, Mould returned the way he had come.

Still hanging down from the window, Victor could feel his feet sliding out of his Wellington boots as Malcolm's grip began to loosen. Looking up, he could see Malcolm place the Wellington boots under his armpits to gain more purchase. But it wasn't enough. Just as Mould was passing under him, Victor felt himself fall. Pulling Malcolm after him, they landed on top of Mould with a loud crash. With about thirty stone of Punch and Judy tumbling down on top of him, Mould was knocked out colder than a store manager hit on the head by a piece of 'Made in England' drainpipe. Mould wasn't the only casualty. Outside came a loud 'Ow!'

With Baz and Rosie's rendition of *Old MacDonald Had a Farm* providing background music, Victor and Malcolm began to disentangle themselves from the jumble of arms and legs and unconscious police inspectors.

'It's Nietzsche,' said Malcolm, pointing down at Mould.

'"What does not destroy you, makes you stronger,"' said

Victor, rubbing his head. Curious about who this stranger was who knew so much about philosophy, he searched Mould's pockets. Inside one he found Mould's warrant card.

Malcolm looked over Victor's shoulder so he could read the details on the card. 'Don't think much of his costume.'

'I don't think he's in fancy dress.'

'You mean…?'

'That's right, Malcolm, he's a real policeman. And when he wakes up and finds out he's been knocked unconscious by Punch and Judy…We better be quick. Where's the ring?' Outside there was a loud groaning sound. 'What was that?' said Victor, looking up at the window.

'I think it's the boss. As you pulled me through the window my foot knocked the ladder and it fell backwards. I think it landed on that part of the wall where Derek was.'

'These things are supposed to come in threes, I suppose.' Victor held out his hand. 'The ring?'

'What ring?'

'Have you noticed, Malcolm, that every time I ask you where the ring is you say, "What ring?"'

'Yes.'

'And then I say something like, "The ring I asked you to keep safe", and you say…?'

'Oh, that ring.'

'You did put it safe, didn't you?'

'Oh, yes.'

'Where?'

'Somewhere no one would ever think to look,' said Malcolm, tapping the side of his nose.

Victor put his arm around Malcolm's shoulder. 'Malcolm, have you ever got up in the morning, looked out the window, seen the sun shining, gone for a walk and halfway into the walk it's started to rain? All around you is blue sky except for the bit directly above you, which is dark and grey and forbidding. It's like you have your own storm cloud following you wherever you go. Well, I've had that for forty years.'

'Buy yourself an umbrella.'

'Eventually, you reach what is known as a tipping point. In climatology that's the transitional point between one stable weather system and another. In physics it's a point of displacement from one state of equilibrium to another. And in Victor it's the point where he has a complete mental breakdown and starts eviscerating his best friend with a pair of rusty scissors. Now, please try and concentrate.'

'What was the question again?'

'Where's the fucking ring?!'

On the ground a still-unconscious Mould seemed to stir. Time was running out. Victor wasn't sure how long police inspectors generally remained unconscious, but he knew it wasn't forever. He also knew that the more pressure he heaped on Malcolm the more Malcolm would become confused.

'I'll look for Angel's bag,' said Victor, in a calmer voice, 'and you think about where you put the ring.'

'Okay,' said Malcolm. 'I remember a wooden ladder…But I wouldn't hide a ring in that. There were those hot cross buns… But I wouldn't put a ring in one of those in case someone ate it. The name Phil keeps coming back to me, but who he is and whether or not I gave him the ring, I can't say…'

Leaving Malcolm to think out loud, Victor ran over to the pile of bags near the sink. With half a dozen runners and riders to pick from he decided to approach the problem scientifically. A person's bag was an extension of their personality. All he had to do was sort through the bags and make a guess based on the psychology of the individual. The easiest ones to eliminate first were the camouflage rucksack and *Top Gear* Stig rucksack, which he correctly guessed belonged to Kurtz and Frank respectively. The owner of the black leather holdall covered in miniature padlocks suggested someone who was the keeper of dark secrets. So, Kevin's then. That left a gold handbag – too fancy, too feminine, too Violet – and a nylon-braided, heavy-duty number of the type used by plumbers, bricklayers and the special forces.

Victor unzipped the bag. Inside he found a canister of mace, a flick-knife, nunchucks, an air pistol and a grenade with the pin still in. Only Angel would keep a grenade in her bag. Confirmation came with the words A.R.S.E. HOLE'S KEEP OWT!!! Written in felt-tip on the inside of the bag.

Bingo!

He held up the bag to show Malcolm. But his friend was standing with his eyes closed, front knee bent, hips turned forward and arms raised.

'What are you doing, Malcolm?'

'The Virabhadrasana – or Warrior – One. It aids concentration, balance and groundedness.'

'Well, is it going to take long?' Victor glanced down at Mould. 'Our friend here is going to wake up at any moment. And when he does…'

Malcolm kept his front knee bent but turned his hips to the side with his arms parallel. 'The Virabhadrasana – or Warrior – Two.' He balanced on one foot, the standing leg straight and the other leg lifted with his arms reaching forward. 'The Virabhadrasana – or Warrior – Three.'

'Malcolm.'

'I'm not a hundred percent certain,' said Malcolm, holding his position, 'but I'm pretty sure I gave the ring to someone called Phil who's up a ladder eating a hot cross bun. All we've got to do now is find Phil. Whoever he is…' He put his raised leg down, bent his front knee, turned his hips to the side like with the Virabhadrasana Two, except this time he bowed his torso forward and clasped his raised hands behind his back.

'The Virabhadrasana – Warrior – Four?' said Victor.

'Baddha Virabhadrasana – or Humble Warrior.'

Victor could feel the panic rising inside of him. Mould was letting out a series of intermittent groans and threatening to come to. He watched on anxiously as Malcolm switched position again. This time by reaching towards the back straight leg with one arm and raising the other into the air. 'The Viparita Virabhadrasana, or Reverse Warrior…Wait a minute…' Malcolm rubbed the hand that was resting on his leg up and down. 'Wool tights?' he said. 'I don't wear wool tights when I do yoga. I only wear wool tights when I think I might be abducted by aliens. Well, you don't want to be hurtling through space without the proper leg protection.'

Victor's outward composure began to fracture. Malcolm bringing aliens into the conversation didn't help. When it came to extra-terrestrials his friend could go on about them all day. And right then they didn't have all day.

'Tights!' said Malcolm. After lifting up a 'Eureka' finger, he stuck his hand inside his tights and brought out the ring. 'Got it!' he said.

'Got it,' said Victor, lifting up Angel's bag.

Malcolm bent down and picked something up off the floor. 'Got it?' he said, holding up a second engagement ring.

II

MALCOLM LOOKED FROM one engagement ring to the other.

'That's three rings,' he said, 'including Phil's.'

'There almost identical,' said Victor, examining the two rings.

'You're not getting married twice, are you?'

'I'm not getting married at all if I can help it.'

'Remember the crocodiles, the sharks and the skunks.'

But Victor was too preoccupied with the two engagement rings to think about crocodiles, sharks and skunks. He pointed down at Mould. 'It must've fallen out of his pocket when we fell on top of him.'

'Maybe he's getting married to Violet, too?'

'After everything that's happened today, anything's possible.'

In the bar Baz, Rosie and the rest had just started up a raucous rendition of *My Old Man (Said Follow the Van)*.

'We better get out of here,' said Victor. Nietzsche here won't be out cold for long. And One Man and His Dog…'

'Effing dog.'

'…won't be going on forever. Besides, if I don't show my face soon I'll be spending the rest of my working life asking people if they want help with their packing.'

'Tills?' said Malcolm. He stuck out a hand. 'Congratulations.'

'Life's just one whole sky full of silver linings for you, isn't it?' said Victor, shaking it.

'All those lovely people you'll get to meet. Don't forget – proper posture and rehydrate every four hours. It's a health and safety war out there.'

Mould let out a loud groan.

'He's coming to,' said Victor. 'Hurry up and put the rings back where they belong – that one in Angel's bag and that one in Nietzsche's pocket. I'll keep an eye on the door.' Opening the door an inch, he peered into the bar area. *My Old Man (Said Follow the Van)* was still being sung loftily from all quarters.

Except Kurtz's. Swaddled in an assortment of makeshift bandages and slings, Victor's nemesis looked like a man who'd just had his laptop seized by the police.

'All done,' said Malcolm.

'Right,' said Victor, pulling down his miniskirt, 'let's get out of here.'

III

As VICTOR AND Malcolm slipped back into the bar, Baz and Rosie switched from *My Old Man (Said Follow the Van)* to *My Old Man's a Dustman*. Baz was trying to drum up a bit more audience participation by telling everyone to 'Join in, you fucking twats!' Soon, the whole room was banging glasses on tables and singing about cor blimey trousers and council flats. Everyone that is except Kurtz, who, as Victor observed as he sat down at the bar, was propped up, fuming, at the side of the stage.

'Drink?' said Malcolm, sitting down next to Victor. 'They're free, remember.'

'In that case,' said Victor, who never paid for a drink when Malcolm was around anyway, 'I'll take a quadruple whisky. No ice.' He looked around at the rest of the room, singing and stamping their feet, and decided to join in. Now that he had rid himself of Angel's ring he could breathe a little easier. There was still the Violet and Kurtz situation to deal with. But with the ring returned to its rightful owner he felt like a great weight had been lifted from his shoulders.

Of course it couldn't last. Not with Violet waving at him from one side of the stage and Kurtz glaring at him from the other. He returned Violet's wave with a half one of his own. Kurtz's glare he responded to with a look that he hoped conveyed sympathy and understanding, but which probably just conveyed fear.

Victor became aware of raised voices at the bar. It was Malcolm and the barmaid arguing. 'I don't care what competition you think you've won,' the barmaid was saying, 'you're not having these drinks until you've paid for them.'

'I'd like to see the referee,' said Malcolm.

'You'll be seeing the back of my hand if you're not careful,' said the barmaid.

Malcolm pulled his wallet out from his tights. 'Someone else must've won the clapping competition,' he said, paying for the drinks. 'Oh, well, good luck to them. Cheers.'

'Down the hat...' said Victor. He felt a big brawny arm grab hold of his neck from behind. Looking over his shoulder he saw that it was Kurtz, who despite all his injuries had managed to lower himself down from the stage and hobble across to the bar. Although one arm was in a sling, the strength of the other was enough to feel like it was an anaconda wrapping itself around Victor's neck.

'Thought you'd done a bunk, me old *bra*,' said Kurtz.

'Just-just-just went out for a breather,' said a gasping Victor. 'And-and-and, just for the record, bra means something very different in this – aargh! – country. Oh, look, there's Violet.' On the stage Violet was craning her neck to see what was going on. Victor gave her an ostentatious wave. He felt Kurtz's arm release itself from his neck and settle on his shoulder. The grip was still vice-like.

A plastered on smile covering his face, Kurtz held even tighter onto Victor's shoulder. 'I hope that other thing's been sorted?' he said.

'Other thing?'

Kurtz slapped Victor on the back like they were old

compadres. 'I mean you and Violet *un*-tying the knot?' he hissed into Victor's ear.

'Oh. That.'

'*Ja.* That. Because otherwise…' Kurtz nodded over at Angel, who was busy downing pints of beer and then crushing them with her bare hands. The last time Victor had seen her drink like that was at a pre-Covid staff Christmas party. She'd ended up being arrested after piling up all the tables and chairs in the restaurant and setting fire to them. Victor remembered thinking at the time that perhaps things wouldn't have been quite so bad if Angel had let the other diners leave their seats first. But it was what happened after the police arrived that he remembered best. It was like the Keystone Cops crossed with Fatty Arbuckle as the police and Angel fought and chased each around the restaurant for half an hour. It took another dozen members of the riot squad to finally wrestle her into the police van.

Perhaps it was the sight of Angel knocking back the pints or Violet blowing him extravagant kisses or having one of Kurtz's arms holding him vice-like by the shoulder that made Victor panic. But panic he did, and without stopping to think of the consequences he turned his head to Kurtz and said, 'It's done. Violet and I are no more.' He felt Kurtz's grip relax a little.

'Then why the *bladdy* hell is she blowing you *bladdy* kisses like some soppy *bladdy* teenager?' said Kurtz.

'Those kisses aren't for me, they're for you.'

'For me?'

'Congratulations,' said Victor, shaking Kurtz's good hand. 'The best man's won.'

Before Kurtz could respond the double doors opened and in staggered a concussed Derek. Stumbling to the bar he said in a breathless voice, 'Whisky.'

'Don't you think you've had enough?' said the barmaid.

'Everything alright, boss?' said Victor, edging away from Kurtz and keeping a hand on his crotch. Derek looked at him with eyes wide with terror.

'Alright, madam?' he said, taking a step back. 'You want to know if everything's alright...?' Derek took the glass of whisky from the barmaid and swallowed it in one. 'I've just felt the hand of the Lord, madam,' he said, handing over the glass for a refill. He lifted his cowboy hat and showed Victor the three bumps on his forehead. 'Thrice He smote me, until, finally, dazed and on my knees, I gave myself unto Him.'

'Amen,' said Victor.

'Amen.' Derek knocked back the second glass of whisky. 'And now I must go and spread the word. There are souls to be saved.' He lurched off towards the stage.

'Hey, what about paying for those drinks?' said the barmaid.

'*He* must've won the clapping competition,' said Malcolm, nudging Victor.

They watched as Derek climbed on to the stage and pushed Baz away from the microphone. 'What the fuck...?' said Baz, nearly falling off the stage. With Rosie pulling on one of his chaps Derek spoke into the microphone.

'For all you sinners out there,' he said, 'I have this message. Turn from your evil ways and repent! Before it's too late. Repent! Before the wrath of God strikes you down like he did me...' Derek lifted his cowboy hat to show the assembled throng the bumps. 'Repent! Because only by turning to Him can you hope to save yourselves. You sir...' Derek pointed at Kevin. '...do you want to spend your life wallowing in the filth and feculence of your Earthly perversions, or do you want to breathe the clean, wholesome air of the Holy Spirit?'

'The filth – and what was that other word? – of Earthly

perversions, please,' said Kevin.

'Hallelujah,' said Victor, dryly.

'And you...? This time Derek pointed at Mould, who had entered the bar rubbing his head. '...is that the Devil's hangover you're nursing or have you been struck by the Hand of the Almighty?'

Worried in case Mould said, 'No, not the Hand of the Almighty, but the hands, feet and all the rest of Victor and Malcolm, who fell on top of me when they were breaking into the changing room', Victor closed his eyes and held his breath.

There was a loud crash. Victor opened one eye to find that Derek had disappeared from the stage. When he opened the other, he saw that a crowd had gathered at the front of the stage and were staring down into what Victor assumed was the abyss. With a good chance that he himself might be visiting the abyss sometime soon he decided to go over and have a butchers at what it looked like. After forcing his way through the crowd he found an unconscious Derek on the floor. Still pulling on one of Derek's chaps was Rosie. It was easy to work out what had happened. Rosie's chap-pulling had dragged Derek off the stage and rendered him unconscious...

Victor looked in turn at the comatose Derek, concussed Mould, crippled Kurtz and blood-covered Kevin. 'A typical Whiting's do,' he muttered to himself. His turn would be next. And when it came it would be worse than all the others combined. Angel was still downing pints and crushing the glasses with her bare hands. Soon, she would be downing Victor and crushing *him* with her bare hands. He glanced over at the double doors. Just a few short steps and he would be free. The image of him sitting on a till scanning tins of soup lodged in his mind. Was it possible for him to work on Checkouts and still write a book? Or would the monotony fry his brain...?

'Victor!'

Imagining for a moment that the person who shouted his name could also read his mind, Victor turned around with a guilty look and said, 'I wasn't going anywhere.'

'Of course you weren't, darling,' said Violet. 'We've our big…' She sniffed the air. 'What's that horrible smell?'

'Smell?'

'Like rotten fish?'

'Erm, probably the drains.' Victor wound the tea towel tighter around his head. 'Or Baz's dog.'

'Yes, well, dogs shouldn't be allowed in pubs. Or at charity galas. I mean, just look at the state of my points.'

Not only did Victor look at Violet's points he felt an instant connection with them, too. Broken, torn and limp, they reflected exactly how he was feeling at that moment. The only difference, of course, was that there were seven of them. Apart from Malcolm and his dead mother, Victor was on his own.

'Now,' said Violet, adjusting her tiara. 'Shall I make the announcement or do you want to do it? Traditionally, it should be the man, but dressed like that…' Victor felt his cheeks blush red as Violet looked him up and down. Not that he didn't have his own complaints when it came to the appearance of his soon-to-be-fiancé. Clad in gold and covered in dog bites she looked like an enormous blob of used butter.

'I think you better do it,' said Victor in a defeated voice. 'Public speaking isn't my forte.'

'Forty?' said Violet, above the commotion of Derek being carried out of the bar. 'You're not forty until next month. One celebration at a time.'

Celebration? With the 'big moment' just moments away, Victor's thoughts on marriage had swung back to total despair. The chances of Violet toeing the line once they were married were about as slim as Kurtz not launching Armageddon against him when the announcement was made. Violet would be tipping chamber pots over him for the rest of his life. Even if it turned him into a philosopher it was a price too high.

He glanced over Violet's shoulder at Kurtz, who was in close conversation with Mould. Pretoria's finest pointed over *his* shoulder at Angel and let out a deep, booming, laugh. Victor swallowed hard. Throw Kurtz denouncing him to Angel into the mix and right then Victor felt about as jubilant as a jilted lover standing on the brink of Beachy Head. Yes, he'd returned the ring. But that didn't mean Angel would see reason. Not after about twelve – Victor watched as Angel downed another pint – thirteen pints.

'Victor!'

'No Plan B, Malcolm,' said Victor, shaken from his thoughts.

'Plan B? Malcolm?' said a puzzled Violet.

'Oh…it's just a silly thing I say sometimes.'

'What does it mean?'

'What does it mean?'

'Yes, what does it mean?'

No one had ever asked Victor that before. What did it mean? It was…both a rallying cry *and* a cry for help. An all-guns-blazing forward charge *and* the white flag of surrender. The reason for getting up in the morning *and* hiding under the covers until midday. What did it mean? Everything. And nothing.

Right then Victor decided to plump for the latter. 'Nothing,' he said. On a different day he might've given a different answer. But with defeat just moments away and reality too real to bear it was time to throw in the towel. He took off the one wrapped around his head and chucked it to the ground. When Plan A has gone this wrong, what was the point of a Plan B? Or a Plan C? Or a Plan Anything? With nothing left in the tank except for a few drops of weary resignation, Victor looked sadly down at the bits of bulging flesh billowing out of his costume and said, 'It means nothing.'

'I think I'd better make the announcement,' said Violet, 'the excitement seems to be getting to you.' She pressed her hands together. 'Oh, Victor, just think, in a few moments the whole world will know about our love! It's so exciting! I feel like Cinderella and you're the handsome prince, who, after searching his whole kingdom for the love of his life, has suddenly found her.'

'Where?' said Victor, spinning around.

'Attention, ladies and gentlemen,' said a beaming Kurtz, into the microphone. 'All acts on stage for the finale, please.'

Victor gulped. The moment of truth had finally arrived. And this time there really was no Plan B.

VICTOR HAD FORGOTTEN about the *Glow-Cop*. If he managed to show Kurtz up as the pilferer of charity money the situation might yet be saved. There was just one problem. Kurtz was still wearing his white gloves. With them on the *Glow-Cop* wouldn't show up. If he could only get Kurtz to remove them…He looked along the line of acts assembled on the stage. At the far end, still sipping absinthe, was Tarquin Travers-Booth. Next to him, still breaking beer glasses with her bare hands, was Angel. Next to her, giving Victor furtive looks, was a wig-less Frank. Next to Frank, with a nose like Rudolph the red-nosed reindeer, was the other half of Whiting's Two Funniest Men, Kevin. Victor himself came next. Then Violet and then Baz, with a lit rollup in his mouth. Lastly came Malcolm, who was busy wafting the smoke from Baz's cigarette away from his face.

Moving like Frankenstein, Kurtz lumbered over to where Mould was standing on the other side of the stage. With Victor looking on, Kurtz took a pill bottle from his pocket and swallowed a handful of whatever was in it.

'Wonder what the big announcement is about?' said Malcolm, pointing to the bottom of the running order that Violet was holding.

'You'll find out soon enough,' said Violet. 'Won't he, Victor?'

Victor gave a strained smile. He was too focused on what Kurtz and Mould were doing to concentrate on anything else. Still huddled together at the side of the stage, Kurtz kept turning around and pointing in his direction. Thinking just how wrong Oscar Wilde had been when he'd said that the only thing worse than being talked about was not being talked about, Victor felt his ears beginning to sting. Caught between the Scylla of getting engaged to Violet and the Charybdis of being denounced to Angel by Kurtz, he decided to meet his fate with Odysseus-like fortitude. But his courage lasted for about as long as it took Mould to retrieve a small object from his pocket and pass it to Kurtz. Beaming even more, Kurtz lumbered back across to the microphone.

'Well, what a fantastic evening's entertainment we've had,' said Kurtz in a muffled, monotone, voice. Like a 78 record played at a speed of 45, he sounded to Victor like Frank giving the daily briefing on Mogadon. 'How about a big hand for all the acts – there they are, ladies and gentlemen.'

Kurtz himself led the ovation, although he was out of time with the rest of the room. But that's not what surprised Victor. What surprised Victor was the emollient, if robotically slow way in which Kurtz had spoken. Maybe a more positive conclusion to the evening was in the offing? The thought was a comforting one and led to Victor joining in with the applause. This started a chain-reaction up and down the line, until everyone on stage – and off – was clapping and cheering.

'And how about a special hand for the lady who put all this together? She's a real *bokkie*. Step forward please, Violet.'

The lady of the hour didn't need telling twice. She was already blowing kisses to the room and waving her wand before Kurtz had even got to the end of his sentence. The infrared lights had been switched on and the room was lit up like a football stadium hosting an evening-time kick-off.

Violet stepped up to the microphone. 'I'd just like to say how proud I am of everybody for making this such a special occasion. You've all made such an effort and gone out of your way to make it a night I'll never forget…'

'Go on, Violet, you fucking bitch!' said Baz.

'Oh,' said Violet, fanning herself with her hand. 'I knew I'd start crying! When you've put your whole heart and soul into something and it's been such a personal success…I did ask some newspaper and TV people to turn up. But they obviously didn't think we were important enough to bother with…'

There were boos from the audience, together with a 'Fucking bunch of cunts!' from Baz. Violet held up her hand for silence.

'It's possible, of course, that Graham Norton was double-booked. But I would've made do with Vernon Kaye. Let's see, what else is there…? Oh, yes, I'd like to thank my mother and father for having me. And the people with Monch…er… Monkhausen's syndrome by proxy for having…something by proxy so we could all dress up and have a good time. We've raised…' Violet opened up the charity tin. Victor looked on as she let out a loud gasp. 'Oh!' She showed the contents to those nearest to her.

'Why is it glowing blue?' said Malcolm.

'There should be a lot more money in there than that,' said Violet.

All eyes (except Malcolm's) turned to Victor. He reacted by raising his hands in a silent 'What?' A few feet down from him Kurtz was shaking his head in disgust. Victor glanced down at Kurtz's white gloves. Somehow he had to get Kurtz to remove them.

But how?

'L-Lastly and most importantly,' Violet said, putting the lid back on the tin, 'I'd like to make a very special announcement about a very special person…' Victor glanced over at Kurtz again. The soppy, drippy look painted across Kurtz's face told Victor one thing: that Kurtz thought Violet was talking about him. '…this very special person, who is standing not a million miles away from here…' A beaming Kurtz adjusted his collar and bowtie. '…is a man…is *the* man,' said Violet to general laughter from the room and a playful, theatrical shake of the head from Kurtz, 'that I have chosen to spend the rest of my life with…' Victor looked on in horror as Kurtz wiped a tear from his eye. '…and there's only one thing left to say. Victor, I do.'

The applause when it came was like thunder. With Malcolm again leading proceedings by clapping his hands together like cymbals. A gulping Victor watched the expression on Kurtz's face change from that of someone trying to work out where he's parked his car, to a look of someone realising that his car has been stolen. It then rested on a look that seemed to combine the bloodlust of a sadistic Saracen with the homicidal determination of a Kamikaze pilot.

'You!' said Kurtz, moving towards Victor.

'I can explain,' said Victor, backing away. As he did he thought how strange it was that every time the Great Director in the sky shouted 'Action!' Kurtz seemed to turn into a character

240

from a Boris Karloff film. Earlier it had been *Frankenstein*. Now, as Kurtz walked towards him with his hands stretched out, it was *The Mummy*.

'I'm not interested in explanations,' said Kurtz, in his Mogadon monotone. 'All I'm interested in is ripping your *bladdy* head off!'

'What's all this about?' said Violet, getting in between Victor and Kurtz.

'Oh, nothing, really,' said Victor, trying to keep things light-hearted and avoid being dragged off to the Isle of the Dead by body-snatching Boris. 'Just a little misunderstanding between a couple of old buddies.' He held out a hand to Kurtz in a desperate attempt to get him to remove one of his gloves. 'Shake on it?' Kurtz knocked Victor's hand away.

'I hope it doesn't have anything to do with our announcement?' said Violet.

Kurtz came to a shuddering halt. With a blank look on his face which Victor couldn't help but compare to the inscrutable Dr Fu Manchu, Kurtz stared up at the ceiling before fixing Victor was an evil grin. 'Announcement,' he said in a sinister voice.

'Announcement?' said Violet.

'Announcement,' repeated Kurtz.

'Announcement?' gulped Victor. He knew the word betokened some evil design, uttered as it was by Kurtz in a portentous, apocalyptic fashion. So portentous and apocalyptic that Victor half-expected Kurtz to throw back his head and go 'Muhahahahahahah!' Instead, Kurtz staggered across to the microphone. Victor braced himself. He didn't know exactly what Kurtz was going to say. But he knew it wasn't going to be anything along the lines of 'Three cheers for the happy couple'. Or a sonorous rendition of *For He's a Jolly Good Fellow*.

'I've got a quick announcement of my own before you all *fok* off and leave me to tidy up,' was Kurtz's starter-for-ten. Victor was tempted to buzz in and point out that he had to stay behind too and tidy up on pain of being sent to Tills. But he decided against it in case he got five bonus punches for his troubles.

'I hate to piss on other people's parade,' said Kurtz, with a smile that suggested the exact opposite. 'But someone in this room has been pulling moves all day. Stealing, you could say.' The room went deadly quiet. 'You see that *bwana* over there...' Kurtz pointed at Mould, or rather, at Mould's back, for as usual Lunestone's finest was facing the wrong way. '... he's a policeman. A real policeman. And he's going to help me nab this *bliksem* low-life, this real-life Gollum, this stealer of engagement rings...'

Victor turned his head to where Angel was standing. Upon hearing the words 'engagement rings' she ceased her glass-crunching and listened closely to what Kurtz was going to say next.

'All that's left for me to do now,' said Kurtz, flashing Victor a Bond villain grin, 'is to reveal the miserable *mompie* and let justice...' To the side of Victor, Angel was preparing herself to pounce. '...let justice take its course. So...'

THAT 'SO' HAD the same effect on Victor as the word 'Aim' must have on someone facing a firing squad. His knees buckled and everything became a blur. But he could still make out the burly figure of Kurtz trudging towards him. Out of the corner of his eye Victor saw a second figure lunge at him. It was Rosie, who no doubt picking up on the smell of rotten fish that still emanated from Victor's costume, launched herself at him. With

Victor moving to one side at the last moment Rosie missed her target and banged into Malcolm instead. As Malcolm jumped back to escape Rosie's lunge he knocked into Baz. Lit rollup still in his hand, Baz then knocked into Violet. Swathed as she was in tissue paper, flammable epoxy paint and solvents, Violet lit up like a Chinese lantern as Baz's fag came into contact with her costume. Flying about the stage like a real shooting star, Violet went from red dwarf to supernova faster than it took Baz to shout, 'Never mind the fucking engagement ring, *her* fucking ring's on fire now!'

Victor ducked down to escape the flames. Those off-stage also took evasive action, while onstage everything seemed to happen at once. Whiting's Two Funniest Men threw themselves underneath a front-row table. Malcolm ran around like a headless chicken shouting 'Don't panic!'. And Angel threw half-full glasses of beer at Violet in a vain attempt to douse the flames....

JUST AFTER VIOLET had been set alight by Baz's cigarette a newcomer found his way into the function room. He wore a crumpled suit, had three-day stubble dotted about his chin and rings the size of Jupiter's around both eyes. Around his neck he carried a digital camera with telescopic lens.

'Violet Dungworth?' said the newcomer to the barmaid. She pointed to the fireball flaming up and down the stage. The newcomer whipped the camera from around his neck and started taking pictures.

'Who are you, then?' said the barmaid.

'Lunestone Gazette. Ms Dungworth invited us down to cover some charity do. Is she supposed to be on fire like that?'

'I don't think so.'

'Shouldn't someone be doing something about it?'

VICTOR WAS JUST thinking the same thing. Before he could react he saw Kurtz grab a fire extinguisher and – using only his good hand – expertly detach the nozzle. Taking aim he covered Violet in a mountain of foam. Within seconds she was transformed from a raging inferno into a badly sculpted snowman. Wiping the foam from her eyes she looked at her saviour, and in a breathless whisper said, 'You saved my life. Now you're going to have to make it up to me.'

Kurtz threw down the empty fire extinguisher and shuffled over to where Violet was standing. Wiping the foam from her lips he gave her a passionate kiss. With the room breaking into applause once more and the man from the Gazette snapping pictures and asking 'When's the big day?', a blackened and singed Violet walked over to Victor. Returning the cheap ring, she said, 'I'm sorry Victor, but it's a woman's prerogative to change her mind. I've decided to marry Kurtz. You must forget all about me now. Perhaps you could join the French Foreign Legion or go on Nights.'

'Oh. Right. Fine,' said Victor. He had no intention of going on Nights. Or of joining the French Foreign Legion. But he did intend to forget all about Violet. Just as soon as he could get to the bar and drink his own bodyweight in whisky. It had been a damned close run thing.

Kurtz was already down on his knees and about to begin his Will-you-do-me-the-honour-ing. Unable to kneel properly because of his injuries, he looked to Victor like Charles I about to have his head cut off. Not that Violet seemed to mind. Standing before him crumpled, burnt, blackened and soaked, she had a beatific smile on her face and – no doubt – an Alice in Wonderland wedding on her mind.

'Violet…?' said Kurtz, taking a ring from his pocket.

'Oh, I do, I do, I do,' said Violet.

Victor could see how much Kurtz was struggling to get the ring on Violet's sausage-sized fingers. Eventually, Kurtz removed one glove, then the other, to give himself some grip. As he pushed the ring onto Violet's finger the room erupted into cheers. With Baz shouting 'Go on Violet, you fucking golliwog' for luck. Still down on one knee Kurtz turned to Victor with a triumphant look on his face and drew a finger across his throat…

…a blue finger to match his blue hand. Two blue hands. With his gloves off Kurtz had unwittingly revealed himself as the thief.

'You!' gasped Violet. She opened the charity tin and showed Kurtz as well as the audience the glowing contents. 'You've been stealing the charity money!'

Boos and cries of shame rang out.

'Now, just a minute, *bokkie*…' said Kurtz. Before he could say anymore a sound like a Tyrannosaurus Rex with toothache silenced the room. It was Angel. She grabbed hold of the hand Violet had been pointing at a spluttering Kurtz.

'That's me ring!' she said.

'It's mine!' said Violet, trying to pull her hand away.

Victor shook his head. Violet was built to last, and against anyone woman-born would've been able to hold her own. But against Angel…It was like a strawweight against a heavyweight. A Greco-Roman wrestler against a Sumo. An oak tree against a General Sherman sequoia.

There was a brief tussle as Angel tore the engagement ring from Violet's finger and then with a single swish of her hand swatted the bride-not-to-be from the stage. Violet flew through the air, hit the far wall – BANG! – and crashed into oblivion.'
With the warm-up act dispatched with such contemptuous ease Angel turned her attention to the main event. Still on

his knees as his injured legs had locked, Kurtz was literally a sitting target. 'Where did you get me ring from?'

'It's my *bladdy* ring!' said Kurtz. 'Ask Kevin and Frank.'

At the mention of their names Kevin and Frank ducked under the nearest table.

'Tell her, Mouldy?' said an increasingly desperate Kurtz.

'Shakespeare put it best,' said Mould, rubbing the back of his still-sore head, 'when he said "Some men there are love not a gaping pig, some that are mad if they behold a cat. And others when the bagpipe sings i' the nose cannot contain their urine." I've lived my whole life by this.'

Victor didn't have to be a mind reader to guess what Kurtz's disbelieving shake of the head signified. That there were probably times and places when talk about piss and pigs was the order of the day. But on your knees before the Angel of Death definitely wasn't one of them.

'The ring, man,' said Kurtz imploringly, 'tell her about the *bladdy* ring!'

'You mean "The bells that ring so clear" or "Bright is the ring of words"?' said Mould.

'I mean the *bladdy* engagement ring I asked you to keep hold of for me.'

'You mean this?' Mould took the De Beers diamond ring from his pocket. 'Funny, I thought I'd already given it back to you.'

Kurtz made a sound that reminded Victor of a pair of exhausted bagpipes, which singing i' the nose and every other part of Kurtz's anatomy rendered him unable to contain his urine. Gaping like a pig, Kurtz looked over at Victor and then up at Angel. 'I-I-It was V-V-Victor,' he said. 'He t-took your ring!'

'This is my ring,' said Angel, 'and you stole it.'

246

'Like the charity money,' said Victor, who thought it was about time to add his own ha'penny's worth. The murmur from the audience told Victor that it was money well spent. For once the crowd was on his side.

Angel moved towards the kneeling Kurtz. 'No!' he cried, trying to back away on his knees.

'I told you what I'd do if I found the person who stole it,' said Angel, hovering menacingly over a cowering Kurtz. 'Rip their bleedin' head off!'

'Help!' said Kurtz, moving like Douglas Bader without his tin legs.

Deciding to round up his contribution to a full penny, Victor threw in another ha'penny's worth. 'Or marry them,' he said.

'Wot?' said Angel, turning her troll-like face to Victor.

On this occasion there was to be no quaking of the boots for Victor. No withering beneath the Gorgon gaze of Angel's threatening stare. 'You said you'd rip their bleedin' head off,' he said calmly, 'or marry them.' He watched Angel's bestial, gargoyle features soften. She looked down at Kurtz with a simpering smile.

'So I did,' she said.

'No!' said Kurtz, holding up two blue hands in a vain attempt to ward off what was coming. Again, Victor could read what Kurtz was thinking. That given the choice of having his head ripped off or marrying Angel, Kurtz would much prefer to have his head ripped off. But Kurtz had no choice, for, beholding not a cat but a twenty-five stone heifer, and with not a single friendly face or port to escape the storm that was about to engulf him, Kurtz had run out of options. And as Angel advanced nearer and nearer, her truck-driver arms reaching out towards him with romantic intent, his eyes widened in horror as he was engulfed in a sea of flesh. Gathering Kurtz up in her huge paws, Angel planted a wet kiss on the top of his head.

'I do,' she growled.

The good folk of Whiting's clapped and cheered and whistled and tore up beer mats for confetti for all they were worth. And with the man from the Gazette busy once more with his digital camera Kurtz exited stage right. Pursued by a bear.

VI

THE AUDIENCE AT the Dog and Whistle began to gradually thin out. But not before going over to Victor to shake his hand and apologise for all the name calling. Sitting at the bar with Malcolm, Victor accepted the handshakes and apologies with all the dignity and magnanimity of the wronged man redeemed. Not for him the bitterness and feelings of injustice of the falsely accused. Instead there settled upon him a peace of mind that brought with it a serenity and new understanding.

'They all thought I'd stolen the charity money,' said Victor, after shaking another hand. 'That's why they were calling me those names.'

'It was still wrong of them,' said Malcolm. 'Two wrongs don't make a right. But at least they're saying sorry.'

'"We all hate a thief", Aristotle, but "nobility shines through when a man endures repeated and severe misfortune with patience, generosity"' – he shook another hand – '"and greatness of soul".'

'Aristotle again?'

Victor picked up his glass of whisky. 'What a time to be alive. Cheers!'

'It's certainly been a long day,' said Malcolm.

'You can say that again,' said Victor, after draining his glass.

'Say what again?'

They watched as Frank and Kevin carried an unconscious Violet out of the room. An ambulance had been called, but one paramedic was attending to Derek and the other was outside chatting up the barmaid. 'And just twelve months to go,' said Frank, struggling under the weight of Violet. With Kevin trying to look up Violet's star they disappeared through the double doors held open by Baz.

'Come on then you,' said Baz to Rosie. 'Next stop, *Britain's Got* fucking *Talent.*' Using Rosie's tail to guide him Mould followed Baz out of the function room. Victor and Malcolm found themselves alone.

'There's one thing I don't understand,' said Malcolm, going behind the bar and pouring himself a glass of lemonade. 'How come Nietzsche had both rings on him? I thought we put one ring in his pocket and the other in, in, in…Where were we supposed to put the other ring?'

'In Angel's bag.' Victor smiled to himself. He knew Malcolm must've mixed things up and put both rings in Mould's pocket. It was just luck that Mould had given Kurtz Angel's ring. 'These things have a way of working themselves out,' said Victor, lifting the refilled glass Malcolm put in front of him to his mouth.

'True,' said Malcolm, taking his glass of lemonade back around to the other side of the bar. 'After all, time and tide wait for no man.'

Victor picked a piece of dead fish from out of his apron pocket. He noticed that there was a folded up piece of notepaper in there too. He lifted it out and unfolded it.

Meet me at the Penny Bank Bridge. Eight o'clock.
I'll be wearing a red rose in my lapel. K.

Victor screwed up the piece of paper. Even a free drink wasn't worth a date with Kevin. 'Well,' he said, letting out a long sigh, 'I suppose I better start clearing up. After all, I don't want to end up on Tills.'

'Tills?' said Malcolm.

'Derek said he would put me on there if I didn't stay behind to clear up, remember?'

The double doors swung open and in ran the man himself. Chased by the paramedics carrying huge syringes he jumped on to the stage. Rushing over to the microphone he started singing *Puff the Magic Dragon* in a high-pitched voice. '*Puff, the magic dragon lived by the sea*…repentance in mine saith the Lord…*and frolicked in the autumn mist in a land called Honah Lee*…repent! Repent!'

One of the paramedics held Derek down while the other took the two syringes and stuck them one by one into Derek's backside.

'Repent!' said Derek. He held a hand up to the heavens. 'Our Clarkson, who art in Diddly Squat Farm, hallowed be your name…' He saw Victor and Malcolm sat at the bar. 'The wild beasts!' he said, pointing over at them. '"I will send wild animals against you to rob you of your children, destroy your livestock and reduce your numbers, until your roads lie desolate…"' *And frolicked in the autumn mist in a land called Honah Lee…*'

Derek fell unconscious.

'I wonder where it is?' said Malcolm.

'Where what is?' said Victor.

'Honah Lee?'

Victor finished off his drink and climbed down from his stool. 'Never mind Honah Lee, I've got a function room to tidy up.'

'Looks like Derek's going to be out it for a while.'

'Probably all those bumps on the head he's had.'

'That's what I mean. I bet he's forgotten about sending you to Tills if you don't tidy up.'

Victor thought for a moment. Malcolm was probably right. Having been hit on the head more times than a used nail and his body pumped full of tranquilisers, Derek probably didn't even know what the like-for-like sales were for the third quarter.

Victor looked around at all the overturned tables and chairs, smashed glasses and ripped up beer mats. It was going to take him hours to tidy up. And he still had that book to finish. Still, with Malcolm to help him and a free bar… 'No, Malcolm,' he said, 'no Plan B.' Picking up one of the overturned chairs, he paused for a moment with it in his hands. 'Aristotle. Aristotle is…'

THE END

Printed in Great Britain
by Amazon

35908451R00145